Men

hairstyles of the damned

joe meno

PUNK PLANET BOOKS
CHICAGO

This is a work of fiction. All names, characters, places, and incidents are the product of the author's imagination. Any resemblance to real events or persons, living or dead, is entirely coincidental.

Published by Akashic Books/Punk Planet Books
©2004 Joe Meno

Punk Planet Books is a division of Independents' Day Media.

Photographs by Laurent Yen
Model: Meghan Galbraith
Book design by Pirate Signal International

ISBN: 1-888451-70-X
Library of Congress Control Number: 2004106233
Eighth printing
Printed in Canada

Akashic Books
PO Box 1456
New York, NY 10009
Akashic7@aol.com
www.akashicbooks.com

Punk Planet Books
4229 N. Honore
Chicago, IL 60613
books@punkplanet.com
www.punkplanetbooks.com

acknowledgments

You rock it: Koren #1 favorite wife of all time, Dan Sinker, Mark Zambo, Meghan Lee, Jimmy Vickery, Jake Silker, Chad Rasner, Meg Stielstra, Lott Hill, Todd Dills, Jim Munroe, Jon Resh, Mike Coleman, Joe Tower, Joe Denk, Meredith Stone, Jenny Norton, Sarah K., Nick Novosel, the cast and crew of "Haunted Trails," Brian Peterson at the Fireside Bowl, Quimby's Bookstore, The Alley Chicago, Charles Everitt, Jenny Bent, Johnny Temple, my family, folks I met through the Phantom Three, Our Missles Are:, *Sleepwalk* magazine, Go Cougars, *Bail* magazine, *Punk Planet* magazine, the all-powerful Columbia College Fiction Writing Department, the *Chicago Tribune*, and the always supportive *New City*.

You suck it: Judith Regan. Badly. And all you other bad publishing corporations. Be ready, the end is nigh.

american nightmare
october 1990

"Whoa, oh, oh oh, sweet child of mine"
—*"Sweet Child o' Mine"*
Axl Rose, Guns n' Roses

"Your penis is king"
—*Graffiti in a high school boy's bathroom*

"The sun shines out of our behinds"
—*"Hand in Glove"*
Morrissey, The Smiths

one

The other problem I had was that I was falling in love with my best friend, Gretchen, who I thought the rest of the world considered fat. We were in her crappy car and singing, and at the end of the song "White Riot," the one by the Clash, I realized by the way I was watching her mouth pucker and smile and her eyes blink and wink, we were way more than friends, at least to me. I looked over at Gretchen driving and she was starting to sing the next song, "Should I Stay or Should I Go Now?" by the Clash again, and I said, "I love driving around with you, Gretchen," but because the radio was so loud all she could do was see my mouth move.

It was a Tuesday around four in the afternoon, the first semester of our junior year in high school, and neither one of us had anything to do, because Gretchen had just recently been fired from the Cinnabon at the mall for flipping off a female customer when she asked for more icing, and I wasn't allowed to work because my mother was very overprotective of me and insisted that I only focus on studying. I yelled something to Gretchen again and she nodded at me and then turned her head back to drive and kept on singing and I guess I looked over at her, at her short blondish-pink hair—some of it hanging in her face, some tucked behind her ear, some dyed brighter pink than the rest—and I watched the way her mouth moved again and I noticed she didn't ever wear lipstick and it was one of the reasons I think I liked her; and also I smiled at how she was holding her small white hands on the steering wheel very seriously, like she was a new driver, which she was not, because she was seventeen and had been driving way before she had gotten her license last year. I also looked at her breasts; I looked at them and they were big, very big, more than I knew what to do with, and I guess the truth of the matter was they were big because she was fat, and it didn't matter to me then, not the way it would if I was like hanging out with Bobby B. or some other guy at the mall, and he'd be like, "Check out that porker," and I'd be like, "Yeah," and then I'd laugh. Gretchen was fat, I mean not like obese, but she was definitely big, not her face so much, but her middle and behind.

Worse than that, she was known for kicking other girls' asses on a regular basis. It was not very cool. There was the awful hair-pulling incident with Polly Winchensky. There was the enormous black eye she gave Lisa Hensel. There was the time Gretchen broke Amy Schaffer's arm at a Halloween party—you know, when Amy Schaffer had rolled her eyes at Gretchen's costume, when she came as JFK post-assassination, with the black suit and blood and bullet holes, and Amy Schaffer said, "You really do look like a man," and Gretchen just turned and grabbed Amy Schaffer's arm and twisted it so hard behind her back that Amy Schaffer's school drama days were ended right there, just like that, so that poor Amy Schaffer had to go around for the next two years milking sympathy, like a fucking martyr wearing her air-cast everywhere, long after it could have possibly been needed for anything recuperative.

Also, well, also Gretchen wasn't the most feminine girl in the world, sincerely. She swore a lot and only listened to punk, like the Misfits and the Ramones and the Descendents, especially when we were in the car, because, although it had a decent stereo for a Ford Escort, there was a tape that had been stuck in the cassette player for about a year now and most of the time that was all it would play, and you had to jab the tape with a pen or nail file to get it to start, and the tape was the same handpicked mix Gretchen had thought was cool a year ago, which according to the label on the tape was what she had called White Protest Rock, version II.

Gretchen's mix-tapes, her music choices, were like these songs that seemed to be all about our lives, but in small random ways that made sense on almost any occasion. Like "Should I Stay or Should I Go Now?" Maybe it meant I should tell Gretchen how I was feeling. Or maybe it meant I should just go home. To me, the tapes were what made me like her, then love her so much: the fact that in between the Misfits and the Specials, she would have a song from the Mamas and the Papas, "Dream a Little Dream of Me" or something like that. Those mix-tapes were the secret soundtrack to how I was feeling or what I thought about almost everything.

Also—and I don't know if I should mention this or not—Gretchen always called other people, even our friends, "douche-bags" or "douche-holes" or "cunts" or "cunt-holes" or "cunt-teasers" or "cunt-wads" or "cunt-heads" or even "cunt-asses," which doesn't even make sense when you think about it, things like that. The way she swore amazed me and again, it probably made me like her a lot more than any other girl I had ever met because she didn't ever seem to mind hanging out with me.

OK, so the thing of it was, the Homecoming Dance was like in three weeks and I hadn't asked anyone and I wanted to ask Gretchen, but I hadn't for good reasons: one, I didn't want her to know I liked-her-liked-her; two, I knew she liked Tony Degan, this white power dude; and also—and this is the worst thing so I hate to admit it—but well, I didn't want the photographs. You know how they make you take your picture and everything? I didn't want photographs of me at Homecoming with a fat girl so that in fifty years I'd have to be reminded of what a loser I was because, well, I hoped things in the future were going to change for me.

"Do you want to go get something to eat?" Gretchen asked. "I am fucking starving, because I don't know if you noticed or not, but I'm a big fat cow."

"Whatever," I said, turning the radio down so we could talk. "Where do you want to go eat? Haunted Trails?"

Haunted Trails was on 79th Street, this monster-movie-themed miniature golf course and video arcade, really the only place we or any of the other stoners and punks hung out. "No, wait, forget it," she said.

"All those kids'll be there and I look so gross. I'm supposed to be on this diet where I only eat white foods, it's like racist or something. Seriously. I am disgusted with myself, you know? I practically *am* a boy. Look at me. I practically have chest hair. I could join the football team or something."

"Shut up," I said. "You just said that so I'd say how you look OK, so I'm not even saying it."

"Oh, you figured me out, douche-bag. No, I mean it, look at me: I'm practically a boy; I practically have a dick." And as she slowed the crappy blue Escort to a stop at the next light, she bunched the front of her jeans up so it looked like she had an erection. "Look, look, my god, I have an erection! I've got blue balls! Oh, they hurt! I need help! Give me some porn, hurry! Come on, let's go rape some cheerleaders! Oh, they hurt!"

I laughed, looking away.

"Forget it, though, seriously. I am so disgusted with myself. Hey, did I tell you that I'm in love with Tony Degan again?"

"What?" I asked. "Why don't you forget him? He's like fucking twenty-six. And a white power asshole. And, I dunno, that should be enough."

"I'm not really in love with him. I'd just like for him to totally de-virginize me."

"What?"

"You know, just have some meathead who doesn't give a shit about you, just get it over with, you know, so you wouldn't have to talk to him ever again? That way, it wouldn't be like uncomfortable afterwards."

"Yeah, I could see how being like raped by some white power dude wouldn't be uncomfortable."

"Exactly," she said. "That's why you're like my best girlfriend."

"Gretchen, you know I'm not a girl, right?"

"I know, but if I think of you as a guy, then I have to worry about what I eat in front of you."

"But I don't care how you look," I said, and I knew I was lying.

two

i am in love with a white power thug. tony degan. tony degan, you're all i can think of. i know you're a burnout. i know you're a racist jag-off. but i can't stop thinking about you. the way you smile, like you're already unsnapping my bra, i don't know, you're all i think about. you make me feel ok. you make me feel less lonely. i think about you and i know i'll never be lonely. no one's going to make me feel gross. no one's ever going to call me fatty again. tony degan. tony degan. the next time. the next time i'm alone with you i'm going to let you do it. i'm gonna let you do anything you want to do.

A N.R.(a new mix-tape) ☐ON ☐OFF	B N.R.(for ?) ☐ON ☐OFF
texas chainsaw massacre by the ramones	hope by the descendents
safe european home by the clash	punk rock girl by the dead milkmen
bottom of the bottomless pit by the dead milkmen	bikeage by the descendents
stuart by the dead milkmen	I'm not a loser by the descendents
police and thieves by the clash	clean sheets by the descendents
a message to rudy by the specials	ask me by the smiths
last caress by the misfits	vampira by the misfits
american nightmare by the misfits	suburban home by the descendents
today your love, tomorrow the world by the ramones	
wasted by black flag	? some other black flag

three

At the video arcade later, Gretchen was crying. It was something I'd never seen before in my life. "What's wrong?" I asked. I was in the middle of a high-scoring game of Phantom Racer and not really listening. I turned and saw her cheeks were pink and shiny with tears, and she was biting her bottom lip to keep from sobbing. She had on her black hoodie and in the light it looked like her bright pink hair was washing away to white-blond again. I hate to say it, but thinking about it now, standing there with her arms crossed and looking sad, looking down, with the flashing lights from Galaga and Bonn Scott from the great AC/DC wailing about "TNT" through the arcade speakers, all of it mixing in with the *click, click* of the air hockey machine and the blips and buzzes and outer space noises from the other video games, well, I dunno, she looked really gentle standing there. Real pretty.

"Tony Degan asked me to go for a ride with him," she finally said.

"So?" I said, looking back at the blinking screen.

"So, I didn't."

"So?"

"So, I just saw some fucking skank making out with him."

"So? Big deal." I shrugged my shoulders and zoomed past a stalled-out race car, downshifting to regain speed, but two red-eyed pixilated demons lurched into my path. I looked over and Gretchen was gone. In a moment then, from the parking lot outside, I could hear someone let out a scream. I finished that level and watched as my score was totaled. Some dick with the name RAD1 had blown all of my old scores and it seemed pretty pointless to even try for first place, because RAD1 had to be some retarded video game genius who worked for the video game company, you know, kind of like The Who's Tommy? I mean, who scores 1,500,200 points anyways? Retarded video game playing geniuses. I dunno. I heard the scream from the parking lot again and since my score wasn't shit, I just turned and walked away.

Outside, it was very bright in the daylight and also very quiet. I had to cover my eyes to let them adjust to the sun, which was just starting to go down. It was around five o'clock. Outside, the Haunted Trails Miniature Golf and Amusement Arcade was pretty much empty. There were all the usual weird horror-themed miniature golf obstacles—the Creature from the Black Lagoon, Hole 3, the green monster rising out of the middle of a blue-green swamp, a coffin with a crappy plastic mechanical hand that rose and fell sporadically, dancing skeletons that you had to putt past—but no one was really around. Some dad and his two little girls were arriving at Hole 8, which was a big wooden haunted castle, in which you had to hit the ball through the drawbridge. The dad was lining up his shot; he had a shiny black patch over his left eye. They all looked like they had been in some kind of accident. Both of the little girls had bandages on their faces and one had a broken arm. It made me wonder for a minute. Then one of the girls kicked a blue golf ball with the tip of her shoe into the hole and they all laughed. *Everything is good when your dad bothers to be around*, I thought to myself. Across from the miniature golf course, some overweight jocks were hitting balls in the "fast pitch" batting cages. One guy had on an American flag baseball hat and a T-shirt that said "One Tequila, Two Tequila, Three Tequila, Floor." He knocked the hell out of an inside pitch and shouted, "He shoots, he scores!" and I decided I did not like that. Across from the batting cages, a Mexican guy was selling hairy-looking hot dogs at the Spooky Snack Shop. There were exactly two fat kids speeding along on the go-cart drag way behind that; they were twins in yellow paper birthday hats. They both had the same joyful expression on their round, tubby faces and I thought how nice it would be to be a kid again. But not fat. At the gates, there was the giant plastic Frankenstein statue rising up to the sky, brandishing his axe. His expression seemed to say, *Yes, I am just as lonely up here*. I waved to him and walked around back.

I lit up a cigarette and looked across the parking lot to where all the stoners hung out. I was trying smoking—what the hell, everyone else did it. I sucked in a mouthful and coughed like a war veteran, then flicked the cigarette behind me, doing my best strut across the parking lot. At the end of the lot there were two or three cool-looking cars: a rebuilt blue metallic-flake Nova, an Impala which was rusty but still sweet, and two decent-looking vans. The guys with the best mustaches and the best cars all hung out in the parking lot. They were kids who were still in high school but because of their fine mustaches and fine cars got some pussy and looked old enough to buy beer. Also, there were older guys like Tony Degan, who had to be like twenty-six but still hung out with high school kids, you know, to sell them dope and talk shit and to try and get some teenage trim. Tony did well, mostly because he was older and knew what to do to get a girl to believe whatever it was he was saying with lines like, "Hey, I really feel like I can open up with you," while jamming his hand down the poor girl's pants. Or so I had heard anyway.

As I got closer to the lot, I saw Bobby B.'s purple wizard van and he and Tony Degan were standing in front of it, leaning against the hood, laughing. Bobby B. was a kid from my street, a senior, a year older than me, with long black hair, gold sunglasses, and acid-washed jeans. He would sit out in his garage all night, smoking and drinking and trying to get the goddamn starter on his van to fire. The van, a '77 Dodge, looked good—it was bright purple and had this magnificent wizard airbrushed on one side of it—but it ran like shit. But it was still a van, his van, a good-looking wizard van. Sitting in the glove compartment, Bobby B. always had about five pairs of girls' underwear, from girls he had made it with. He called it his "trophy case." I would open the glove box and the panties would all seem to sing a hymn to me—*Hallelujah!*—glowing with golden light. Also, with much gratitude, I must mention Bobby B. was the one who had turned me on to AC/DC when he loaned me *High Voltage* in eighth grade. For that, I would be eternally grateful.

Beside Bobby B. was Tony Degan, who, on the other hand was, like I said, maybe twenty-five, twenty-six, tall but lanky, wearing a yellow T-shirt that said, "My grandparents went to the Bahamas and all I got was this stupid T-shirt." He was smoking and nodding and shaking his head. That was what he did: nodded to himself and smiled, like there was a joke about you that you weren't really getting. He looked high most of the time—maybe he was, I dunno. He had blond hair, which was longer in back, combed-up with grease of some kind, and two black wristbands just above his hands, though he wasn't a jock or in a band, but he had that look, like 1-2-3, he could kick your ass.

As soon as I made it around the corner, I heard the scream again and saw Gretchen holding some girl I didn't know in a headlock. Like always, Gretchen was winning. The other girl's eyes were big and bugged-out with panic. She was very skinny and very slutty-looking. She had on spiderweb nylons, which were torn, and a black jean jacket with a huge Megadeth patch. She was on her knees and having a hard time breathing. Drool was pouring over Gretchen's forearm and onto the cement. It was not very cool.

"Dude, what's the malfunction here?" I asked.

"Brian Oswald, what's up with you, dude?" Bobby B. asked with a nod. He had a nice mustache coming in: thin, but it extended around his narrow lips all the way down to his chin, biker-style. I had been trying for months to grow a mustache but there was nothing; not anything: no stubble, no shadow, not anything. I was a junior in high school who still looked like a junior-high kid. "So what's fucking going on?" Bobby B. asked again, slapping my hand.

"You know, nothing," I said.

"You break that high score on Phantom Racer yet?" he asked.

"Not yet."

"Fuck. They must have some fucking expert come in and reset it every week."

"Yeah," I said. "So what's the deal here?"

With an amazing thud, Gretchen slammed the girl's head off the side of a parked LeBaron. "Ohhhhhh," everyone moaned.

"Fucking chicks," Bobby B. said.

"Yeah," I said. "Chicks." I turned to Gretchen and shouted, "Dude, Gretchen, fucking relax."

Like always, she just ignored me.

"Aw, let her go already," Tony mumbled, still grinning. He ran his hand through his dirty blond hair, which was thick with grease, and rubbed his own neck. "She didn't do nothing."

Gretchen's chubby face was pink, turning red, and she gave in finally, shoving the girl against the hood of somebody's station wagon. She held her finger up to the girl's face and said, "The next time . . . The next time, your ass is grass."

Everybody standing around said, "Ewwwwww," and clapped,

and Gretchen picked up her hoodie and wiped her nose, which was running. The other girl limped away, her mouth bleeding, while Tony Degan kept on laughing and nodding.

"You're fucking dead," the girl shouted from across the safety of the parking lot. "I'm gonna get my friends and we're gonna kick your ass."

Gretchen just turned to me and said, "Let's fucking go already," and I nodded, without a word, which was my way at the time, because I chose to live my life like fucking Zatoichi the blind samurai, you know, the samurai dude from the '60s movies? I was going through that phase, watching nothing but samurai movies and horror flicks. That was some serious metal, you know, the blind swordsman with his flashing sword. If you don't know, you need to check those movies out. Anyway, I was deadly fucking silent—*deadly fucking silent*—most of the time. I was a shy kid and I was afraid what I said sounded stupid, so I hardly ever said anything. I was the third wheel. Fifth wheel? I was the fucking wheel you didn't really need, but I still hung around. I thought maybe my silence would one day impress somebody. As of yet, it hadn't done much for me. Most people, when they thought of Brian Oswald, probably said, "Who?" Then someone might say, "That dude, the quiet one that is always hanging around." Then the other person would probably say, "Who?" again. I was invisible to most people, I guess. For example, when Gretchen and I hopped back in the Ford Escort, the radio was working—a one-in-a-million chance—and we motored away to the tune of "Dirty Deeds" by the great AC/DC, before Gretchen switched the radio station on me without asking.

four

American History

10/3/90

I. Causes of the Revolutionary war were many
  A. results of the French and Indian War, 1755 to 1763
    1. American colonies think they helped British defeat French
    2. King George III thinks colonies owe the British for protection
  B. taxation without representation
    1. No elected representatives in Parliament
    2. Boston Tea Party, 1773
  C. the Intolerable Acts and the Quebec Act
  D. also many funny fucking stupid white powdery wigs were fought over
  E. 1775: minutemen vs. the redcoats
  F. Bad-ass names for a metal band, if I ever have the chance to be in one
    1. The Unwieldy Hammer of Thor
    2. Your Rotting Fucking Oracle
    3. The Corpse Kings! Must Unite!
    4. Fear the Thunder and Lightning of the Master Druid
    5. The Most Deadly Spells
    6. Hail Skeletor, like the skull dude from He-Man
    7. The Lansdale Barbarians
    8. Operation: Headwound
    9. Dr. Killbot
    10. All of Maggotkind
  G. the Bad-ass covers set list
    1. opening song? has to be Iron Man by Ozzy

2. Back in Black by AC/DC

3. Search and Destroy by Metallica

4. Communication Breakdown by Led Zeppelin

5. Paranoid by Ozzy

6. if you had a fucking amazing guitarist,
   then Sweet Child of Mine by GNR

7. Highway to Hell by AC/DC

8. Too Fast for Love by Mötley Crüe

9. again, if you had an amazing guitarist,
   Hot for Teacher by Van Halen

10. end the set with Cum on Feel the Noise by Quiet Riot

five

At her high school, Gretchen was punk rock and had a reputation for beating other girls up. We all got into trouble back then, but Gretchen was known as the girl who liked to fight. It was why I liked her so much, maybe. Being punk back then for most kids meant the way you dressed mostly, not what records you played—maybe that's the way it still is in some places, I dunno. All the kids who had been geeks or fags or nerds or wastoids in junior high started dressing fucked-up when they hit high school, with the torn clothes and safety pins and makeup and dirty hair, and not one of them had ever heard of the MC5 or New York Dolls, but what it gave some of them was a group identity and also some courage, maybe. Kids in junior high who had once gotten the crap kicked out of them on a daily basis, well, now they would get pointed at and laughed at, but no one would fuck with them and so they didn't have to take anyone's shit ever again. Being punk meant having something to fight against. That's what happened with Gretchen. By her junior year at Mother McCauley Catholic Academy for Young Women, she had been involved in at least five full-on fistfights and suspended three times already. She routinely received detentions for her failure to adhere to the uniform; she had been sent home several times to change her hair and makeup and clothes. She was still serving demerits for having her hair dyed pink, and had to spend time in detention every Tuesday. It was what made me like hanging out with her, I guess. She did the things I wished I could do but didn't have the guts to, maybe. Like with everything.

OK, so the fourth in-school suspension Gretchen got—the one she always talked about—was for fucking up Stacy Bensen. Stacy Bensen, the girl who had run for president of student council under the motto *Stacy Bensen—why? Because you're too lazy to do it*, and had won. Stacy had made the bad mistake of calling Gretchen "a fat dyke." After it happened, Gretchen told the fucking story so many times—at the counter of Snackville Junction, in a booth at Wojos, in the crappy Escort, at parties, to her sister, to my brother, to my little sister, to her dad, in the parking lot of Haunted Trails, to people we didn't even know—that I could tell exactly what happened, probably better than she could tell it, maybe. Also, when she told it she usually left out the most important part, which I will not do, I promise you. OK, so it went down like this:

One day after remedial English class, a period in which all Gretchen did was write her favorite band names in black ink on her arms and legs—ramones, the descendents, the clash—Gretchen decided that she'd had it, she did not like school. None of us liked school—well, I did, but I would have never admitted it to anybody—but for Gretchen it was worse. Why? Because of the way she looked. That's what she said anyway. Other girls hated her, even just the sight of her, not just because she was punk, but because she was punk and got away dressing that way a lot because her mom had died two years before so all the teachers and school people kind of left her alone.

In Catholic high school, that was crucial, the way you looked. As Gretchen was stomping down the hall—her fucking black combat boots clomping along the tile, her boot chains rattling, the sounds of her plastic and leather bracelets making noise like ringing bells, sweeping up and down her arm like a lot of loose change—one super-prim girl in a Catholic school uniform after the other stopped at their lockers to stare and shoot back dirty fucking looks. What they saw when they saw Gretchen was this: an overweight, baby-faced junior, seventeen years old, with long blond and pinkish-red bangs and the sides and back of her head nearly shaved, heavy black eye makeup and safety pins and patches for The Exploited and DRI, bands she didn't even listen to, but the patches looked cool, so anyway, patches and combat boots and a black leather jacket with the Misfits skull logo which had been hand-painted on with a bottle of Wite-Out stolen from her dad's desk, and hands, hands full of silver, spiked rings, clenched at both sides, anticipating a fight, like always.

After class, Gretchen always met Kim, our friend, at her locker. Kim was also punk rock: a short girl with long bony arms and a sharp narrow face, always with at least five or six hundred hickies on her neck and along the top of her chest, blood red hair, and a dozen piercings in her ear, and now in addition to all that, an adorable red sore at the corner of her lip which she proudly called her "herpe." I liked Kim a lot, but she scared the hell out of me. She was very attractive but a little fucking crazy. OK, so Kim turned to Gretchen, putting on her jean jacket, and asked, "What's your malfunction, douche-bag?" which was what she always said when you met her someplace.

"I fucking hate school," Gretchen said, and they headed down the hallway. Gretchen always walked with her head down; Kim always kind of skipped and whistled and knocked books out of other girls' hands when she had the chance. Gretchen curled her lip and glared at two beauty-queen freshmen, their perfect fucking blue kneesocks pulled up high, their green sweaters tied about their waists, and their young, soap-opera-star faces already glowing. The two freshmen were reapplying lipstick in their compact mirrors and laughing and pointing behind their reflections at Kim and Gretchen. Gretchen did the balk to make them jump, taking one step in their direction. The girls turned away quick, hiding behind their locker doors. The shorter one, with darker hair and these recently plucked eyebrows, made a mousy squeak. Kim flicked them off and Gretchen let out a laugh—Ha!—and turned, glad she had done it. It was in that moment—that second—that she took a left down D hall and accidentally bumped into Stacy Bensen.

Stacy Bensen.

Stacy Bensen, a senior; a student council snob, blond hair, dyed a shade blonder, always in a bouncy bob; thick red lipstick with black lip liner that accentuated supple lips that every dude couldn't help but notice, which made you feel kind of sad for her, the way you feel sad for strippers and girls who do porno flicks because they're so pretty that no one will ever see them as anything more and it begins to destroy them maybe; blue eye shadow with matching blue sparkle nail polish that was always flawless and hinted at the fact that Stacy Bensen had never worked a part-time job, or any job, a day in her life; a green cardigan sweater, tied neatly about her neck or waist; and the most fucking darling brown penny loafers, perfectly accessorized with two bright copper pennies, which sparkled just less than Stacy's glowing, makeup-ad, all-around-American-girl, picture-perfect face. Also, leg warmers of various patterns and colors. Also, as I was often told, her remarks in ethics class about how girls who got abortions should be prosecuted as child-murders. Also, as overheard, her tendency to address other girls in school as "girls," as in the sentence, "Girls, we need a couple of more volunteers for the blood drive." Also, and altogether her worst feature: her buttons. We had gone to grammar school together and even then she wore a different homemade button almost every week: *Proud to be a Princess. Go with God. Sensible and Celibate.* Here was a girl who, in her fucking over-emphatic, rehearsed tone of voice, seemed to say, *Everyone around me is a fucking subhuman.* Here was a girl who, in small, measured, perfect movements—a blink of her glittering fucking blue eyes, this smiling wistful sneer, her giggle sweet as someone ringing a tea bell —seemed to whisper, *I am better than you in every way.* And maybe she was right because her looks and smarts and charms always dared you to argue, but you never did because what did you have to argue with when you looked the way you did?

That day, Stacy Bensen was wearing a button that said, *Beam me up, Scotty, there's no intelligent life down here.* So in the hall there, at the end of the day, between the noise of last classes—*Are you going to play practice?* and *Pick me up at seven,* and *He gave us so much homework again*—the smell of hair spray and fucking perfume thickening with repeated after-school maintenance, Gretchen turned and bumped into Stacy Bensen and Stacy Bensen stopped and looked at Gretchen and said, "Why don't you watch where you're going, you fat dyke?"

OK, cut.

OK, if you knew Gretchen and could like read her mind, here's what you would know already:

Cut to:

Five years old, Gretchen, a ballerina in this tumbling class. OK, Gretchen, five years old, tumbling. She couldn't do a somersault because of her weight, you know, and all the other little girls would laugh, and there was this mean-faced little brunette doll in her class in particular, who one time pointed at Gretchen and said, "She's fat," and when it was time for the ending recital, Gretchen was told to just run across the stage while the other girls did their handsprings and windmills and front flips and shit like that. Instead, backstage,

Gretchen bit the other little girl and was sent home crying.

And:

Eight years old this time, Gretchen shopping for a Halloween costume in the aisle of Osco Drugs, the rows and rows of plastic masks attached to plastic one-piece suits—Superman and Batman and Wonder Woman and a Fairy Princess and Frankenstein and Dracula and all the rest—and her mother suggesting that perhaps Gretchen would prefer a Frankenstein to a Princess costume because the Frankenstein had just a little more room.

Then:

In junior high, someone spray-painting *FAT-ASS* on the side of her garage and Gretchen watching her dad, Mr. D., trying to hide his embarrassment by quickly painting over it with a shade of brown a little too light, and Gretchen and me and everybody seeing the spot every day as she came home until the day she moved, everyone knowing the spot was there, still there, and why.

So:

So when Stacy Bensen said, "Why don't you watch where you're going, you fat dyke?" Gretchen turned around and grabbed for a part of Stacy's head, getting ahold of her fucking golden-yellow ponytail, and pulled hard until some of it came out, some of the hair tearing loose from the soft white scalp like the magical golden thread used to stitch together some lucky princess' enchanted fucking wish, and then Gretchen, holding the girl by the front of her blouse, began pummeling Stacy Bensen's face, breaking the fancy aquiline nose in one pro-nounced crack, followed by a dollop of bright red blood, over which Gretchen yelled, as loud as she could, "Why don't you suck my fucking dick, Barbie?"

In a moment, the lezbo gym teacher in her blue jogging suit, Mrs. Crone, tackled Gretchen around the waist and then the elderly school nurse hurried to Stacy Bensen's side and all the girls stood around shocked, their tender and holy virginal hearts beating hard, all of them open-mouthed and struck dumb. Here, here was the part Gretchen almost always left out: For all the fights she had been in before with tough stoner chicks, heavy mascara streaked down angular faces, in random basement parties, or in the back of deserted parking lots while their boyfriends hooted or clapped or looked on frightened, maybe; or with the preppy girls, strangleholds around long, elegant necks and noses that would later have to be retouched by expensive plastic surgery; or with that one tall, gooney girl from the volleyball team who had tons and tons of brown hair all along her forearms and who was so overly fierce and manly; for all that scratching and swearing and hair-pulling, for all that punching and hissing and biting, this was the first time—the very first time—Gretchen had ever felt bad about what she did, the first time she felt worse after it all had happened, and still, she didn't know the reason. But to me, looking back on it now, it's easy: Like Gretchen being born fat, it wasn't Stacy Bensen's fault she had been born pretty.

six

American History can suck it. The U.S.A. can suck it. The Thirteen Colonies can suck it. George Washington can suck it. The British can suck it. The Red-coats can suck it. Muskets can suck it. That's good. Muskets can suck it. Cannons can suck it. Benjamin Franklin can suck it. Roanoke can suck it. Jamestown can suck it. The Quakers, the Pilgrims, and the Indians can suck it. Early American trading posts can suck it. The Boston Tea Party can suck it. The Intolerable Acts can suck it. Bro. Flanagan and his bald liver spots can suck it. His bald liver spots can suck it separately, also. Bro. Flanagan's overhead projections can suck it. His timelines can suck it. Billy Lowery in the front of the room who has to ask fifteen million fucking questions can suck it. Jim Gallagher behind me, jabbing me in the back of my neck with his pen can SUCK IT! These walls can suck it. These desks can suck it. These books can suck it. The ceiling can also suck it. The other jags in this classroom can suck it. This whole school can suck it. From top to bottom, they can suck it. The teachers can suck it. The Holy fucking Brothers can suck it. The sportos and jocks can suck it. The football players, baseball players, soccer players, wrestlers, runners, the meatheads and their varsity letters can suck it. The student council wanna-be fag politicians can suck it for being on student council and being fag politician wanna-bes. The rich, suburban kids with their brand-new cars can suck it. The dirty, inner-city dope dealers looking me up and down like I'm a pussy can suck it. The other marching band kids can suck it. The stoners, the burnouts, the metalheads, the druggies, the gangster black kids, the gangster Hispanic kids, the whiggers, the nerds, the geeks, the fags, the dweebs, the dorks, the wusses, the pusses, the flamers, the jag-offs, the chronic masturbators, the freaks, all of them can all suck it.

The whole fucking school can just fucking suck it.

I looked down at my digital calculator watch, then I looked up at the clock at the front of the classroom. Both of them said 1:13. American History, 6th Period, Bro. Flangan's room, Brother Rice Catholic High School, Chicago, IL, USA, North America, Planet Earth. Two more hours of this fucking shit. I sighed, then dug into my back pocket and checked out the mix-tape Gretchen had made me:

(I am a) Rabbit/The Lemonheads

Devil's Whorehouse/The Misfits

Gimme Some Head/GG Allin

Dear Lover/Social D.

Lover's Rock/The Clash

Day After Day/The Violent Femmes

I got it suddenly. All of the songs were about fucking. I looked at the side of the tape, where the title was: I Got Pubic Lice. I kind of laughed out loud in class, then covered it quick with a cough. I looked at my watch and then at the clock once more. I started at my list again.

seven

Like I said, I heard about everything after school. In the parking lot of Mother McCauley, where Gretchen parked her crappy blue car and where I'd meet to bum a ride home every day after class, I sat on the hood and listened, watching as Kim and Gretchen re-enacted the whole Stacy Bensen fight thing: the other girls giving them looks in the hall, Gretchen remembering being a fat kid, even with her shouting the "Suck my dick, Barbie" thing. I just listened and nodded. Whatever happened that day, I'd have to hear recounted in minute detail before we could go home. I really didn't give a shit about Stacy Bensen. I knew her but I didn't have a problem with her. I wasn't punk rock at all; I didn't go looking for fights. Like I said, I was into metal and hard rock like AC/DC, Mötley Crüe, Metallica, stuff like that mostly. I guess I was kind of a pussy. In high school, I dressed the same every day: lame—blue flannel shirt over the white button-down shirt and black tie I had to wear, black pants, and black dress shoes that were scuffed almost gray. I had dirty-brown hair that hung in my eyes, like a mop I guess, and also my huge brown plastic frame glasses which I needed to wear because my eyesight was so weak. Also, I had a wicked-bad case of acne—on my face, on my neck, even down my back. Like I said, I guess I was a quiet kind of kid. There wasn't anything punk about me in the least. I always thought the punk kids were a bunch of fucking phonies; I thought they tried too fucking hard, maybe. I mean, I had grown up with Gretchen and Kim—we had been losers together in junior high on the Bloom Junior High Math Team, in which Gretchen had been the club president—and that was the only reason we hung out anymore, I guess: We had gotten used to being losers all together, maybe.

"And I got a note sent home," Gretchen bragged, digging in her school bag, "and a three-day in-school suspension." She rifled through her folders and pens, found the blue paper note, and held it up proud—over her head, like it was a scholarship or an aced test or something. I just nodded and looked away.

"Are you guys going straight to Gretchen's house?" I asked.

"I got to go to work," Kim said.

"Well, I dunno. I don't really wanna go home," I said.

"What's your malfunction, Brian, you pussy?" Kim asked, and shoved her finger into my chest. I looked down at her shiny black combat boots, then over at Gretchen, who was wearing dark black sunglasses and still waving the letter up high, and then I lowered my head.

"I've got a serious problem," I mumbled.

"What's *your* serious problem?" Gretchen asked, laughing.

"Nothing," I said.

"What? What is it?" she asked.

"Nothing."

"Just fucking say it," Kim hissed. "What's your fucking problem?"

"My dad. It's kind of weird. He started sleeping down in the basement," I muttered, and then lowered my head.

"Well, what the fuck does that mean?" Kim asked.

"I don't know. Before I went to bed, like a few nights ago, it was late, you know, and I saw him on the couch and then he saw me and he said, 'It's OK, Brian. I'm going to be sleeping down here for a while.'"

"Well, do you think they're going to finally get split ?" Kim asked.

"I dunno know, I guess so," I said.

At night, my pops, who worked at the Tootsie Roll plant and who, no matter what, always smelled like chocolate candy, had started sleeping downstairs, where my room was also located. I liked my dad a lot; he was quiet like me. When I was a kid, and even now, he'd come home from work and hold his hand out and make me guess—*which one?*—and then he'd drop a few Tootsie Rolls into my palm. My mom said that was why my acne was so bad. My dad had acne, too. It didn't bother me, because my dad was always singing and telling corny jokes. He would come home with bags and bags of Tootsie Rolls and we'd build these enormous structures—the Eiffel Tower, the Sphinx, all from Tootsie Rolls—for their annual Employee Father and Son Contest. Sometimes, he'd take off his glasses and wipe them and stare off into the future like he had something important to say, but then he wouldn't say anything, just like me. And now he was sleeping in the basement, alone and lonely, and it made me feel awful. I didn't know what was going on with him exactly.

About my mother, well, I don't want to say too much except this: When I was in grammar school at Queen of Martyrs, there was this pumpkin-carving contest every year. And like every year my older brother Tim and I would win, because our mother had carved the pumpkins for us. We really didn't want her to, you know, she just kind of made us. So there is this black-and-white photo of me in like third grade and Tim is in sixth grade, and our picture is being taken for winning the pumpkin-carving contest again and he is standing on one end of this long table and I'm standing on the other, and there's all these other kids in between us, and Tim's pumpkin is this really beautifully hand-painted Indian Chief and mine is Dracula with bared fangs and they have exactly the same features, the Chief and Dracula, because my mom did them both, and no one, none of the teachers or principals or whatever, noticed or wanted to say anything. That was just how my mom was about a lot of things, I guess.

"Dad, aren't you going to get lonely sleeping down here?" I asked him, standing in the dark, watching his face switch colors with the flicker of the TV.

"It's OK, Bri, thanks for asking. There's plenty of room down here, son. I bet there's a good movie on tonight."

"All right. Well, I mean, what about mom?"

"Oh, well, she keeps getting those hot flashes. It'll just be easier to sleep down here for a while."

"Oh," I said. "Well, OK, goodnight."

"Goodnight, son."

That night, I heard him out there snoring, watching an old Western, the sounds of shootouts and gunfights on TV echoing with him mumbling in his sleep. I felt kind of bad for him. I mean, there he was, his soft face, his dirty-blond hair, his work boots standing at the foot of the couch, him breathing through his nose, snoring loudly the way I did. I saw that he still had his glasses on, so I kind of crept out there and just stared at him and slowly, I guess, lifted off his glasses. For some reason I tried them on; they fit my face, but the prescription was too strong. But it was funny, him and I having the same size frames, and then I folded the glasses closed and set them along the arm of the couch as carefully as I could, still trying not to wake him. I looked down and felt something under my bare feet and there were like five or six Tootsie Rolls lying in place all around my dad's folded pants, which was kind of funny, and I stood over him for a minute more and I wondered why nothing seemed to be good for anyone over the age of eighteen.

"So, is he gonna move out or what?" Gretchen asked.

"I dunno. He's just sleeping down there for now."

"Did he say anything to you about it?" she asked again.

"Nope," I said. "Not really."

"That's really fucking weird," Gretchen sighed, patting my back.

In a gesture completely unlike Kim, she turned and hugged me, wrapping her thin arms all the way around my neck. I felt her spiky bracelets against the side of my cheek; I smelled the fruity, sticky odor of her styling gel; the bubble-gum sugar of the wad of Bubblicious in her mouth; I felt her small, firm, full-packed breasts against the front of my chest as she squeezed. To be honest, I had lusted after Kim all throughout junior high. I had fantasized about getting in her pants and worse, much worse, but it didn't even feel hot when she was hugging me. It felt bad. It felt bad because she had done it, which must have meant I looked pretty fucking pathetic. I closed my eyes to keep from crying and she just stood there, hugging me like that. And then it happened: She breathed right beside my ear, accidentally, but it was hot and moist, and right away I began to get a full-on erection.

"Dude," Kim said, "are you getting a chubby?"

"No," I said.

"Well, that's what it feels like." She let go of me and leaned against the Escort. "This is why nobody's nice to you, Brian."

"Thanks anyway," I said, and we all climbed inside to get Kim to the mall to work on time.

eight

At school, most of the time all I ever did was make plans for band names of superstar hard rock groups I would one day be part of, coming up with set lists and song titles and making rosters with various band members and everything. Even during band class, a class I was truly embarrassed for having ever taken, because, *Come on, man, marching band? Have you ever seen the Q-tip hats? And funny jackets?* It was also awkward because it was a class we shared with girls from Mother McCauley, girls who, nine times out of ten, were more nerdy and socially retarded and gangly than me, because, *Come on, what hot teenage girl plays the oboe or coronet in her spare time,* right? It was the only reason I had signed up for the class, the girls, I mean, and I couldn't have been more mistaken. So when I was supposed to be playing the xylophone, following along to the bass clarinet, I would hear the crappy, corny carnival music rising from the worn and misplayed trumpet section directly behind me and be thinking of me, rocking out, with a superstar backup band, in front of a huge stadium of screaming, braless, well-endowed female fans.

Like my new masterpiece, which was so good it begged to be committed to the page: *In Gods We Thrust,* the greatest hard rock album by the greatest hard rock band ever, The Young Gods, featuring Tommy Lee on drums, Eddie Van Halen on lead guitar, Izzy Stradlin on rhythm guitar, Cliff Burton on bass (if he had been alive, but since he was dead, Geddy Lee would have to play bass even though RUSH fucking sucked), also Eddie Van Halen on keyboards, and Brian Oswald, lead vocals/xylophone.

1. Rip it Like You Should
2. Something Wicked this Way Comes
3. In Gods We Thrust (title track)

4. Everyday Survivor, the ballad
5. Lay Down for My Love
6. Nobody Has to Know (You Like It)
7. Under the Gun (the controversial suicide song)
8. Beauty is in the Eye of the Beholder And You've Got my Eye
9. Ain't Nowhere to Go, Ain't Nowhere to Run from my Love

nine

I had bad feelings. At the time, we were driving back from dropping Kim off at the mall. I was looking through Gretchen's bag for some gum or candy when I found this fucking note Gretchen had written and I held it up and started reading it, Tony Degan. Tony Degan. The next time. The next time I'm alone with you, I'm going to let you do it. I'm gonna let you do anything you want to do, and Gretchen fucking flipped out and began screaming. "I Want to Be Sedated" was playing on the crappy Escort radio as Gretchen pulled up to a stoplight, tearing the note from my hands, punching me, still yelling.

Just then, two fucking motorheads in a red Trans-Am pulled up beside us at the stoplight and started blaring "Smoke on the Water" by the most god-awful classic wanker rock band of all time, Deep Purple, and then, like always, they started making comments about Gretchen's hair, which was a very fucking bad idea.

"Nice hair!" the driver laughed, giving Gretchen the thumbs-up, elbowing his buddy. The driver had a fantastic mono-brow and an acid-washed jean jacket that was cut at the shoulders to fit like a real super-looking vest—except it wasn't super-looking, it was lame and trashy.

"Did you do that to yourself on purpose?" the other guy shouted, raising his hands in feigned confusion. He was taller, with mirrored sunglasses and an American flag bandana. The comments these two meatheads made were typical fucking south side Chicago: totally obvious, totally pointless, even a little hypocritical, considering both of the dudes had serious shoulder-length, well-coiffed mullets any carnie operating a Tilt-a-Whirl would envy.

"Go back to fucking California!" the one with the mono-brow shouted, revving the engine a little.

"Freakshow!" the other added, pointing at us, as if we didn't know who he had been fucking with; as if he was saying, by pointing his finger, *Yes, you! I am making it clear now that I am insulting you! Even though I am only a night stocker at the Radio Shack; even though I am twenty-eight and have an illegitimate kid and bills from the white T-top Camaro I wrecked; even though I am a glue-huffing idiot who blows all my cash on coke whenever I can get it, you are the ones who are to be made fun of because, to me, you are funny-looking, and this is the best thing I can do to insult you: me, pointing my finger like this, so I will keep pointing.* And he held his finger out like that, jabbing at us and pointing again and again until I turned my head and looked back at Gretchen.

The reason it was such a fucking bad idea to make fun of Gretchen's hair was because it had taken four months for her to dye it pink, because the Manic Panic she had bought wouldn't take, and she had tried everything—bleached it, peroxided it, we even drove out to this mall an hour away in the suburbs to a Sally Beauty Supply to get this crazy industrial strength whitener, but she had left it in too long and pieces of her hair had broken off—and finally, after months of trying, she had gotten it right and now it was a cool-looking, bright, outer-space pink.

If you want to go through the trouble and if you want to know how to dye your hair right, here's how, for fuck's sake:

First off, you really need two people. Don't do it alone. Why? Because that makes a fucking mess and is stupid. Also:
    a. A rag or shitty towel.
    b. Some plastic baggies.
    c. Some nail polish remover or Sea Breeze skin cleanser.
    d. Vaseline or some other petroleum jelly—this is fucking key!
    e. A disposable brush or comb.

It's simple enough once you know how to do it:
    1. Do it in a place with tile floors, like a bathroom or basement or garage.
    2. Take off all your good clothes and maybe go topless.
    3. Put the towel around your neck to keep the shit from dripping all over and making a general fucking mess.

4. Put the Vaseline all around your hairline, put globs of it on the top of your ears, back of your neck, and along your forehead all over, especially.

5. If you've got blond hair, cool. If not, you've got to strip your hair first. Dark hair doesn't take that Manic Panic ultra-color hair dye. You can try, and waste your time, but it won't work. Gretchen tried everything—I mean everything: Kool-Aid, food dye—and none of it would take because her hair was too dark. Like I said, we got this industrial stripper at Sally's Beauty Supply at the mall. Do not leave that shit in too long, it will kill your hair. Follow the directions for the hair stripper, wash it once, dry it, etc. It should be almost whitish-yellow. Now you can either buy hair dye gloves or make them out of ziplock bags, using the bags and rubber bands, whatever, just don't be dumb and use your bare hands—Gretchen did and her hands were pink for like three weeks.

6. Put a glob of the color dye on the top of your head and start combing it through. This is where the second person is really helpful, otherwise the back of your head will look like shit.

7. Once it's all rubbed in and your hair is saturated, blow-dry it. Why? I dunno, this is what Kim said to do. Maybe it is supposed to cook it in or something. Wait like an hour.

8. Rinse it, but when you do, stick your head under the faucet instead of taking a fucking shower. If you take a fucking shower, the run-off dye will get all over your face and shit and stain you like a dumbass. Then the next day at school or the mall or whatever, you will look like a fucking poseur. Hold the towel over your face and wash off the shit. Don't shampoo, just rinse it.

9. Use the skin cleanser or nail polish remover to clean up the color stains around your hair line. You're probably gonna have to scrub pretty hard.

10. Take a Polaroid now because it will never look as good as it does right after you rinse it the first time. Expect that your fucking pillow and bed sheets will be ruined, like Gretchen's, which were stained pink, permanently.

11. Why do you want to dye your hair, anyways? To look punk? Don't you know, everyone dyes their hair to look punk? Duh.

OK, back to the mulletheads: Just before the stoplight could change back to green, the driver of the Trans-Am shouted, "Faggots," and Gretchen shouted back, "Douche-bags!" and then she did it: She jumped out of the car and went right up and snapped the Trans-Am's antenna right in two. Their loud, riffing wanker rock vanished immediately—"Come Sail Away" disappearing, the radio going totally silent, totally quiet. The two motorheads, one of them in a black Alabama concert T-shirt, the other in his acid-washed vest, jumped out, flexing their mullets, and both of them began pulling on these black leather weightlifting gloves—they actually had them, these fingerless black leather gloves. When I saw them pull out the gloves, I thought, *Oh shit*, and I didn't know if I should start laughing or start getting very fucking worried. But just then the traffic light turned green and a brown station wagon, which had been cruising along pretty fast, being driven poorly by an old, glassy-eyed man, slammed hard into the back of the Trans-Am. The Trans-Am, which had been idling, spun and screeched and its plastic red fender got crinkled all to hell, the whole car being knocked sideways, totally, completely.

As Gretchen hopped back into the superbad Ford Escort and we sped off, I had one thought and one thought only: *This year. This year everything's fucking changing for the worse for me.*

ten

We lived on the south side of Chicago at the time. Our neighborhood was in bad trouble: brick bungalows in straight, arranged lines, appearing block after block with their small tidy lawns hiding this very quiet intent no one said out loud. You could see it in the uniform mailboxes and many statues of the Virgin Mary and repeated pots of matching flowers; in the white kids playing on their front lawns, parents talking over the fence, retired people raking up their leaves: the same kinds of faces and same kinds of last names, street after street, block after block, house after fucking house. The message to me was clear: *If you're not white, don't fucking cross Western Ave., heading west. Do not do it. Don't come into this neighborhood. Don't drive through, or you're gonna end up hurting bad.*

We lived on the south side, me in Evergreen Park and Gretchen in Mt. Greenwood, two neighborhoods set side by side but split by 103rd Street, in a city world-renowned for its dangerously racist history. There were huge race riots on the south side in the summer of 1919 that left 38 dead, more than 500 injured, and a lot more homeless, that were started by the killing of a black teenager at the 26th Street beach. That seems kind of random and historical, but it wasn't, although I did have to do a history report on it freshman year. Then there was the exploitation and dehumanization of the Pullman porters, poor black youths who were treated so unfairly by the railroad boss that he demanded a slab of concrete be poured over his coffin, out of fear his grave would be later pillaged by angry south side workers. In the last decade Harold Washington, a smart-talking black politician, had run and won the mayoral office, but only after months of all kinds of racial animosity, including an incident in which St. Ben's Catholic Church was defaced with the word "nigger" the night before he came to deliver a campaign speech.

Both of the neighborhoods Gretchen and I lived in were OK, both pretty similar, I guess. They both had houses that were mostly small, brick bungalows in the style which was made popular on the south side in the 1940s. Both neighborhoods were mostly Irish Catholic, both home to the notorious St. Patrick's Day Parade, in which lug-heads from all over would gather to puke green beer in the street. There was an Irish bar every few blocks along 103rd and 111th. I'd see kids all the time, in grammar school and high school, from both neighborhoods, wearing T-shirts and jackets that proudly declared, "South Side Irish."

Evergreen Park was this small town bordered by Chicago on three sides, but it wasn't considered part of the city, even though the same kinds of people lived in both neighborhoods, all of them white and working class, Irish Catholics mostly—not bad people, but not tolerant people either.

The thing was, there were no black people in Evergreen Park and none in Mt. Greenwood either, even though it was still considered part of the city. They were not wanted there or allowed there—nothing. Why? Mt. Greenwood was full of the homes and families of white Chicago firemen and Chicago cops, who always had a real bad reputation for being racist. But it wasn't just a reputation, it was the fucking truth. And that wasn't in 1919 and shit. It wasn't even the '40s. It was fucking 1990. I don't know how they did it, honestly, besides intimidation and threat of force. Maybe that's all they needed.

There were these racist cops and then their kids, growing up on their parents' racial prejudice and increasing frustration—*nigger this, nigger that*—who were running around calling themselves White Power. White Power? These kids had no idea what White Power was, really. At least, I didn't think so. To me, it was a name these idiots associated with the anger they felt, the ignorance. Like calling yourself *punk*; it was just one other label to help create an identity, to give you a sense of purpose. But the White Power kids were tolerated—not only tolerated but fostered, looked past, ignored completely, even when they put some black kid in the hospital for walking past the imaginary racial dividing line that ran along Western Ave. There were some tough kids there, kids who had played football and gotten bored, or had wrestled for a year or two before getting turned on to smoking dope and buying used vans and Cutlasses and Novas, growing their hair long in the back, wearing their acid-washed jean jackets, Nike high-tops, S.O.D. T-shirts, that sort of thing. Most of them were into metal or hardcore—you would hear it blasting from their cars as they howled past you, "Kill Yourself!"—though none of them looked any different than any of the other burnouts we knew. The White Power kids tolerated the other stoners and the punks in our neighborhood as long as they were white, I guess, even if they looked like fruits, and for the most part none of them ever bothered Gretchen or Kim or said anything about how they dressed. I guess they thought the punk kids were all pretty harmless. We listened to some of the same music like the Misfits and Samhain, and some girls dated some of the punk guys and some of the White Power kids, so they didn't have a problem with me, or Kim or Gretchen, considering how goofy they looked. But when I saw Tony Degan and his other cro-mag thugs, I don't know. I'd dig my hands into my pockets in fists of kung-fu-movie-type rage, but not say anything and eventually just walk away.

Sometimes driving around in the blue crappy Escort after school, we would see black people who had been stopped by the Evergreen Park cops and were being hassled, their cars searched and them being frisked, just for driving through. I am not lying about this shit, seriously. Once, I had gone with my older brother to play basketball up at Hamlin Park—basketball, which I sucked at but my older brother Tim made me play because he said I had to do something to prove I wasn't really turning into a girl, which I think my dad made him do. Well, while my brother and I were playing, two Evergreen Park cops came up and said, "You better not steal those basketball nets like a bunch of niggers," and one cop hit his nightstick into his hand and the other nodded, and then both walked off. And that story is fucking true.

The class thing in our neighborhood was very important to Gretchen because of all the fucked-up punk music she listened to. "The world is racist and chauvinistic by nature," she said. "How come every person with a shit job, like at McDonald's or at the 7-Eleven, is like black or Mexican? Do you ever see a white kid working at McDonald's? Maybe. Maybe at the register, but they sure ain't back there frying the fries." She'd say this nodding with herself and it would make me want to kiss her even more, her believing in things I had never even taken the time to think about.

eleven

At school, again.

Bad-ass horror movie titles for those direct-to-video horror films which could include at least two partial sex scenes, like all those knock-offs they have at Evergreen Video of Halloween and Friday the 13th, in which I could star as the slasher, possibly:

1. A Night of Agony, A Night of Pain
2. Enchanted by Evil
3. How the Undead Weep
4. The Hangman's Hand
5. Kill for Thrill
6. Night Seductions
7. The Game of Deadly
8. Beware the House that Bled
9. Lethal Injection
10. Sleepover Party Camp
11. The Crypt Has Spoken
12. Brother Mooney Speaks with his most sinister discussion of anal-ass grammar which eats your fucking soul for one hour every fucking day nonstop and there is no end in sight ever never ever until your fucking eyeballs bleed out of your skull and they have to clean it all up with that motherfucking red sawdust stuff and even then you have to fucking listen, so you have to jam pencils in both your ears and I'm sure you'd find a way even then, wouldn't you, Bro. Mooney? you baboon.

twelve

OK, this is another mix-tape Gretchen made me which was all about the summer before, which she titled, Better Days, when it seemed everything was all right, so listening to it was kind of like going back in time, even though it was only a year ago when Gretchen first got the Escort and I had been seeing this girl Colleen, not actually seeing her like dating, but seeing in the sense that I saw her at the Chinese Wok counter in the food court at the mall, and I had found out her name and she knew who I was and, well, like I said, it seemed like there were these secret messages on the tape that reminded me of when everything was still good for me:

Police and Thieves/The Clash

We sang this one in the parking lot of Arena Lanes, this bowling alley, after we had each stolen a pair of bowling shoes some night that summer.

Panic/The Smiths

Wow, this one seemed to be about our lives that summer for sure, because it was when Gretchen first got the Escort and even though it was used, the tape player still worked but there was never anything good on the radio, it was all crap all the time, and there was this line in the song where the singer sings, "Hang the DJ, the music that constantly plays says nothing to me about my life," and when I first heard it, I thought, *That's exactly right, man.*

Hateful/The Clash

Another sing-along song, this one though, was, to me, about the time Gretchen thought it would be funny to drive really fast behind a student driver—you know, the kids who drive around with the big sign on top of the car—and so Gretchen was like swerving and riding the poor kid's tail and kept honking her horn at different stoplights until finally the driver's ed teacher got out, and she was this crazy-looking woman with permed hair who was screaming like a fucking banshee, and Gretchen tried to back up, but she backed into a parked car and had to pay two hundred bucks to get the other car's headlights replaced. The song that was on when she backed into the other car? "Hateful."

Ball and Chain/Social D.

Social Distortion was one of Gretchen's bands that I actually liked because they were kind of just rock'n'roll. When the singer sang, "I even got me a little wife," I always thought of Colleen, the girl I had been seeing at the food court at the mall, because in my mind she was my girl that whole summer and she was like 4'5", very tiny.

Ratt Fink/The Misfits

OK, I had no idea what this song was really supposed to be about, but it reminded me of the time Gretchen got arrested for shoplifting at this department store, Venture, and when they had her empty her pockets, all she had were like ten bags of Gummy Bears, and she said when they tried to find out her name, all she kept saying was, "R-A-T-T-F-I-N-K," because some old lady had spotted her shoving the candy in her pockets and the same lady was just standing there, watching from outside the security office as Gretchen was interrogated or whatever. This was a good sing-along one, too, I think.

I turned the tape over and read the track listings, and got very sad, suddenly.

I Know It's Over/The Smiths
Please, Please, Please Let Me Get What I Want/The Smiths
Heaven Knows I'm Miserable Now/The Smiths
Straight to Hell/The Clash
Asleep/The Smiths

One, they were almost all by the Smiths, and two, they were all slow songs about dying, I think. I think maybe she was trying to tell me something like, *My mom is dead and I am still sad about* it, or something like that, because the title of the second side was just Carol, her mom's name, and that was it. I didn't know what to say to her, so I just called her and said, "Thanks," and she said, "Yeah, no problem," and for some reason, I ended up listening to the second side all night, thinking about Gretchen lying in her room. I guess it made me feel better somehow, like her making this tape for me and saying she felt bad a lot, too. It just made me feel a lot less worse, maybe.

thirteen

Other than that, I would sing gospel out loud, really loud, in church, and that made me feel OK. Really. Every Sunday to get out of my house I'd go to mass, by myself even. The church I went to was Queen of Martyrs on 103rd, where I had gone to grade school, and it was nice, all baby-blue inside with these shiny stained-glass windows and light-wood pews and with all the gold of the altar shining and these nice wood Stations of the Cross posted along the wall everywhere. Everyone in the neighborhood went to church, I guess, even if they were pretty shitty. My mom went by herself early in the morning. Me, I usually went to 11 o'clock mass and I would sit somewhere in the back, usually with the old people, their white hair like wisps of cotton candy, their grubby clothes smelling like mothballs and the thrift clothes Gretchen would buy at the Salvation Army—old people, who, like me, were there by themselves, maybe. I guess if you go to church enough, you just go and say the things and kneel and pray without even thinking, because that's what I did. I mean, I had been going to Catholic school all my life and I never really thought about what I had been taught; I just kind of went through the motions of it all. Worse than that, I would kind of check the women out—you know, high school girls, hot-looking moms, stuff like that. I would have all kinds of weirdo fantasies—nothing satanic, you know, but pretty involved anyway. Most of the fantasies involved me imagining what the hot girls would look like as they walked up the aisle to get married, their hair all done-up, their soft faces behind white veils, smiling nervously. I dunno why I fantasized about that. Sometimes I would take the time to think about what was going on with my mom and dad and some-times it would make me so sad I'd have to excuse myself and go to the bathroom to keep myself from fucking crying.

But like I said, the thing I liked best was the singing. I mean it—I would go there and really belt it out like a total retard, you know, because I was there by myself and didn't have to worry about looking dumb for doing it, and it felt nice to be singing the same song as everybody—you know, belonging—and, well, all the old people around me loved me for it; they would nod and smile and I would shout, "Amazing Grace" or "How Great Thou Art," thinking that some day, one of these old ladies would be interviewed for some rock'n'roll documentary about me and in the film the old lady would nod and wipe her glasses and say, "That boy had a voice like a saint. Like a saint," and have to look away from the camera to keep from crying tears of joy at the thought of me.

Get this, though: One time Gretchen and I were in the car, and she was smiling and watching me only mouth the words along to "Hope" by the Descendents, and she said, "My dad told me he saw you singing in church," and I said, "No, man, I just mouth the words," and she said, "No, he told me you were really singing," so I stopped singing when I went there, from then on, and I went back to just thinking about my mom and dad.

fourteen

Dinner at Gretchen's was the best. When I was an "invited" guest and not just standing in the kitchen, watching until I made my way over to begin working on whatever leftovers had been left, it was nice to sit at their table and eat like a member of their family. It was very sad at her house since her mom had died a few years back, but it was better than at my house, I guess. I tried to be very polite because Gretchen's dad always looked very, very worn-out and very heartbroken, like he might start crying at any minute. He was a sad-looking guy, eyes like runny eggs, with a narrow face and dark tidy hair, but he was always very generous to me. Usually, Gretchen would be silent. She would just stare at her dinner plate and move her food around, you know. Her older sister, Jessica, a fucking super-fox, would completely ignore me. I'd try to talk, tell everyone about my day, but since they weren't my family they weren't very interested. My family didn't ever really eat together. Like I said, my dad hadn't been around much lately and my mom was always working, my older brother Tim was always some-where doing jock stuff, and my little sister Alice was usually staring at herself in a mirror. So I guess I went over to Gretchen's whenever I was invited for the sense of belonging I thought I was so desperately lacking. It felt nice to pretend to have some kind of normal family.

Tonight's meal at Gretchen's looked iffy. I mean it looked bad. Like meat. But not meat maybe. Something brown and black on the white plate with something green on the side. To me, the whole kitchen was out of date and worn-out looking, like it was from the '70s. The dull yellow light overhead made everything look gray, sad, somber, much worse. Like the faded blue in the crisscross kitchen wallpaper and the brown from the tile floor, whatever was on the plate looked drab and totally unappetizing.

"It's imitation steak," Mr. D. said. "We're trying to market it. It's called Imi-Taste-Y! Try it." Mr. D. was in advertising or marketing or something—a white collar job, my dad called it—and he drove downtown into the city every day and back home to make sure he had dinner with his girls every evening.

"I'm not hungry," Gretchen sighed, folding her arms in front of her chest.

"Well, what do you think, Brian?"

"I think it's sensational, Mr. D. In fact, I think *you're* pretty sensational," I said.

He nodded and gave me a wink.

"Well, then, what about this in-school suspension, young lady?" he asked. "Have you been making amends?"

"It's no big deal," Gretchen said. She hung her head low and pushed her fork into the mysterious black mound then withdrew it slowly.

"No big deal? One more and they said they'll have to toss you out," Mr. D. mumbled, blinking behind his glasses nervously. He was still wearing the blue flowered apron, the front of which read, "Kiss the Cook." He was short and nervous-looking, his eyes big and twitchy. After fourteen years of wearing a mustache, he had decided to shave it recently. His face looked empty without it, even if you had never seen the mustache. He had been single for two years and he had shaved the mustache to seem younger, more attractive, since his wife, Gretchen's mom, had passed away from lung cancer. Gretchen's mom was the best. I mean it, she was the nicest and the most fun and she smoked and played video games with us; I dunno, I had grown up wishing my mom had been like that. The kitchen smelled the way I remembered Gretchen's mom smelling; the yellow outdated wallpaper held a hint of her brand of Virginia Slim menthol cigarettes and I hoped they'd never change it.

"Like I said, it won't happen again, Dad, I promise," Gretchen said, taking his hand and shaking it as a pledge.

"That's what she said before, and the time before that," Jessica chimed in. Jessica was known as a slut, but she was super, intergalactic hot. She had a reputation for making out with other girls' boyfriends, you know what I mean. I had seen her do it a few times at the parties she would throw when Mr. D. would go out of town on business. At one of those parties, I overheard her say this to some other girl:

"Duh, he's such a nimrod, he doesn't even know how to fuck."

Which to me meant Jessica did know how to fuck and since then I had these elaborate fantasies about her, you know, teaching me. Also, she was a sloppy kind of kisser and didn't care who she made out with, which is what got me. There was a rumor she had given gonorrhea to Mike Estevez, who almost died because of it. What had really happened was Mike Estevez was dating Katie Camden and Jessica decided she liked Mike and made out with him at a party and Mike got mononucleosis from some other girl named Tricia a few weeks later and he lost like thirty pounds and had to go to the hospital and so everyone blamed Jessica and made comments to her like "cocktease" and "tramp." But it didn't matter because, like I said, Jessica was hot. She was a year older, a senior, short like Gretchen, but thin. She was hot because she was petite, with big green eyes, hot like a cat hot, and a sharp chin, like a hot Dungeons and Dragons princess elf. Boys found her very hot. Men found her very hot. I found her extremely hot. I masturbated thinking about her a lot. She was one of the few girls around who would actually put out, or so she said anyway, and did not make you beg for it and then act like you were married or cry afterwards about it, maybe. Or so I had heard. Or so she had told Gretchen. She also said she liked sex and was not afraid to admit it. Another time, she told Gretchen that she would become a hooker if she could. She shaved her legs every day just in case, that was the rumor. Also, Jessica had a secret—or what she thought was a secret—she sold pot to her boss at the Yogurt Palace. She also had had sex with him. Twice. His name was Caffey and he was married with three kids, all beautiful blond boys which Jessica said would someday be hers. That's what she told Gretchen anyways. Until recently, Jess had been a member of Key Club and in French Society and a football cheerleader, then out of the blue, she quit all the activities she was enlisted in and started buying dope off of our friends to sell to all the adults she knew. The worst part of it all was that she wanted nothing to do with me, no matter how I tried, even when I was like a foot across the table. I did everything I could to get her notice, and then I just gave up and decided I would just worship her from afar, maybe.

"More Imi-Taste-Y, Brian?" Mr. D. asked.

"I'm cool, Mr. D."

"I just want to say Mom would never put up with Gretchen's

lousy behavior at school," Jessica announced, nodding her head. "It's pathetic."

"Fuck off," Gretchen hissed.

"Language," Mr. D. stammered. "Let's watch the language."

"I'm done anyway," Gretchen said, standing up slowly. I watched her stand and made no move to follow.

"What about dinner?" Mr. D. asked.

"I'll eat something later."

"I'm sure you will," Jessica said.

"Fuck off, cunt-head!" Gretchen shouted.

"Language," Mr. D. whispered.

"Fuck off, yourself," Jessica replied. "That comment doesn't even make sense, sewer tramp."

"Language! Let's have some respect here. Gretchen, I want you to know I'm serious about this. No more trouble at school, do you understand?"

"Yes," she said. "Come on, Brian." As Mr. D. looked down to scoop up his imitation hamburger, Gretchen flipped off Jessica, who only smiled back. I felt a small pain of sadness, thinking about my older brother, as they both eyed each other and laughed. I hadn't talked to my brother in a few weeks, it seemed like anyway.

After that I followed Gretchen up to her room and I laid down on her bed as she began doing her chemistry homework, sitting cross-legged on the floor. I loved the smell of Gretchen's room, like vanilla incense, even though it was a typical fucking mess: clothes all over, shoes, boots, notebook paper strewn around with the names of songs to make mix-tapes with, homework half-finished, boots without laces, record albums, broken cassettes, a bottle of glitter nail polish left leaking beside the bed. There was a Ramones poster and Misfits poster on opposite walls and then a poster of two cute cats in which she had put X's over the eyes of the poor animals, knives and bullets and nooses encircling them in a ring of panic and flame. On another wall were all kinds of photos—from her junior high Math Team days, from her older sister's parties, photos of her and Kim, of her and her mom, who was thin and beautiful, and like I said, the nicest lady ever—all of the photographs taped or glued directly to the wall. Then there were all kinds of horror and monster movie stuff, like masks and fake butcher knives and videotapes of almost every Hammer film ever made, including a rare *Dracula 1972* which she had ordered from the back of *Fangoria*. The best part of her room was her bed, which was big and white and soft and which smelled kind of like baby powder and kind of like her. I might have literally made out with her pillow if I had been given the chance.

I thought about asking her right then, like just blurting out, "OK, so do you want to go to Homecoming with me or not?" but I couldn't because I still didn't have the guts. I turned on my side and began staring at her—her soft round face, her small ears, the tiny pursed lips that mumbled words as she read to herself—and the more and more I looked, the more and more I realized I really, really liked her, not like other girls, you know, like Kim or Jessica, because I knew the only reason I liked them was because they looked hot, and, well, I could just stare at them and imagine boning them. I liked Gretchen as like a person and it was killing me that I couldn't say anything and she looked up just then and said, "What? What is it?" getting all self-conscious, straightening her white school blouse, brushing some blond strands of hair out of her face. "What?" she asked again. "What is it?"

"Nothing. You just look nice."

In a minute, her face went bright red and she got all uncomfortable and flipped me off. "Well, just stop staring at me, you fucking freak."

"I wasn't staring. I was just, you know, looking at you."

"Well, don't you have to go home at some point? Don't you have homework to do?" she asked, sitting up, stretching out her legs. Out of the corner of my eye, I glanced up her soft, plump thigh toward the spot where her plaid skirt began, searching, searching for that dark shadowy spot . . . but she crossed her legs and starting talking again. "Well, don't you?"

"I was thinking I could just tell all my teachers that my parents are getting split and I'm too, um . . . bereaved to do anything."

"Bereaved? That's when someone dies, douche-bag."

"Well, then whatever I am. Upset or whatever."

"Are you upset?" she asked.

"I don't think so. I think I might even be happy about it."

"Why?"

"Because both of them are fucking miserable and maybe it's better if he splits."

"Maybe," she said, looking down at her notebook. "It's cool you're not pissed at him."

"Yeah."

"Are you pissed?"

"I don't know. Maybe I will be later."

I climbed off the bed and sat down beside her. I could hear her breathing and me breathing and I was feeling all clammy and I tried to swallow but my mouth was all dry and I was kind of getting an erection and I turned and stared down at her ample breasts and I could see her flowery bra through the spaces in between the buttons of her blouse and I didn't know if I should try to hold her hand before I asked and just then Jessica barged in, blowing my big fucking chance.

"What's going on here, fuckers?" she asked, lighting a cigarette as she soon as she entered. "You guys making out? Smooch-smooch-kiss-kiss."

"Fuck off," Gretchen said, standing, pulling the pack of cigarettes from her sister's hand. She slipped a single cigarette out and lit it, then exhaled a long drag.

"Listen," Jessica whispered, shutting the bedroom door. "I need you little fuckers to do me a favor."

"What? What is it?" Gretchen asked, annoyed. "We're busy."

"Can either one of you guys get me a dime bag?"

"A dime bag? Of what?" I asked.

"Of what? Of weed, you spaz," Jessica said, laughing, shaking her head.

"Right, yeah, weed. No problem," I replied.

"No problem?!" Gretchen said with a snort. "Where are you getting a dime bag, Mr. Asshole?"

"Don't worry about it," I said. "I'll get it, no problem."

"He doesn't even know what a dime bag is, for fuck's sake," Gretchen said.

"Is that true?" Jessica asked, standing over me. "You're just fucking with me?"

"I know stuff," I said, and pretended to be very involved in reading *Fangoria* magazine.

"Thanks but no thanks, losers," Jessica said, closing the door and shaking her head. I turned to Gretchen and she was looking at me funny like I was an idiot and not funny and I didn't like it so I grabbed my coat and said, "See you later, losers," even though it was just her and I thought I had pretty much blown my chance, right about there.

I was riding the bus, then, and I got scared in a weird way because the bus was all empty and alone, and I started worrying if anyone would be there when I got home, and my mom was asleep already and my older brother was gone and I thought about going to talk to my little sister, but she might think I was high or something, and so instead I chickened out and went down to the basement and saw my dad there on the couch sleeping, so I didn't talk to anyone about anything. I sat on my bed and wondered what the hell I was doing and what I should do and then I got the greatest idea ever:

I'd make Gretchen a mix-tape. And then she'd fall for me. And then she would fall for me.

fifteen

The only other friend I had in the world beside Gretchen and Kim was
a kid named Rod, who was black and maybe even a homosexual, I
didn't know. I did know that he had the largest record collection of
anyone I knew and was like retarded about music. I met him in my
chemistry class at the beginning of the year because he sat next to
me, and right away you could tell he was not like the other black kids
in school. He was nervous, kind of glancing around the room, folding
his arms across his thin chest. He always had the look of a very
scared rabbit, maybe. Also, the way he dressed was very white: white
dress pants and a white button-down shirt, and he always wore this
red, button-down cardigan sweater. And he was white-acting, what
other black kids called an "Oreo"—you know, black on the outside
but white on the inside—because he was in honors classes and hung
out with all the nerdy white kids who were very into role-playing
games like Dungeons and Dragons, and also he stayed after school
to participate in the Young Scientists Club. He was the kind of friend
I'd hang out with after school, when other dudes weren't around. He
had this thing about him, and that thing was that he was an even
bigger pussy than me, maybe.

    The first time I met him he sat down next to me and then he said,
"I like to walk in cemeteries alone at night."

    "Yeah?" I asked.

    "I am a ghost. *Only you can see me* . . ." he whispered, scary like
a ghost.

    "That's cool," I said.

    "Don't you think that's weird? That I walk in cemeteries at night?
That I think I'm *a ghost*?" he whispered in the ghostly voice again.

    "No," I said. "It seems like you're the kind of kid I'd hang out with."

After school the next day, we went to his house and you could see why even though he was black he had turned out white. His mom had long, black, straightened hair and his dad wore a very clean business suit and tie and they all spoke with perfect white-people English and the sight of them made my dad look like a real slob who had dirty hands and used the word "jag-off" at the dinner table all the time. Well, these people ate dinner at exactly six and there was absolutely no swearing—or Mickey-Mousing around, as my dad called it. Rod had the perfect family and when he introduced me to them, you could see his mom's eyes light up. Here her boy had made a white friend and she couldn't be happier.

Mostly all Rod and I did was listen to records. Sometimes we'd go to the mall or video arcade, but mostly we went to different record stores looking for old vinyl. On Saturdays, we'd go to the flea market and he'd search for some obscure soul album like Curtis Mayfield or some ABCO Rolling Stones title and I'd go there to try out the Chinese stars and butterfly knives. Rod was very into music, all kinds: pop, R&B, rock, even jazz—which, for a high school kid, was weird. I mean, I always figured it had to do with his dad, who had this immense record collection. You saw it as soon as you walked into their living room—the living room which looked like it belonged on a television show, with white curtains and yellow furniture and all of it was perfectly clean with plastic on the sofa cushions and lace coasters under everything—and there, set inside wood shelves all around the room like a library, were hundreds and hundreds of vinyl records—blues, ragtime, modern jazz, bebop, soul—and his dad would be sitting in his soft red chair with a cardigan sweater and black slippers on, smoking his pipe and nodding his head and listening to Don Cherry. And Rod would walk in and say he'd found some B-side of a Marvin Gaye song and his dad and him would high-five each other, and then gently, like parents of a newborn baby, they'd lift the record out of its paper sleeve and place it on the hi-fi to play. Rod would take a seat on the couch and I'd just stand there, wondering, *Who exactly are these people*? and then the music would come on—a song like "Underdog" or "Living for the City"—music I had never heard before in my life, and yet after just a few notes, they were songs so simple and pure and full of joy that they'd make their way into my heart. Me, a dumb white kid humming Motown and not caring, and I'd sing them all, one after the other, on the bus ride home, maybe.

Once we walked into the house and Rod's dad, who insisted I call him Burt, was sitting in his red chair with his black slippers on, and said, "Boys, boys, listen to this one," and just then the needle met the small vinyl grooves of the record and "Time After Time" by Chet Baker began playing, the strange haunting voice of a man that to me sounded like a woman, so that I asked, "Wow, who's this lady?" and Rod's dad nodded and laughed and said, "That's Chet Baker, son, the trumpet player," and I said, "He sounds spooky," and Rod's dad said to Rod, "This was the first song your mother and I ever made love to," and I thought that was a little strange for him to say, but I didn't say anything. I just listened, and the more I heard that ghostly, quiet, night-time voice rising, the more I was thinking about Gretchen and kissing her to a song like that, and then it was over and we were all standing around silent and Rod's dad said, "That's how you should feel after you hear a good song. Like a brand new man," and I said, "Burt, I know what you mean," and we walked off into Rod's room, still kind of listening.

The only record I could listen to straight through was Guns n' Roses' *Appetite for Destruction*. When everything else was wrong, that record made it right. I could go back to it, always. No matter what, that record would make me feel all right. *Appetite for Destruction*. Guns n' Roses. That was it. That was my record. "It's So Easy," "Nightrain," "Out ta Get Me," then classics like "Paradise City," "Welcome to the Jungle," and probably the greatest song ever, of all time: "Sweet Child o' Mine." What was it about that song? I loved that song so much it sometimes made we want to kick a hole in the wall. If Gretchen and I were driving and if her stereo was working—which it did once every ten million years—and if that song happened to come on, I'd have to get her to pull over so I could listen to it, without having to hear the engine running or traffic going by. She always pulled over; she understood, I guess. That one part, where the song kind of slows down—"Where do we go now? Where do we go now? Where do we go now?"—I didn't even know what Axl was talking about, but if I was in the car with Gretchen, or better, at home alone in the basement where my room was, I would have to stop and crank it or just stand there and do the air guitar parts. In the car, I'd try to get Gretchen to sing along, but since it wasn't punk, she wasn't having it, though one time she did do the "Where do we go? Where do we go now" parts, but to get her to do anything else was almost impossible where GNR was concerned.

When I brought the record over to Rod's to try to get him to listen, all he did was roll his eyes and shake his head. It was the first time I had played a record of mine for him and he just folded his arms over his chest, raising his eyebrows, and laughed.

"Lame," was all he said.

"What? How can you not like this?" I asked.

"It's just so lame," he said.

"Lame? Stevie Wonder is lame."

"Seriously. I'll take Stevie over this any day," he muttered, getting up to switch it off.

"Dude, you've got to listen to the whole thing. At the end. It gets all quiet and pretty and everything."

He stood up and walked beside the deep mahogany record player, his hand on the record arm, and I thought, *If he touches that needle, I am going to kick his ass* and *Maybe white kids and black kids can't be friends* and *If he turns this fucking record off, I am never going to talk to him again*, and just then Slash began his solo and the song began to build and Rod waited, closing his eyes, and listened, and sat back down on the bed. We listened to the whole song together and then when it was over he nodded and said, "That was a jam. I was wrong. That really was a jam."

"Like I said." He handed me back the LP, gently sliding it into its paper sleeve.

"Hey, man, I need to put a mix-tape together for this girl. Can you help me pick out some cool songs she's never heard before?" I asked.

"Why do you want to put songs she's never heard on it?"

"Because she does that for me. Plays songs I've never heard, you know."

Rod frowned, crossing his arms in front of his chest.

"Don't be lame, man," he said. "That would be like writing somebody else's love letter."

"No it isn't," I said.

"I'm not helping you out. If you like this girl, you should be able to pick the songs out you want her to hear yourself."

"But I'll pick fucking rock songs. I need sexy songs like that shit your dad listens to. Like Chet Baker and shit."

"Man, forget it. I'm not doing it."

"You're screwing me here, Rod," I said. "You're blowing my chance with love."

"No, man, you are," he said, and I knew I was on my own from there.

sixteen

At exactly that same strange time in my life, I began getting these massively raging erections for no real reason—sometimes right in the middle of class or walking down the hallway at school—and they would be so painful that I would have to go into the men's room and masturbate right away or I would get these very intense stomach aches. I'm not kidding. Anything might set me off. I would masturbate for no real reason, thinking about anyone, any girl I had ever seen. Once after school, when I was watching *Star Trek*, some alien lady with blue skin and tight pants came on the screen and immediately I had to go jerk off. It got really bad. If I had a female teacher—any kind of female, skinny, fat, hot, ugly, whatever—I would immediately get an erection if she even called on me. If she was like, "Well, what do you think, Brian?" I would be like, "I think I have an erection now and so I have to go deal with it." It was worse in, like, math class, where I had to sit close to the math teacher Mrs. Daniels's desk. Once during a quiz, she spilled her perfume all over—that "White Fantasy" perfume stuff—and I had to run out of class in the middle of the quiz, which I failed, because I practically blew my load in my pants.

The only thing I had going for me romantically at the time was cable TV, which meant Cinemax After Dark on Friday nights, where they'd show these soft-core porno movies, like *Emmanuel 5*, *Emmanuel 6*, and *Emmanuel 8*, or *Lady Chatterley's Lover*, tame stuff like that. I wasn't brave enough to try and buy a porno magazine so all I had was the cable and my mom's fashion magazines, like *Cosmo*, which if I wasn't careful, were always left with a suspicious crease.

Also, there was this guy at Evergreen Video, a few blocks from my house, who'd let me rent rated-R horror movies. He was a fat guy with a greasy white forehead and big brown glasses, and it seemed like he was always eating when I came in to rent something. "How's *Sorority Party Massacre*?" I'd ask, holding up the video box, which was full of blood and gore and photos of beautiful co-eds in pink lingerie, screaming.

"That one's so-so," he'd say, licking his fingers from fried chicken, maybe. "The one next to it, *Prom Queen from the Dead,* well, there's some full-frontal nudity in that one. Girl in a shower scene—little red bush. Almost burned out my slow-motion feature on that one."

"How's this one?" I asked, pointing to a copy of *The Curse of Dr. Fang*.

"That one borders on straight porno."

"Really," I said, bringing it up toward the register.

In the film, which was Spanish, I think, with English subtitles, Dr. Fang is this scientist with big pop-bottle glasses and a Fu Manchu beard and a white lab coat and he invents this ray to get girls to have sex with him. Within the first ten minutes of the film, I had nearly blown out a nut, sincerely.

So in school at about the same time, I began to sign all my tests and assignment sheets as "Dr. Fang," just screwing around, and also because, like I said, I hadn't gotten laid yet and I thought this might grant me some kind of individuality. I thought that was what I was missing, you know: a cool identity. I asked Gretchen and Kim to call me "Dr. Fang" and they just laughed. In my mind, though, I started to think of myself as a super villain who could make women fall in love with me, but instantly, like that guy from *Charles in Charge* in that one teen movie, where he would like blink and then *bam!* women's brassieres would pop open. I imagined I would have some word, some secret phrase, like "Shazam!" or "Activate!" and I would like whisper it with a nod and women, like the ones I would ogle in the poster section of Spencer's Gifts at the mall, all of them tan and yellow bikini-clad, would stop taking their soapy bubble baths or washing their cherry-red Lamborghinis or whatever they were doing, and become helpless sexual slaves to my most wild desires, which would have been a whole lot of making out, because that's all I had done so far. It seemed Gretchen had no idea I was interested in her and all she could ever talk about was Tony Degan. I had no idea how to make a mix-tape that would, like, capture her, so I decided to put off asking her to Homecoming and I began waiting to see if my new persona might capture the hearts of a few other unsuspecting ladies.

In band class, which, like I said, was just one other thing to be embarrassed of, there were the geeky girls from Mother McCauley. They were also fledgling band members, socially awkward and ultra-nerdy. But there was one girl out of all the creepy, bifocal-glasses-wearing types that was super fine: Suzy Lee Siler. As I sat pretending to play the xylophone behind Suzy Lee Siler—first chair clarinet, brunette, tall, very tall, and at age seventeen already very sexually aware, which I could tell because she never walked home from school, always riding in the passenger seat of some mullethead's rusted-out red Camaro or Firebird, with her feet resting on the dashboard—*on the dashboard!*—which to me meant she and the guy had already done it because, *Come on, look, her feet are up there on the dashboard*—well in class, right behind her, I would trace the narrow crisscross of her bra strap which was visible under her white uniform blouse, all the time whispering, "Dr. Fang, Dr. Fang, you are under the spell of Dr. Fang," knowing at any moment Suzy Lee would turn and wink at me, just once—*wink*—falling under the wicked, perverse charms of the most fearsome Dr. Fang for all eternity.

I didn't know any girls other than Gretchen and Kim, really, and like I said, I hadn't ever had a real girlfriend, so to take up time between watching horror movies and hanging out with Rod and jerking off to photos of Suzy Lee in the high school yearbook I stole from my younger sister Alice, and *Suzy Lee was in the French club and on the volleyball team and there was this one shot of her leaping in the air to spike a volleyball and her bare, long legs were like the blades of two magnificent scissors cutting through the air and my heart—oh, my heart, snip, snip*—so after school, I asked my mom if it was OK if I could start mowing lawns again for a few families in my neighborhood like I had in junior high, and she said as long as I left time for studying; so I did, cutting lawns and nodding along on my headphones to Mötley Crüe or Guns n' Roses or Slayer.

On the other side of the block around the corner was a girl a year younger than me, a sophomore named Carrie Steeple, who everyone called a skank because her parents put her on the pill in eighth grade, and everyone knew she was on the pill because the little plastic thing had fallen out of her purse during homeroom—that's what Kim had told me—and her dropping the pill compact made a lot of people think she was full of shit, because it seemed like Carrie was advertising, and also, it had been rumored that she had been knocked up twice before she was on the pill, which to me didn't make any sense, considering she didn't have any babies, but that just goes to show you how much I knew about abortion and condoms and the pill and all that kind of sex-stuff. Well, Carrie Steeple would sit in a yellow plastic lawn chair right on her front lawn and watch me mow her neighbor's grass and she wouldn't wear nothing but a bright yellow two-piece bikini, and it was like October, and this girl was still young, younger than me, and not very developed—I mean, her chest was as flat as a cutting board and the only thing remotely curvy on her was her very large, swooping forehead. Also, her shoulders were always covered in bright red freckles. Her hair was kind of brown and dirty and long and stringy. She would sit there in the yellow chair, purple sunglasses on, with a boom box playing Paula Abdul or Madonna or whoever, tapping her foot along, and to be honest, her sitting there scared the hell out of me. One time, she uncrossed her legs when I was looking, and I could see the soft folds of her privates held tight against the stretchy yellow fabric and just the faintest line of black stubble where she had shaved and it made me feel sick and excited all at once. This other time, I remember I had run over a stone or rock or something, and the mower had jerked forward suddenly, and Metallica was blaring in my head-phones, and I looked up and Carrie Steeple was sitting there in that chair, leaning forward in her tiny yellow two-piece with her elbows on her knees, and she was staring right at me and I think she was mouthing some words at me and I said, out loud, "What?" switching off the mower, and she flipped her stringy hair over her shoulder and said, "Take off your glasses," and I didn't understand what she was saying, and then she said it again, "Go ahead, take off your glasses," and I said, "I've got to get back to work," and I started the lawn mower and finished the side of the Foster's house, not looking her way again.

About three days later, it hit me: I was in the middle of a chem-istry test and, of course, I had signed my name at the top of the page as *Dr. Fang*, and right then I began to play that moment over and over, again and again, in my head—Carrie looking up and saying, "Take off your glasses"—and I'd be at school, or at home, or lying in bed, or at dinner when my mother would ask me to pass the mashed potatoes, or when I was being called on in class, or when I showered, or when I went to the bathroom, or when I walked down the street, I'd be thinking about Carrie—her flat chest, her stringy hair—saying, "Take off your glasses. Take off your glasses." In that moment, anything could have happened. Anything could have happened, but I had chickened out. I had chickened out, and this might have been it, my big chance, and I had blown it. I had blown my chance to just get it over with and now nobody was going to ever have sex with me—not Carrie Steeple, certainly not Gretchen—and I'd get all worked up about it and swear to myself that no matter what, the next time, I'd do it, no matter what, and I'd decide to masturbate right then, sure that that was the closest I'd ever get to sex before some kind of nuclear war or Soviet radiation destroyed me.

seventeen

Bad-ass possible songs for the Gretchen mix-tape:

1. **I Won't Forget You** by Poison
2. **Every Rose Has its Thorn** again by Poison
3. **Home Sweet Home** by Mötley Crüe
4. **Don't Fear the Reaper**, Blue Oyster Cult
5. **Feel Like Making Love**, Bad Company
6. **Freebird** by Lynrd Skynrd—all-time number one making out song
7. **Separate Ways** by Journey
8. **Rocket Queen** by GNR
9. **Patience** by GNR
10. **Sweet Child o' Mine** by GNR

eighteen

Out of nowhere, at school, I got a fucking egg busted on my head for no real reason. I was going to the bathroom in a stall in the washroom on the second floor, and it was just after third period began and I was feeling sick because I had milk with my cereal for breakfast, which I shouldn't have because I was lactose-intolerant, but Tim was down at the table eating breakfast and the gallon of milk was sitting there and it looked really good on his Cap'n Crunch instead of plain fucking water, which is what I usually had, so I put some milk on my cereal—and not just a little, a lot—and by third period, I was all cramping and everything, and when I asked Bro. Hitler—a.k.a., Bro. Paluch—if I could go to the bathroom, he said yes, because he must have saw how bad and green and sweaty I looked, even though usually he never let anyone go to the bathroom, which is a little fucking crazy because what the fuck are you supposed to do? Crap your pants? If you are at a job and have to take a dump, they will let you because that's common fucking courtesy.

The bathroom smelled like Pine-Sol and cigarettes and I was in the stall closest to the wall, because I was uptight about that kind of thing. I didn't like taking dumps when someone was sitting in the stall next to me. I'd sit there and wait if I had to. I did not enjoy hearing other people take a dump and I didn't like it when people could hear me taking a dump. Why? I dunno. Common fucking courtesy, I guess. So I picked the stall farthest from the door—I mean, the whole bathroom was empty, but it was just in case someone came in to piss, that kind of thing. I went into the stall, pulled down my pants, then remembered and wiped the black toilet seat with some toilet paper, then sat down on it. I didn't fucking squat, I sat down. Why? Because I had been sick like this my whole life and you just get very fucking tired of squatting your whole life. So I sat down and was waiting, which I had to because it would be like this hour-long buildup until it shot through me, and so I started looking around the stall. The walls of it were dull green marble, the floor tile was greenish blue, pretty clean-looking. Toward the front of the john, one of the sinks was dripping. It was pretty quiet because everyone was in class, I guess, and then I started reading the graffiti.

EVERYTHING TODAY IS AS BAD AS MY SPELLING
come here to suck my cock at 1:30 every day

COLLEEN CHANDLER WILL NOT FUCK

I was sitting there trying to make out some line that started with, *IN CASE OF FIRE, EVACUATE YOUR BOWELS AND STROKE YOUR*, when the heavy wood door swung open and two pairs of feet stumbled in. I could tell they were bigger dudes from the way they were laughing and shoving each other; they didn't give a fuck about anyone hearing them. Someone lit up a cigarette—I could hear the sound of the wheel grinding against the flint. Someone farted, then laughed and shoved someone else. Then someone crouched down on the floor. I could hear it. I could hear the sound the rubber soles of his shoes made as they squeaked and the sound of him breathing and laughing and the sound his knees made pressing against the floor, and then he whistled and said, "Dude, McDunnah, someone's shitting in there," and right away I got a flash of this kid, John McDunnah, this big cro-mag senior on the wrestling team, who I once saw de-pants some honors-class fag in the gym locker room like two years before. This kid, John McDunnah, was big, like over six-feet tall, square-shouldered, square-faced, square-chinned, and probably square-brained, his face hidden under a dark, monolithic eyebrow ledge. In that moment, all I remembered was the look on that one kid's face—some squirrelly pockmarked kid with enormous bifocal glasses—as John pinned him against a row of lockers, first tearing down his dress pants, then his scabby white underwear. It was all *Animal Kingdom* strongest-of-the-jungle kind of shit, John McDunnah's laugh like a brooding and very feral hyena.

"Someone's in there?" I heard a voice respond and then that same cackling-hyena laugh. Just then, I kind of started getting nervous and decided to pull up my pants even though my stomach still felt sick as hell, and then the heavy door opened and either someone else came in or someone left, and I heard the same voice again—slow, deliberate, stupid with laughter—say, "Someone's in there taking a fucking dump," and I buckled my pants and heard the door open again and one of them was laughing, then another, and then I heard the quick squeak of someone's shoes against the tile and I could hear someone on the other side of the stall door, very close by, and then I felt something hit my fucking head. It hurt, just for one quick second— a slight sharp sting from how hard it was thrown—and then another sensation, like I was bleeding, but it was not blood but egg yolk running down my face and neck, down the crook of the collar of my shirt, and there were pieces of egg in my hair and I didn't even stand up or say anything. I picked some of the shell out of my hair and waited for them to leave. I heard the squeak again of their feet and the heavy door finally slam and I opened the stall door and went to the mirror and it made me think: Did they know who it was, or could it have been just anybody and *I mean, who brings a fucking egg to school?* What kind of people do those kinds of things? The answer: John fucking McDunnah. I knew it was him for sure, at least he had been part of it. But why? Why did they even bother? What do those kinds of fucking people grow up to be? It seemed like shit Gretchen would bitch about. Seriously.

nineteen

Going to the mall with Gretchen was a lot of fun because sometimes she would steal. Mostly we just walked around, giving the uptight suburban home–type mothers and grandmothers our dirty looks, but every so often, when she was complaining about how oppressive corporate America was to the rest of the poor undeveloped world—which usually coincided with her listening to a lot of Minor Threat or the Dead Kennedys—Gretchen would grab me by the hand and pull me into Kohl's, this big middle-class cheeseball department store, with the intention that both her and I would score something for free, in the name of revolution and international equality.

"You're just a loyal, thoughtless consumer, aren't you?" she whispered one day as we made our way through the clothing racks of bright pink and green Ocean Pacific swimsuits in the preteen section.

"I'm not a consumer," I said, "I don't buy anything."

"You don't buy anything?" she replied, shoving me.

"I don't have any money."

"What about movies? Don't you rent movies?" she shouted, shoving me into a rack of preteen nylon slacks.

"So?" I said. "That's renting, not buying."

"Well, what about your clothes? You buy clothes, don't you?"

"No," I said. "My mom buys that shit."

"Well, what about music? You buy records and cassettes, right?"

"Duh," I said.

"Well, those people are trying to control you!" she shouted, grabbing my wrist again. She tugged me through the young miss section, which was all stone-washed jeans and color-changing T-shirts flying past, bright color after bright color. "They want you to buy stuff so you don't think about anything."

"That's cool," I said, "the less I have to think about shit, the better."

"But that means you are under their fucking control. THEY tell you what movies to rent. THEY tell you what records to buy. THEY tell you what clothes to wear. And, like a dumbshit, you spend all your money on buying stupid things that don't even make you happy. Like this"—she grabbed a white, lacy, see-through-type bodysuit—"do you think girls even want to wear this shit?" she asked, shoving it in my face.

"I dunno. Hot girls, maybe," I said, and she grabbed my hand again.

"Don't you know about classes and shit like that? Don't you ever think about that stuff?" she asked.

"I've got to go to classes eight times a day. That is where I do all my thinking."

"You're working class, and they're trying to control you so you don't overthrow them," Gretchen whispered, as if THEY were somehow listening in an empty corner of the store, directly behind a sale rack of reduced puffy red ski jackets.

"I can't even worry about that shit," I said. "I'm just trying to get through fucking school without going fucking crazy."

"That's how they get you, though," she said. "First you don't have time to worry about it because of school, then you've got a job, and a wife, and kids, and a family, and so you just keep going on buying and buying and you never ask why you're so fucking miserable about everything."

"I know why I'm miserable," I said, staring up the long, shiny, sensuous plastic legs of a topless female mannequin. "I need to get laid."

"Is that all you fucking think about?" she asked, and I looked up, and we were in the middle of the intimates section, which was nothing but hot bras and hot panties, and I glanced around at the vast, endless beauty, rows and rows of lace and silk and tiny delicate flowers and garter belts and stockings and nodded once, without thinking.

"Yes, I can safely say that is all I think about," I said as she tugged me by the arm again. "What? Where are we going?" I asked, and we stopped in front of the last rack in the row, which was a row full of big white bras and big gray pairs of panties, and she said, "The fat-ass section," and pointed to a packaged pair of nylons decorated with a shadowy photo of what was a hefty model tastefully shot from the back, and the name brand, "Just My Size."

I stared at the package and kind of shuddered, thinking these droopy gray stockings were what old-ass senior citizens wore, and I was going to say something and make a joke but Gretchen stopped me and said, "See? See how bad they make you feel? 'Just My Size'?" and I looked at her, under the twitchy florescent light, her pink hair soft and no longer so bright, and it seemed like, for a minute, I got what she was saying, because when she started stuffing handfuls of the puffy gray packages under the waist of her black leather jacket, I turned to make sure no one was watching and followed her out of there running, and even when we were in the Escort, flying away, I was still thinking about it all and I still hadn't said a word about anything.

twenty

The Mole People and other monster movies were what my dad and I would sometimes watch together without having to say anything. Like one night, I came home late and my dad was asleep on the couch and his face was all blue and white because it was dark downstairs and the TV was still on and I could hear sirens and shooting from whatever it was he had been watching—*Hunter*, probably, that was his show, the one with that dude, fucking Fred Dryer, because he liked that Fred Dryer had been a linebacker for the Pittsburgh Steelers and now was on TV—and I was sneaking into my room and my dad snored and then he sat up and said, "Hey, Brian. Brian, is that you?" and he shoved on his glasses quick, pretending that he had been up waiting and not totally asleep.

"Yeah, Dad, it's me."

"Where have you been all night, kid?" he asked, smiling, and I said, "Gretchen's. Out with Gretchen."

"Out with Gretchen, huh?"

He sat up, took off his glasses, rubbed his face, and then put them back on, smiling again. "Guess what's on tonight on cable?" he asked. "At midnight."

"I dunno," I said.

"*The Mole People.*"

"*The Mole People*? I love that movie." *The Mole People* was this weird sci-fi movie from the '50s, probably one of my favorite movies of all time. It was about these scientists who climb the Himalayas, or some mountain range in like Asia or wherever, and they discover this secret passage to this underground civilization that is like hundreds of miles down and like thousands of years old. It's kind of like this world of these beautiful secret super-pale Egyptians—they all dress like that, with the pharaoh kind of helmets and belts and buckles and whips and male-dresses or whatever you call them—and they are all albinos because they haven't seen the sun, like ever, and they are the rulers of the civilization. But there are these other people, the monsters, the Mole People—who don't look like moles at all, but kind of like lizards, but not lizards—they are blackish with scales and they have these big white eyes and small narrow mouths and huge, huge four-fingered claws, and they are forced to work in these mines or caves and to serve the albino people. So the monsters were actually the good people and the good-looking people were bad. Also, one young stud scientist discovers this hot, normal-looking girl, with dark hair and a regular complexion, who is considered a freak because she isn't an albino, and the scientist and the normal girl fall in love and the scientist helps the Mole People revolt and then there is some fight of some kind and an earthquake and somehow sunlight makes its way down there and it generally freaks all the albinos out and that was all I could basically remember. I had watched it a few times when I was really young, with my dad, when it played on the late Saturday night horror show, *Son of Svenghoulie*, this local program that ran old black-and-white monster movies every Saturday night. That was our thing, my dad and me. We would watch these monster movies every Saturday night and how long ago had that been?

I looked over at my dad and smiled. "Yeah, that one part where the monsters help the scientists out, I love that."

"I know it. So can you watch it?" he asked, smiling big and nodding. "Or do you got homework to do or something like that?"

"No, I can watch it," I said. I threw my coat in my room and sat down in the soft green chair beside the couch and watched as Hunter tackled a suspect, flying over the hood of a car and landing in a pile of cardboard boxes.

"So, Dad, how long do you plan on sleeping down here?" I asked.

"I dunno," he said, staring straight ahead. "Am I cramping your style?"

"No. I was ... I guess I was just worried about mom and everything."

"You let me worry about that," he said. "We're having problems. We'll work it out. I promise."

I turned and looked at him. He didn't look too hopeful. He had a long red pillow mark on the side of his cheek and he was still wearing his work clothes because my mom had stopped doing his laundry, apparently. He switched the channel and stretched out his feet and I noticed his socks were looking gray and dirty. I was going to say something, but decided not to. I just sat there and watched as the titles began appearing over a cavernous, murky cave, the foreboding music rising.

"Well, here we go with *The Mole People*," my dad said, "you can always count on them."

"You sure can," I said back.

twenty-one

Weird as it was, for fun, Gretchen and I would always go eat some place after school, even though she had this really big problem with being overweight. It was kinda fucking crazy. Like maybe I knew what we were doing but didn't want her not to be fat or she'd stop hanging out with me. I dunno. We usually went to Snackville Junction, this diner on like 111th and Western that had a big linoleum counter in the center of it which was shaped like half a circle and had toy train tracks on it. A toy train would come out with your food in a basket on a little train car. The restaurant was meant for kids, but it was our favorite place to eat—that and Rainbow Cone, which you could only go to in the spring. At Snackville Junction, Gretchen always got the same thing: a chili dog and a Green River, this bright green soda-pop drink. Also, they let Gretchen smoke there which was a big deal to her, because clearly she was underage. Me, I always got a grilled cheese or a vanilla shake, and if I got a vanilla shake I knew it would make me sick because, like I said, I was lactose-intolerant, but I'd get it anyway for some fucking reason.

Today I was eating a pizza puff with crinkle-fries and a vanilla shake, so diarrhea was pretty much a definite for me. Gretchen was looking very pretty, which sometimes she did and sometimes she didn't, depending on her mood, I guess. Her hair was up in these two small bluebird barrettes and she didn't really have any makeup on— her face was soft and clean and her cheeks looked scrubbed and pink—and she was eating the chili off her chili dog with the crinkle-fries, scooping it up and then sliding the fry and chili into her mouth quick, which was her way of eating, I guess, and the afternoon sun was like a hundred-watt light bulb in my chest, coming through the window behind her and lighting her hair really nice, making it seem soft white and blond. She was not talking, it was just the two of us eating together, which was nice, and I thought, *What's so wrong with this?*

"Listen what happened today," she said and I nodded. "I'm in the locker room after gym class, right, sitting on this wet wood bench, changing as fast as I fucking can. I usually leave my blouse already buttoned, so I can slip it on, you know, without showing too much of the bulk, right? And so I'm sitting there and I turn and look down the aisle to be sure it's safe to pull off my shorts, so I can finish changing before anyone has the time to comment on my fucking fat thighs, you know?"

"Your thighs aren't fat," I lied.

"My legs are my least favorite feature."

"Really?"

"When I was a kid my dad would call me *Miss Plumpkins, Miss Plumpkins, my pumpkin.*"

"But that's cute," I said.

"I know. He wasn't trying to be like oppressive or anything. Anyway, so I start pulling up my skirt and then I pull down the shorts and begin sliding on my socks, and my fucking legs are so hairy and it's all steamy in there and everything, and guess what? At the end of the aisle is Stacy Bensen. Fuck. Stacy fucking Bensen. So I think, *Fuck, hopefully she won't notice me,* you know? And I try not to look, but I can't help myself. Stacy fucking Bensen is just sitting there on this other bench and both her eyes are black and blue and her fucking head is covered in these huge white bandages and there's a bald spot at the top of her head where her hair was."

"Wow, you fucked her up bad, huh?"

"I guess. But here's the thing: She was changing, right? And her shoulders were all bare and pale and everything, and her blouse was in her hand, and her face was pressed into the fucking blouse, and for some reason, she was fucking crying."

"She was just crying?" I asked.

"Yeah, but listen. She's sitting there in a black fucking bra only, with the white bandage on her face, and crying, and the bra is this shiny black satin thing—fucking trashy."

"Don't you still wear the same bra from eighth grade?" I asked. "The one with the tiny blue flowers?"

"Yeah," she said, nodding. "But listen, she's down there, Stacy Bensen, with her hands over her face, sobbing. And I dunno, I opened my mouth to say something, but hell, I didn't know what to say, because, well, Stacy Bensen is so thin and fucking confident and she's got these long perfect legs, like a lingerie model."

"Yeah, she's hot," I said.

"But that's not it. Everything about her is lovely. The way she sits, the way she smiles, the way she speaks; she's lovely."

"Huh," I said.

"Even with the black eyes and the fucking bandage, she's still so lovely."

"I guess," I said.

"It made me happy to just watch her and imagine what it must be like to be Stacy fucking Bensen just for a minute. You ever do that?"

"Not Stacy Bensen. Vince Neil from Mötley Crüe: I think about being him a lot."

"Well, I was looking at her and wondering, *How can anyone be so pretty?* And you know she's probably had sex once or twice already, or even a few times."

"How do you know?" I asked.

"She's always so sure of everything. And she never asks questions or acts meek and she shows off her body in the locker room. I heard she flirts with the male teachers bad. Well, I was looking at her, thinking, *Does that girl ever feel ugly?* And like that, she starts crying again."

"Yeah?"

"'Are you OK?' I ask her. But she just kept crying. 'Are you sure?' I asked again, and then she says—and listen to this—'I think I'm fucking pregnant.'"

"Really?" I asked. "She just said that?"

"Really," Gretchen said. "So I ask if, I dunno, she wants me to get a teacher and she says to leave her the fuck alone, and so I put on my shoes quick to leave and then I hear her cry again, and I turn back and I see Stacy lift her head—and this is where it gets weird, OK—and she looks like one of those pretty mass cards; there is this string of tiny silver tears in the cups of her hands and it's like all the tears together spell out, 'HELP ME, GRETCHEN,' and I take a step closer and try to think of something to fucking say, but Stacy shouts, 'Leave me the fuck alone!' And I want to say, *But you're just so pretty*, but I knew that out loud it would sound gay, which wasn't how I meant it."

"I know what you mean," I said.

"Right. So I just sat there for a minute and then I stood and began wobbling out. I was feeling kind of woozy, and I remembered I hadn't even finished changing. Like she was that pretty, even when she was crying—even more pretty, you know—that I forgot to fucking finish changing. What do you think about all that?"

"I think being a girl is sort of fucking crazy."

"Yeah," she said. "Yeah." She finished her hot dog, wiped the corner of her mouth with a small white napkin, and said, "So, do you want to drive by her house?"

twenty-two

OK, it was like this incredibly strange and wonderful secret we knew but the rest of the world didn't. Stacy Bensen was pregnant. Stacy Bensen, of all people, with her *Go with God* buttons and abstinence contracts and abundant *Mothers Against Drunk Driving* brochures. So we drove past Stacy Bensen's house at least three times that afternoon, slowing down, just staring. Up the block, down the block, and back again. Gretchen slowed down each time she passed. Why? I dunno, maybe hoping for a glimpse, a flutter of the yellow curtains, a frown in the window, some message, some sign of life, something. I dunno, really. Stacy Bensen was the only girl we ever knew to get knocked up. Only girl our age, at least. I mean, we had heard about it, we had seen it on TV, but this, this was something momentous. We slowed down in front of her house again. Stacy Bensen's house was big and white-bricked and square, about twice the size of my house or Gretchen's. There was a lovely yellow awning above the porch and a pool, which was now covered, around back. Stacy's red fucking convertible Mustang was in the driveway beside a brand-new black sedan. There was a tiny garden out front as well, wilting brown and dull green with the season, guarded by all kinds of magical cement animals: two blue bunny rabbits sitting up on their haunches, smiling; a small elf playing a mandolin; a white swan, its neck curling back on itself; and a large brown deer, nestling its nose to the ground. I noticed the animals the last time Gretchen drove by and smiled.

"Man, do you see all those animals in front of her house? What's that about?" I asked.

"She's like fucking Snow White," Gretchen whispered.

"I guess."

"We should do something to them," Gretchen said.

"OK," I said, and all we could think to do was stop the fourth time, leave the car idling, grab the two bunnies, then the elf, then the swan, and put them all on the front porch as quick as we could, then punch the doorbell before we hurried back to the Escort and drove off wildly.

twenty-three

In his garage, Bobby B. had the AC/DC cranked up, as he tried like hell to get his van to start. I was watching, sitting on the hood of an out-of-commission Chevy, its black-and-chrome nose peeking out from under the dusty beige tarp. It was around eight at night, still real warm, Indian-type summer and all, but getting dark quick. Bobby B. had a work light hung from the lip of the garage and it made long, weird shadows on the empty white garage walls around me.

"The fucking radio's working," Bobby B. mumbled, scratching his head, "so it's not electrical. Maybe the alternator?" He had the front end of the purple wizard van edged beneath the open door of the white aluminum-sided square garage. His brown hair was raggedy and was hanging in his face as he wiped his hands on his gray Megadeth shirt, which was cut at the sleeves to reveal his muscular arms. He turned and picked up a screwdriver and began jabbing at the battery. "Start, you fucker!" he shouted. "Just fucking start."

I gave a little laugh and he glared over his shoulder at me.

"Dude, what are you laughing at?" he asked, sorely.

"Nothing. Sorry," I said.

"Well, fucking stop grinning and come over here and hold this screwdriver for me."

I hopped off the hood of the Chevy and took the screwdriver and pressed the contact wire down at the contact point on the top of the battery. "But hold it down there, so the headlights stay lit. Good," he said, watching the big rectangular bulbs resume shining. "Now fucking keep it pressed down."

He climbed into the driver's seat, wiped his hands on his gray shirt again, and turned the ignition. I could hear a strange, mechanical *click-click-click* as Bobby B. began swearing.

"Dude, are you holding it down?" he shouted.

"Yes."

"Well, what the fuck?" he said, shaking his head. "Try it again."

I pressed down hard on the screwdriver and it gave a little spark as he hit the gas, turning the key, and then *BLOOOOM*, it roared to life, the enormous engine shaking right at my chest, the belts and fans turning with a whiny speed.

"Fuck yeah!" Bobby B. shouted. "Looks like I'm gonna get some pussy tonight after all!" He hopped out of the van, mussed up my dirty hair, and said, "Is there somewhere you need to be dropped off, dude? Because I owe you."

"No, man, I'm cool," I said. "But listen," and I took a seat on the hood of the Chevy again. "Listen, OK. Um, say you like this girl, right, and you're not sure if she likes you. What can you do to get her to, you know, like you?"

"Well," Bobby B. said, pausing in his answer as he walked over to the corner of the garage, opened a small, red plastic cooler, dug out a can of Pabst Blue Ribbon, cracked it open, took a long drink, then drained the entire can. He crushed the can in his hand and threw it out the open garage door. "Brian Oswald, you can't do shit."

"What?"

"The more you like a girl, the less she likes you. It's like fucking scientific."

"What about you and Kim?"

"That's what I'm talking about, little dude. If I start being nice and acting cool and saying things and being on time, she starts acting, you know, fucking uninterested. But if I act like a total dick, then she calls me all the fucking time. It's fucking crazy, because I really like her and all, but when I say nice shit to her, she gets all freaked out and says she needs some fucking space and all. So I just act like I don't give a shit, you know? It's all part of God's plan," he said, nodding.

"Really?"

"What the fuck do I know?" he said, smiling. "All I'm saying is that if I was into a chick that wasn't into me, I dunno. I would play it safe and act like a dick."

"Huh," I mumbled. "Well, thanks, Bobby."

"No problem, little dude. Good luck with that shit. Listen, I got to split. I got a lady to meet."

I hopped down off the hood of the Chevy and watched as Bobby climbed into his van, blaring "Hell's Bells" as loud as the van's stereo could crank it. I watched him back out into the street, the van stalling for a minute, then the lights coming on bright, and him tearing out, leaving a length of rubber as he disappeared into the dark. I wondered about what he said and then thought hard. I could never be a dick, not to Gretchen anyway, so I guess I was doomed; doomed to go for this girl that didn't go for me. But that was OK as I long as I did everything I could. So I crossed the street and headed down to my room and got out all my records and cassettes, found a blank tape under my bed, and started making it, the mix-tape, you know, totally ignoring what Bobby had just said. In about an hour, I was done with it and I stared at the little plastic thing and punched out the tabs so it couldn't be recorded over, and after I did all that, I decided Bobby B. was totally right and there was no way in hell I was going to hand it over to her, knowing how she felt. Like always then, I decided I would wait and see, and hope something in the next few weeks would change for the better for me.

twenty-four

Bad-ass ideas for Kung-Fu movies in which I could star in:

1. A teen helps save an old man ninja who teaches him the way of the ninja and he goes around kicking the other kids' asses in school before he learns the true ninja way in a Chinese star showdown at a video arcade.

or

2. A teenage boy inherits these magical camouflage nunchucks from an ancient council of mysterious assassins and he must learn to use their powers to defeat a series of strange, masked killers, hired to steal the magic nunchucks in their quest to rule the world.

or

3. The boy's father, before he dies, hands him this mysterious book, The Way of the Samurai, and the boy learns many important ninja skills before saving a female ski team from Soviet terrorists bent on upsetting the Olympics. He falls in love with one of the girls from the ski team who is from Sweden, maybe.

Yes, I ordered two Chinese throwing stars and a set of camouflage nunchucks from *Ninja* magazine and that shit still hadn't come yet. It'd been four weeks—why was everyone in the world trying to keep me from realizing my dream of becoming a shadow assassin? I ask you, Bro. Dorbus, why you think it is OK to stand in my way. Yes, you are teaching me in "Religion Class" what spirituality is, which will help strengthen my inner-spirit if I am ever captured and tortured by my countless faceless enemies, but not even you forcing us to watch the entire *Ten Commandments* movie will calm my undying rage and need for the ninja's kind of unending vengeance. You may very well be Numero Uno on the hit list, Bro. Dorbus, and if not Numero Uno, a very close Numero Two.

Numero Uno? John fucking McDunnah. I had seen him in the cafeteria and in the hallway after school. He was bigger than I fucking remembered, in his maroon and orange varsity wrestling jacket, moving between freshmen and sophomores like a motherfucking Aryan mountain range, surrounded by two weasel-faced sportos in their matching varsity jackets. I was standing at my locker and he walked past and I heard that high-pitched jungle-hyena laugh, him shoving one of his fellow goons, and I looked up from putting my books away and made eye contact with him and he just grinned like he knew that I knew it had been him and he also knew that there wasn't shit I could do about it and he just kept staring at me, nodding, until he disappeared down the hallway.

It was hard not to imagine: ordering the Chinese stars and nunchucks, leaping out of a tree on a dark, windy night, busting out his kneecaps or something hardcore kung fu like that, and leaving him there to squeal in pain. I made a solemn ninja oath that somehow, John McDunnah, some way, you will get yours, some day.

twenty-five

It was bad going for Rod at school too, not just because he was black but because he was also a nerd. He got it worst of all from the other black kids in school, I guess. In between 7th and 8th period one day, Rod got his assed kicked by two big black kids, Derrick Holmes and Mike Porter, both of them stiff-necked seniors on the varsity football team. They told him it was because he was so fucking light-skinned. "Hey, white chocolate," one of them said, knocking Rod's chemistry books from his hands. It was just after two o'clock, at the end of the second floor hallway, so no one but other jocks, who got out of class early to work out, and the janitors, who hid beneath the stairwells smoking, were around.

"How come you so white, boy?" Derrick Holmes asked with a laugh. Derrick was a huge kid, with a massive chest and forearms and a face as wide as a bull's.

"Looks like your moms must a gave it up," the other kid, Mike Porter—slighter, ganglier, with a loose, fluid kind of coolness—said, and then shoved Rod against his locker by his neck. "How come you think you're better than all the rest of us, huh?" Mike tore off Rod's clip-on tie and spat. "Prancing around with fucking white kids." He swatted the side of Rod's head and laughed.

Rod wasn't the kind of kid who would fight back. He just closed his eyes and let Derrick Holmes dump a plastic garbage can full of papers and trash all over his head. "Go home to your whitefolks, Oreo."

When I asked him about it that Saturday, we were on the bus heading to the flea market. Rod was looking for the Velvet Underground on vinyl and I was looking for the guy from Chinatown who sold switchblades and butterfly knives, the things that were illegal to sell in the back of kung-fu magazines. I had been eyeing this one silver pearl inlaid butterfly knife for weeks. I was convinced what Rod needed was some sort of weapon he could flash and not another out-of-date record from some group that no one had heard of except his dad.

"How come you didn't fight back?" I asked. "You could have done something."

"You don't get it. Even if I fought back, they wouldn't get it."

"'Get it'? Who cares if they 'get it'? If someone is out to hurt you, you got to fight back, man."

"That's not the way me and my dad see it. He's been hassled. He says they just want you to act like an animal, you know. But if you do, then you're no better than them."

"Yeah," I said, "I don't know about any of that. I just know if someone knocked my shit out of my hands, I'd start swinging."

"Maybe that's why no one fucks with you."

"Maybe," I said, thinking of getting hit in the head with the egg in the stall. I never told anyone about it. Why? Because it was fucking humiliating and I never really knew if they had done it to me on purpose or if they would have just done it to anybody, and, well, like I said, it was pretty fucking embarrassing.

"Yeah, maybe," he said.

"Hey, you thinking about asking anyone to Homecoming?" I asked. "It's coming up quick."

"Who? Who am I going to ask?" he said, shaking his head. "The only other people I talk to is you and my mom and dad. And I ain't asking any of you."

At the flea market, we ended up stopping at this booth where this man had all kinds of weird, foreign horror flicks. The guy was tall and thin with a brown ponytail that ran down his back. He was wearing a Blizzard of Oz T-shirt and was smoking, nodding his head to some Dio he had playing.

"You guys wanna see something scary, check this one out—it's from Italy," he said, sliding a videotape of Lucio Fulchi's *Beyond* across to me.

"Dude, I've seen that one already. It's garbage," I said.

"OK, how about *Evil Dead*?" the guy asked.

"Man, that came out like ten years ago. Do you got anything, like, unknown?"

"Have you ever seen El Santo, the masked wrestler from the '50s?"

"Duh," I said. "I was asking about serious horror."

"Well, OK, how about this," he said, sliding a blank VHS tape toward me. "It's a VHS transfer from an old 8mm."

I picked up the videotape and read the title: *Lion vs. Tiger!*

"What the hell is that?" I asked.

"Five bucks to find out," he said. I had the five bucks I was planning on spending on the butterfly knife, but *Lion vs. Tiger!* How could you resist it?

We went back to Rod's house, locked his bedroom door, slid the tape inside, and waited. A black screen came up:

THIS DOCUMENT IS A WORK OF FACT: SADLY, WHILE FILMING A SHORT FILM WITH THE VERHOEVEN CIRCUS IN FINLAND, OUR CAMERA CREW BECAME WITNESS TO THIS TERRIBLE ACCIDENT.

Then it cut to a grainy black-and-white shot of a lion swiping at the bars of its cage. A strongman in black tights strikes his whip at the animal, trying to get it to perform, maybe. He turns and closes the gate to the cage. The camera follows him as he smiles, says something unclear, and flexes his muscles for the camera. He lifts the bar for another cage and leads a magnificent tiger out by its collar. And then, from out of frame, the lion attacks, escaping from its cage somehow, knocking the man on his back. The strongman rolls to his side, catching a meaty claw to his neck. The tiger lunges, hissing and growling, snapping its claws near the lion's head. The lion snaps back, leaps forward, and sinks its mouth into the tiger's neck. The tiger turns and catches one great paw into the lion's throat and then quickly, with one movement, has its enormous jaws around the lion's neck and begins snapping wildly. The tiger retreats as a gunshot goes off, limps into its cage, and stops moving. From out of frame, two cameramen help the strongman to his feet, and the lion lies there, its black eye blinking, before you can tell that both animals are dead.

"Shit," I whispered. "That was intense."

"Yeah it was."

"It's just like fucking high school."

"Nope, it's the whole fucking world," Rod corrected.

"Yeah. Shit," I said. "Listen, I got to use your can."

"Sure," he said.

I crept out of his room and went down the hall to the bathroom, shut the door, then double-backed around to the front room. I didn't know what I was doing. It was just happening as I was doing it. I knelt down as quietly as I could before those hundreds and hundreds of records, looking nervously for the Chet Baker one. I found it, slipped it out of its place, and started to open it. Why? I dunno. I think I was going to try to steal it. Why? I dunno, really. I mean, I could say it was because I wanted to give it to Gretchen, but then again, I dunno. Maybe I was just jealous of his dad and everything, I'm not sure at all. I do know I looked up to be certain his parents weren't around and there was Rod, standing there, silent, watching me just like that, not saying anything.

"What are you doing?" Rod asked.

I closed my eyes and felt my heart drop like a hammer in my chest.

"I dunno, I'm sorry, man. I was just looking."

"Why are you doing that?" I looked up again and it seemed like he might start crying. His face was dark and his eyes were shiny.

"I . . . I'm sorry, Rod."

"I would have given it to you if you asked."

"Oh, man, I'm sorry. Really."

"I think you should leave," he said.

"OK," I said. "I'm sorry."

He opened the front door and looked at me. "I thought you were my fucking friend."

"I am," I said, and knew how dumb that sounded even as I was saying it.

twenty-six

OK, I was an asshole. A real, total, super fucking asshole. I sat in my bed all night feeling like shit, like crying—but I didn't—and I thought about calling Rod up and apologizing, but for some reason I couldn't do it. I just sat in bed with the pillows over my head. For some stupid fucking reason I just couldn't do it; I couldn't say I was sorry because I was so fucking embarrassed and everything. I put on a mix-tape Gretchen had made for me like a year ago, Things Been Bad, and the first song that came on was by the Lemonheads, when they were punk, and it was called "Fucked-Up," where the singer sang, "I fucked up, I don't want to hear it." The next song was by the same band, and it was called "Hate Your Friends," and he sang, "When you got problems you can't solve, it's enough to make you start to hate your friends." I rewound that song and played it over and over and over again all night, twitching and convulsing like an epileptic in my bed.

twenty-seven

At Gretchen's, what we did sometimes was go through all the rooms in her house, just kind of snooping. It was something we did a lot, I guess. We'd get so bored that we'd go through her sister's and parents' rooms, looking for stuff to either laugh at or take. We'd go through her dad's clothes looking for money, or her sister's hope chest to find silly shit, like condoms and love letters. We usually started in her parents' room, lying on the floor, searching under the four-poster bed which was made-up perfectly with pink pillows, the white sheet taut and wrinkle-free on one side, but totally ruffled and unmade where her father slept, which I thought was sad and kinda strange, I guess, how he still only slept on his side of the bed.

"Wow, look at this." Gretchen pulled out her parents' photo album from their wedding and smiled. It was opened to a particular page already, a photo of her mom from her wedding day. It was very pretty but it made me feel sad, right away.

"My mom's a ghost now. But she was pretty, huh?"

"Yeah," I said.

In the photo, Gretchen's mom was laughing, just a very small parting of the lips, and from the picture you could totally hear the sound of it, a small burst of giggles—very delicate, very tiny—which usually ended with her mother pardoning herself, raising the back of her hand to stifle her happiness. It made me feel very awkward and sad, staring at it like that. I hadn't seen much of her mom's stuff around, only one or two pictures really, since she had been gone, I guess.

"You miss her bad still?" I asked.

"Yeah," she said.

In the photograph, Gretchen's mother was wearing a long white veil made of the thinnest lace you could imagine, her face covered

completely, her dark eyes only spots of very delicate softness, making
the veil wet with tears. She looked like a tiny, beautiful angel all in
white, sitting there at a table with a white plastic tablecloth, posing
demurely in a metal folding chair, her own father in a dark suit and her
own mother in pale blue standing behind her, looking grim and looking
down. Gretchen's mother was smiling up at the camera with the small
fairy-tale smile her sister now had, her immaculate fingers reaching up
to press a small sparkling of tears of laughter away, always, always
with the back of her hand. She looked like a ghost, like Gretchen said;
otherworldly, you know, that was her kind of beauty: so lovely, so pre-
cious you felt bad for seeing it, knowing it wouldn't last. Gretchen
didn't look anything like her mom. She looked like her dad, I guess,
short and stocky. I glanced from the photo over to Gretchen. At the
moment, Gretchen's arms and legs and the tops of her hands were
covered in black ink that declared, *"I am a prisoner of class politics,"*
and her forehead had broken out in a number of unexplainable black-
heads. But there was still something there from her mom—maybe her
laugh or that look in the eyes; maybe mischief, I guess.

We went to Jessica's room next. In there, on her white wood
dresser, Jessica had had a framed photograph of John Denver since
she was like seven. It was fucking lame, but hilarious. In the photo,
John was holding a guitar and singing. Jessica loved John Denver.
Once, their parents had taken both of the girls to see him in concert.
There wasn't anything about it that Gretchen ever told me except that
after the concert, her dad had carried her up to bed.

Jessica's room was the opposite of Gretchen's: mostly pink and
white, with framed photo collages on the wall of Jessica's cheerleading
friends, pressed flowers, teddy bears, other miscellaneous girlie crap. The
room was a big fucking sore spot between the sisters. Since Jessica had
been born first, she had been given the bigger room. The worst part wasn't
that it was bigger, it was the tree: a big oak that ran right up to the window.
Jessica had been using it to slip out at night since she was fifteen.

"So?" I said.

"So," Gretchen said. She stole a tube of glitter lipstick from the
dresser and quickly applied it. Gretchen looked around the room for
a minute, wondering, and then there was John Denver, grinning hope-
lessly back, his plain, smiling face and guitar and long hair looking so
out of place and Gretchen leapt at it, laughing.

"What are you gonna do?" I asked.

Quickly, Gretchen slipped off the back of the framed picture, removed the photo of John Denver, set it back down on the dresser, and very carefully, only touching the edges of the picture of her mom laughing, placed it within the silver frame.

"Now what?" I asked.

"Let's take my mom out for a ride," she said and I nodded, not knowing what to say.

After a little while, listening to the Escort strain to turn over, the Clash blaring "Spanish Bombs," Gretchen got the car started. She pulled the framed photo from her purse and placed it along the dash, the ghostly reflection of her mom staring back at us.

"That's a little creepy," I said.

"You don't have to come with," she said, and I nodded again, keeping quiet.

Gretchen jammed the pen into the cassette player and fast-forwarded to "Straight to Hell" as she turned up the volume and drove off. The radio gave a sputter and then stopped working altogether. It made a whiny, clicking sound, then a low buzz. Gretchen turned the volume down and said, "Fuck it."

Outside, I watched the neighborhood as we quietly went past. It was sunny out, just before sunset, and the leaves in the trees were beginning to lose some of their greenness, giving over to fall, allowing for these bright patches of blue sky. Kids were playing football on their front lawns, shouting, running out in the street.

"Very American," Gretchen said with a laugh. "All of them are future rapists."

A mailman was delivering the mail, whistling as he went, the wheels of his mail cart turning, one of them wobbly. We knew him. He had short gray hair and wore shorts well into the winter. We had seen him once sitting on someone's front porch smoking. There had been a black mailman for a few weeks, but then somebody said something and now there was this white old guy who smoked on people's front steps. *Fucking south side,* I thought. Gretchen started to light a cigarette but stopped, smiling at the photo on the dash. She tossed the lit cigarette out of the window and began pointing out the way the world looked as we passed. "It's real sunny today," she said to the photo, "and that asshole mailman is leaning against somebody's fence."

Some time later, the radio switched on, the cassette became unstuck again, and Momma Cass from the Mamas and the Papas began singing "Dream a Little Dream of Me."

"Man, that's real pretty," I said, and could not fight the feeling that it was her mom's voice from the photograph, but talking about stuff like that just sounds weird, unless it's happening at that minute, I guess.

As usual, we drove around with no direction, and ended up finding our way to Stacy Bensen's. We screeched to a halt in front of the white brick house. "What are we doing here?" I asked.

"Just wait here a minute," she said. "You too, Mom." Gretchen jumped out, ran up to Stacy Bensen's garden, lifted the two blue bunnies, then the elf, then the swan from where they rested, and placed them on the front porch again. This time she placed the two rabbits on top of one another, and the elf beneath the swan, as if they were all doing it together. She nodded, then rang the doorbell and booked back to her car, too out of breath to laugh.

"Dude, there is something seriously wrong with you," I said.

At the Yogurt Palace, where Gretchen's sister Jessica worked, we sometimes found ourselves killing time, asking for different samples, staring at the real customers, until Jess demanded we leave. Gretchen would shout, "I am an American! I can do what I damn well please!" then knock over the straw dispenser and we would run out, screaming.

We came in and Jess sighed and then she saw Gretchen with the framed photo of their mom. Jessica was behind the counter, in a bright pink apron and pink blouse and pink and white Yogurt Palace painter's cap, and she just shook her head. There was nothing she could do about us. She was there alone until seven when Caffey, the boss she was nailing, came in.

"What the hell are you doing?" Jess asked, folding her arms in front of her chest.

"Hanging with Brian and Mom," Gretchen said, winking.

"That's not even funny. If Dad sees you doing that, you're gonna send him to the loony bin. Don't you guys have something better to do with your lives?"

"No, not really," I said.

"This one's my favorite." Gretchen handed the frame to her older sister. "But doesn't she look like she's just gonna die early?"

Jessica stared at the photo, touched the thin glass, and nodded. "Yeah, she does, I guess."

"Look at Grandma and Grandpa. Do you think they ever looked happy?"

"Nope. Wow, look at her eyes," Jessica said. "She's laughing so hard she's crying."

"You got her smile," Gretchen said, taking the picture back. Jessica blushed, I dunno, maybe wanting to say something nice, but all she said was, "You guys want anything to eat?"

"Yeah," Gretchen said. "I'll take a raspberry blast for Mom and a chocolate vanilla twist for me."

"Brian, you want anything?" Jess asked.

"No, I'm cool," I said. "I don't eat ice cream."

Jessica nodded and began filling two small Styrofoam cups with each flavor, pulling down on the lever until each one was filled properly.

"Why don't you get a new job, Gretchen?" Jessica asked. "You guys seem bored as hell."

"I'm spending quality time with my family," Gretchen replied, sinking a spoon into the bowl of raspberry.

"Well, where you headed after here?" Jessica asked.

"I dunno. We might go shoplift something."

"Well, be careful. If you get arrested, you two'll have to sit around for a while. Dad's working late and I don't get off until seven."

"OK," Gretchen said. "Hey, Brian and me were talking. How old were you when you lost your virginity?"

"What?" Jessica took a step back, folding her arms in front of her chest again.

"How old were you when someone popped your cherry?" Gretchen asked.

"Why are you asking me this?"

There were no customers in the yogurt shop and the sound of the fans overhead just kept on spinning.

"Forget it," Gretchen said.

"Well, how do you even know I'm not a virgin?" Jessica asked.

"Because we saw the rubbers in your dresser."

"Oh."

"So?"

"I dunno. Sixteen, I guess."

"With who?"

"Bill Paris."

"The kid with the blue Camaro?"

Jessica nodded. "Yeah." Then she asked, "Why'd you want to know?"

"I dunno. We just wanted to know. For comparisons."

"Well, what about you guys?" Jessica asked.

Gretchen's face went red. "I dunno. Last year," she lied.

"With who?"

"My hand," Gretchen sighed.

"Brian Oswald, what about you?" Jessica asked.

"I haven't found the right girl yet," I said. "Why, are you offering?"

"No," she said, then looked down. "Well, that doesn't mean anything. All the people I know who started having sex when they were young are all fucked up now."

"You don't have to lie," Gretchen said, looking up. "We don't mind. Really."

"It'll happen, and when it does, it'll be nice because you waited."

"I guess." Gretchen looked down at the framed photo. "Mom and me and Brian are gonna go meet some sailors. See you later."

"OK. See ya," Jess said.

"*See yaaaaaa*," Gretchen whispered in a ghostly voice, holding the photograph of her mother up, shaking it. "And Jess?"

"Yeah?"

"Thanks for not being a douche-bag."

twenty-eight

Going to somebody's basement party that Friday night, I decided I would totally have to make my move on Gretchen, do or die. It also meant three things:

1. I would try and tell Gretchen how I felt, but I would probably puss out.

2.. If Bobby B. came with Kim, he would hit someone in the back of the head.

3. Something would happen and Gretchen and I would get in some sort of argument by the end of the evening.

I had been walking around the mall to avoid being at home because my mom had the day off of work, and I was just strutting around, heavy-eyeballing the hot chicks with their light-blue eye shadow and glitter lipstick, in patent-leather high heels and black turtlenecks and mini, mini jean skirts, all of whom worked at the hot-chick stores like Express and Benetton; and also, I had been busy getting a boner in front of the Frederick's of Hollywood, staring at all the red and purple and black bras and panties, wondering if it might not be so bad making it with one of those mannequins as long as they were wearing those hot panties; and also killing time at the Aladdin's Castle video arcade to check on a high score of *Rampage* I had made the week before.

In between all that, I called Gretchen at the pay phone and asked what she was doing and she asked if I wanted to go with her to this girl Esme's party and I said, "Why the fuck not?" and decided: *This. This was most definitely it*. There was only like two weeks left before fucking Homecoming and it was a Friday night and still like summer outside, warm and clear, and it made you feel kind of reckless, like you didn't have a care in the world—which I did, but you know, I was trying to outsmart myself, maybe. I went and bought like a bottle of Drakar, this bullshit Euro-cologne and doused myself in it and took the bus over to Gretchen's and we went together from there.

OK, have you been to a basement show before? I had been to a couple with Gretchen. It was loud, usually. The way it usually worked was someone's parents went out of town and someone got a friend's band to play and then another and another and so about a hundred kids all crowded into someone's basement to listen to some shitty punk rock band do Ramones covers, while someone else would start moshing and someone else would start making out and someone else would break up with somebody.

Like I said, the punk kids usually annoyed the fuck out of me, with their green liberty Mohawks and ripped-up jeans and safety pins and spikes and shit, because it was all a put-on. The joke was they were supposed to look beat, like scummy and fucked-up and scabby, but if you've ever waited for a girl to fucking dress like that, well, it takes time, because none of it is an accident. By the time Gretchen was ready, with all her get-up and gunk in her hair and shit, it was already after eight and we headed over to this girl Esme's house in the suburbs—Palos Hills, I think—about a half hour southwest of the city.

"Do you know whose house we're going to?" Gretchen asked.

"I guess," I said.

"You guess? Brian Oswald, this girl fucking loves you," she said, laughing.

Which wasn't exactly true. At a party, I had once made out with this girl, Esme, and I had kind of gotten nervous and blown it by being stupid. When she gave me her phone number to call her, I did. But on the phone I was more uncomfortable and awkward than I was in person, and so I started lying my ass off and said I was a singer in a metal band. When she had asked the name, the best I could come up with on such short notice was "Ramrod" and she said, "Cool," and she asked if we had any shows coming up and I said, "Sure," and then she asked if she could come check us out and I didn't know what the hell to do, so I just stopped calling her.

"Brian, maybe you can sing for her tonight," Gretchen said with a smirk.

"Maybe you can fuck off for mentioning it. That still is the longest relationship I've ever had," I said, kind of pouting.

We followed the long, winding, tree-lined subdivision road around and around until we found the right house. We pulled up out front, Gretchen and me, her pink hair all spiked-up and shiny, a black spiked choker around her neck, her silver chains dangling from her wrists, all kinds of black mascara and lipstick and glittery eye shadow on her lids. She looked hot—not pretty, but hot like a porn star maybe—but she had to check herself in the mirror again. We were sitting in the magnificent Escort and Gretchen was fixing her lipstick and more than anything in the world I wanted to grab her and kiss her; I wanted to make out with her right there, but I didn't. Instead, I watched as she took out a piece of Kleenex from her purse, put it between her lips, and then crinkled it up, the imprint of her hot mouth, the kiss I could have had if I wasn't such a pussy, maybe. It was weird and it made me feel weird to be noticing things like that, but that was what I was thinking. I was thinking about getting her to kiss me. But that was it; I had blown a good chance. We got out of the car and headed up toward the house, me with my hands in my fucking pants.

About this suburban home: It was big and white—about three stories, it seemed—with a two-car garage and a perfect, newly sodded lawn with its own fancy, built-in sprinkler system, which I noticed right away because, hey, I mowed lawns and *this was the suburbs* and everything. There were like about twenty shitty punk rock cars parked up and down the street which was, like I said, this winding cul-de-sac, which was surrounded by this thick, black, metal, shiny suburban subdivision fence. There were about eight more cars parked in the girl's driveway, with kids pulling amps and guitars and cases of beer out of their back-seats and trunks. The two-car garage door was open and we followed some kid who looked like he was eleven—short, skinny, pimply, with orange spiked hair and a NO FX T-shirt—through the garage, past a pristine black Lexus, into a small hallway and down into the unfinished cement basement.

It was like every other basement I'd ever been in, suburban home or not: one long wood flight of stairs down, a few single light bulbs hanging from single wires, and a washing machine and dryer beside some bed sheets hanging on a line. There were about fifty kids there already and it was hot—real hot—down there, with a few fans blowing, but not much air getting in.

Like I said, I knew the girl whose party it was, Esme, and shit. I didn't know if that was her real name or not, but I always thought it was hot, and she was a sophomore at Mother McCauley and kind of friends with Gretchen and she had her dyed-red hair cut in a Chelsea—you know, with the long bangs but the rest of her hair shaved? Also, she wore these cool, retro black cat's eye glasses because I think she was slightly cross-eyed. Like I said, I had made out with her once, kind of by accident. We had been at another party, like a year before, and we were sitting on a couch talking about bands, and she said her first record was *Appetite for Destruction* by GNR and I said that was my favorite record of all time and soon enough we started kissing. Then she giggled and said, "Your name's not Darren, is it?" and I said, "No, it's Brian," and we both laughed and she wrote her name and number on the back of my hand, and then, like I said, I called her and got nervous and lied. More than anything in the world at the time, I wanted to feel her up because she had very small breasts but never wore a bra and always had on these very tight T-shirts, which drove me fucking crazy. I dunno. Now, I guess Esme was only interested in guys who were in punk bands, which is the way it usually goes with those kinds of girls, I guess. I thought the only way to a woman's heart like that was by being a somebody, and I wasn't even close to being a somebody. I mean, fuck, I was in the marching band if that says anything.

Like I remembered her, there she was: Esme, sitting on top of the washing machine drinking a bottle of beer, her red Chelsea looking lovely, talking to Kim, who was there with Bobby B., who, like always, looked bored with everything. They all waved to us and smiled, Bobby B. flashing me the devil sign. As we came down the steps, I could hear a brittle-sounding guitar pounding out power chords from a cheap-o practice amp and tinny drums that seemed far away and muffled, like one of those windup monkeys. At first I thought someone was playing a record on a stereo that had blown its speakers, but when we got to the bottom of the stairs, I saw some band was already playing.

The band was called the Morlocks! with the exclamation point and everything. It was this guy Jim's band, a guy who we all knew, a sophomore at Evergreen Park, the public high school. The name Morlocks! they got from the *Time Machine* by H.G. Wells, which I had read myself. They couldn't really play too well and didn't have a bass player; it was just a singer, guitar player, and a drummer, and they didn't have any real equipment, but to me it was still a band, because to me a band isn't anything but an idea, good or bad, and once you get the idea it's only a matter of time before it either happens or it doesn't. I had been thinking about being in a metal band for years and it was almost as real to me as if it had already happened. Jim had an idea and it was the Morlocks! and he wrote the name *MORLOCKS!* very satanic-looking all over his jean jacket and shirts and on the white rubber tops of his Chuck Taylors with black magic marker. I always thought that it was cool that he wrote his own band name all over everything, even though no one had ever really heard of them. The Morlocks! played about seven songs, one after the other, three of them by the Ramones; the rest were songs Jim had written about this girl we had known, Sheryl Landry, who shot herself when we were in junior high, songs with real subtle titles like "Ricochet Baby" and "I Wanna Be Your Bullet." Mostly the songs were pretty bad, pretty uninteresting, but Jim had a lot of energy and kept spraying beer at the kids who were standing up close. I felt jealous for a good ten minutes watching them play. Not because they were good, but because they were not good and still people were loving them. Especially the girls. Especially Gretchen.

OK, it kind of broke my heart but I looked over and saw Gretchen was up close to the corner where the band was playing and she was dancing with her eyes closed like she was alone and she had her hands over her head and she wasn't moshing like some of the other kids—dudes, mostly, who were karate-chopping the air and kicking and shoving each other; they were younger kids mostly, with recently dyed hair that left color splotches along their necks because they hadn't been told to use Vaseline, or skater kids in their favorite band T-shirts, like Naked Raygun or the Circle Jerks, with their one long strand of hair that hung in their faces like Glenn Danzig. All of them were sweaty and laughing and dancing hard. When we went to these basement shows, I never danced because I didn't know what the hell to do, so I just sat beside Kim and Bobby B. near the washing machine just watching, like always.

Like I said, it wouldn't have been a real party if Bobby B. had not tried starting a fight. See, Bobby B. hated punk music. He would bitch about it all the time. "There's no fucking guitar solos. Those fucking bands should learn how to play their instruments," he'd tell me while working on his van or at some other basement show. The only reason he came was because of Kim, who he was on-again/off-again with anyway. Punk music was just another thing for them to argue about, I guess. I turned to see what Bobby B. was thinking of the Morlocks! and he gave me the devil sign again, followed by a thumbs-down, rolling his eyes. "This is fucking noise," he yelled as loud as he could. Kim covered his mouth, shaking her head, but not before two skinny straightedge suburban kids had heard, their bald heads glistening on their bumpy crowns with sweat. The straightedge kids were all straight: no drugs, no smoking—no sex? I'm not sure about the last one. They were like a weird, hard-core kind of cult that was very fucking arrogant, because they didn't ever get fucked up. They were like the student council kids of that scene. They were dressed in matching Minor Threat T-shirts, which was kind of fucking weird, and they had black bondage pants on, with the four hundred zippers, all tapering down to their twenty-hole combat boots. They also had black magic-markered X's on the back of their hands, you know, to let you know who they were, I guess. It was like being punk wasn't special enough, so they had to be a group within a whole fucking group. Those kids kind of irritated me. Well, the two straightedge kids turned and gave Bobby B. a dirty look, elbowing each other and crossing their arms in front of their chests; and Bobby B., looking at them, just laughed. He moved Kim's hand aside and stood, pushing himself off of the washing machine, patting down his hair, which was getting kind of long and almost unruly. "Do you two faggots have a staring problem?" he asked, pointing his finger back and forth between them. I sat up stiffly, watching it all happen but not doing anything.

"You're the one with the problem, man," the taller of the straight-edge kids said, giving him a dirty look again and turning back around to watch the band. Bobby B. laughed, looking around, and dug into the back pocket of his dirty jeans. He pulled his right fist back out, slipped a pair of brass knuckles over his fingers, and began flexing them, pounding the weapon into his other fist. He strode up behind the taller straightedge kid, looked back at me, and then—*BAM!*—snapped a quick blow to the back of the guy's head. The kid went down like the power company had shut off his lights; one shot, that was it, he was laid out. The other straightedge kid, who was a lot shorter than Bobby B., made a move to maybe swing at him, but didn't. Some punk girls we didn't know gathered around the kid on the ground, whose eyes were weak and flickering, and Bobby B. went back to standing by the washing machine, winking at me.

Fights like that weren't too frequent at the shows because, for the most part, the punk kids we knew were kinda wimpy. They were the ones who had been picked on or hassled in junior high, so most of them were pretty well-behaved. Bobby B., on the other hand, had been a bully his whole life. I thought he was a good guy, but it was like, by exposing him to all these geeky punk kids, he kind of reverted to being the bully. Kim and Bobby B. started arguing, her with her arms crossed in front of her chest, and him smiling and shrugging his shoulders and shaking his head, then he would roll his eyes and wink at me. It seemed like Bobby B. punching someone in the back of the head was just an eventual part of us going to a party, say, around the middle part of the evening.

By then, some of the kids had taken off their T-shirts because it was so hot down there; they were these little skinny punk kids who didn't even have armpit hair yet, but they didn't care, going crazy, dancing and jumping up and down as Jim from the Morlocks! shouted and threw himself against the guitar player, a mulatto kid named Darren who I was told had very rich parents. Then some kids slung their T-shirts on their heads and some were whipping each other with them and some had thrown them in the air and then Gretchen, still with her eyes closed, started taking her black Blanks shirt off, and threw it to the ground and kept on dancing and I couldn't fucking believe what I was seeing. Gretchen was getting fucking naked and there she was, dancing in her white bra with the tiny blue flowers, and I felt myself move away from the wall to get a better look. But there were so many kids it was hard to see anything—anything but the soft sloping lines of her bra strap along her creamy white back.

I turned to ask Kim if she was watching but she was already making out hard with Bobby B., who had his hand down the back of her pants and I could see Kim's thin, lacy red underwear, and they were kind of just dry-humping right there. It seemed like the whole world was making out already, kids pressed against the smooth concrete walls or sitting on the steps or behind the bed sheets, which were hanging. Esme passed by and offered me a bottle of Bud and I said, "Fuck yeah," and drank it down as fast as I could and started dancing around by myself, and it felt good for a minute because I was feeling so fucking lonely. When I looked back, Gretchen was dancing with some dude—it wasn't even someone we knew—and I stopped dancing right then, and Jim from the Morlocks! was holding the mike up to the crowd for their last song, "Rock'n'Roll Radio," another Ramones tune.

OK, then I saw it. I saw this kid—this nobody with long brown skater bangs and baggy skater jeans, with his little narrow bare chest and little grubby scabby hands—making out with Gretchen, kissing her with his tongue and she was kissing him back hard, and they were both sweaty and both of them had their eyes closed, and he was fucking feeling her up and everything, and she was just letting him, in front of everybody. And it seemed everyone in the world around me was making out with somebody—Kim and Bobby B., this tall gangly girl with an Operation Ivy T leaning over this short freshman dude I didn't even know, completely eating each other's faces—and I couldn't take it anymore, so I grabbed a beer from the cooler and headed up the stairs from the basement through the kitchen and out the back door to get fucked up by myself. Totally.

I don't know what time it was already, but outside it was pretty quiet, still very warm, and when I walked out through the back kitchen door I found a beautiful silver and aqua in-ground swimming pool, the sound of the filter still running, but the rest of it quiet and secluded and completely empty. It smelled great, the chlorine, like being a kid in the middle of summer all over again. Downstairs I could hear Jim through the basement windows yelling, "OK, OK, this is our last song, for real," and they went into "Last Caress," a Misfits song I really liked, but they kind of fucked it up, but it was OK because the song was just that good. I looked up and the stars were out and the rest of the neighborhood was deadly fucking silent and I thought about jumping in the pool and drowning myself right there, but I didn't want to die without making it with somebody and so I cracked open my second beer and started drinking. I almost started crying for some reason. I walked toward a set of white plastic lawn chairs and just then I noticed Esme was lying in one, wearing a white terry-cloth towel wrapped around her narrow middle. She had her eyes closed and she was smoking. She opened her eyes suddenly and noticed me standing there and jumped, startled, I guess, maybe.

"You scared me, Brian Oswald," she said.

"Sorry," I said back.

"Well, Brian Oswald, no one's supposed to be back here," she said.

"Sorry," I said.

"I don't want my neighbors to, you know, find out."

"Dude, you have like eight cars in the driveway," I said.

"Yeah, you're right, Brian Oswald," she said and nodded, then laughed. She sat up, adjusted her cat's eye glasses, and lit up another smoke. She was barefoot and her legs were stretched out. Her small shoulders were totally bare, also. There was a tiny silver toe-ring on one of her toes and that was it. I was staring at it for a while and she seemed to notice me staring, but didn't care, and then she reached over and took my beer. She took a sip and handed it back to me and I took a seat in a plastic chair across from her, promising myself not to speak no matter what happened here.

"So what are you doing back here, Brian Oswald?" she asked.

"Nothing," I said.

"You don't like parties, Brian Oswald?"

"I dunno. Hey, why do you keep saying my whole name?" I asked.

"I don't know. It's funny. You have a funny-sounding name. Brian *Oz*-wald. It sounds like a funny name."

"Yeah, I guess," I said.

"Does your band have any shows coming up, Brian Oswald?" she asked, smiling.

"I don't have a band," I said.

"I know," she said. "Brian Ozzzzzwald."

I sat up, frowning. "You of all people shouldn't be making fun of people's names."

"What, you don't like my name?" she asked, defensive, sitting up and crooking her thin eyebrows at me suspiciously.

"No, I like it," I said. "But it's pretty funny."

"I got it from a J. D. Salinger story."

"Wow," I said. "That's cool."

"Yeah. I'm going to change it when I become eighteen, legally."

"Cool," I said. "I was thinking of changing my name too."

"To what?"

"Vince Neil," I said, doing my best now to try to be funny.

"You're pretty funny, Brian Oswald," she said, nodding, taking another sip of my beer.

"That's Vince Neil," I corrected.

"Do you want to know my real name?" Esme asked, leaning in close to me. I could smell her: her hair apple-scented but dusted in cigarette smoke; her skin, some kind of luscious skin-conditioning soap; even her sweat, which was salty, little droplets along her neck.

"OK," I said, leaning in closer again. Esme put her small pink lips beside my ear and I could hear and feel her breathing.

"It's Gladys," she murmured, giggling against my neck. "It's my grandma's name."

"Gladys?" I whispered back. "Really?"

"Don't tell anyone, Brian Oswald," she said, and now we were staring at each other and we were very close and I thought for sure we were going to kiss, but we didn't. We were sitting beside each other, our legs stretched out, face to face, and we were so very close I could see her nose move as she breathed. Then she went and did the most lovely thing ever: She went and took off her glasses and folded them up carefully, then, leaning forward and holding herself up by her fingertips, she went and did the same for me. I looked down and I could see my eye glasses and her eye glasses, folded up neatly side by side along the arm of the plastic pool chair—which was a little wet for some reason—and then she pursed her lips a little and said, "Now don't laugh," and slid out her retainer, which was small and hard and pink and plastic, and set it down beside the two pairs of glasses.

"Now I'm ready," she said, and I could have cried. And so we started making out and

out of nowhere, we were making out and I felt her lips against my mouth and her tongue against my teeth and we were leaning forward uncomfortably, and as she grabbed me by my T-shirt

the soft baby-powder smell of her cheeks and the sweet peach schnapps in her kiss and strange chlorine of her hair and the pool and the summer-y taste of her mouth and spit

vrmmhhh, went the pool filter and the singing heat and the cymbals from "Last Caress" still ringing and kids downstairs shouting and a small dog somewhere barking and the wetness, the smooching of lips against lips

OK, so this is it. This is what it feels like to be really liked by somebody, and *I really like this girl and I hope she really likes me* and *I hope I am doing it OK*

and Esme pulled me on top of her and we were really, really kissing and I felt her arm go around my neck and we were really going at it now, like a couple of rabbits, and then she just stopped and looked up at me and one of her eyes, the left one, really was kind of slower than the right, and she straightened her lips and looked very serious and said, "Are you with Gretchen?" and I said, "I came here with her," and she said, "No, are you going out with her?" and I said, "No, we're just friends," and she said, "If you tell me the truth, I won't be mad at you," and I thought about that for a second and said, "We're just friends," and she nodded and we started making out again.

One hot minute later, some goth kid with long black hair stumbled out back through the kitchen screen door, looked around, nodded, and shouted, "Pool!" then pulled off his shoes and jumped in without getting undressed from his black man-dress. In a couple of minutes, all these sweaty punk kids were tearing off the rest of their clothes and cannon-balling in the air, doing trick moves like front-flips and jack-knives—maybe like sixty kids all going fucking crazy in the pool, someone shouting, "Marco!" and someone else shouting, "Polo," and girls on guys' shoulders chicken-fighting, and kids starting to make out again, and Esme said "Do you want to go inside?" I nodded and we stood up and someone was pointing at us and just then I took a look around for Gretchen and I couldn't find her and I started thinking the worst, like she was taking it from that skater kid, but then she came out, flicking the ash of her cigarette into a beer can, kind of sad-looking. Esme must have noticed me watching because she let go of my hand and said, "Go talk to her if you want, Brian Oswald," and then, like that, she disappeared into the fucking house and that was the end of that.

The truth was I did want to talk to Gretchen, but I didn't know what to say, and so I walked over to where she was standing alone, leaning against a tiny pool shed which someone had busted open to steal some floaties and rafts.

"So what happened to your boyfriend?" I asked, being all shitty.

"He said he had to go to work."

"Did you even ask him his name?"

"Duh," she said. "His name is Jeremy. He goes to school out here."

"Oh, he's a fucking rich kid," I said.

"What the fuck do you care?" she asked.

"I don't care," I said.

"Great," she said. "I heard you were making out again with your scam."

"She isn't a scam."

"If you scam with a girl and never talk to her because you're a pussy, then it's a scam," she said, flicking the ash again into the beer can. "I know. I don't think I'll ever see that kid again. Big deal."

"I dunno," I said, kind of whispering.

"What?" she shouted.

"I dunno," I said again, quieter this time, so that in that one moment Gretchen and I were standing by the pool shed, very close, very close, and it all smelled like chlorine and kind of like suntan lotion and someone somewhere was smoking dope—that kid and that girl on the other side of the pool, maybe—and the night was all sparkly and light-blue, and some kids were naked now, skinny-dipping, and the stars were all reflecting and drifting along with them at the bottom of the pool, and I dunno, I just said, *Fuck it. Fuck it. Why not go for it?* And really quick I sucked in a breath and grabbed the side of Gretchen's face with both hands and kissed her, sticking my tongue in her mouth for one brief instant and feeling her teeth and gums and tongue, and then she punched me in the gut hard, then wiped her mouth with her arm and punched me again and said, "What, are you, fucking drunk too?" And I said, "No." The wind was still knocked out of me and I looked up and she was still wiping her face and then she said, "Well, then stop being fucking stupid."

twenty-nine

OK, I had no special song so I was fucked. Because now all I had was the mix-tape. But to make the perfect mix-tape you had to reveal how cool you were, how interesting, without being obvious that the person you were making the tape for was someone you were completely and totally in love with. That's what Gretchen said anyway.

"The point is not to be too obvious," she warned, inking a tape cover of a smiling skull, knives projecting from his saucer-sized eyes, with her black magic marker. We were in Gretchen's room, both of us working on tapes. I was trying to make another one for her but it was still mushy and lame, and she was making one for none other than—you guessed it—Tony Degan. I was watching her work and wondering how long it would be before she finished the tape, gave it to him, and ended up being mauled, sexually, by him.

"That's my whole problem," I said, staring at her with longing on me like a stink. "I am too obvious."

"What songs do you have picked out?"

"I dunno. I can't think of anything good."

"Let's see what you've recorded so far," she said.

"'Every Rose Has Its Thorn'! 'Home Sweet Home'? What the hell is the matter with you? What girl even likes this shit?"

"I dunno. I can't think of the right songs without being mushy."

"Who are you even making this for?" she asked, squinting.

"Some girl in my band class," I lied.

"Is she a skank?"

"No," I said. "She just likes rock."

"The point is to show her you're cool, not to be all fucking whiny. That way it's like a secret that you like her."

"Well, Tony Degan's going to know you like him anyway," I said.

"Nope, I have a method."

"What method?"

"I'm putting on very fast, very loud songs."

"So?" I asked.

"So it's not all lovey-dovey."

Gretchen pressed the record button and started the next song, the Dead Kennedys' "Holiday in Cambodia." She had a few from London Calling, then a few from the first Black Flag—"Wasted," etc.— then the entire second half of Operation Ivy. The bedroom door opened and we looked up and Kim stepped in smiling and wearing a black Misfits T-shirt and a red flannel skirt. Her red herpe had not gone away and she had used a lot of the wrong color cover-up to try and hide it. She leapt on the bed and pinched Gretchen's side smartly.

"You ready to go, douche-bags?" Kim asked.

"I guess. How'd you get here so fast?" Gretchen replied.

"You know that kid with the mohawk, Mike, that one kid that works at the movie theater in the mall? He dropped me off."

"Oh yeah? Is he cool?" Gretchen asked.

"Yeah. Well, I dunno, he's kind of a faggot. He just, well, kind of dry-humped my leg."

"He seemed kinda nice."

"I thought he could get me into the movies and shit, but all he does there is sweep up. So, you guys ready or what?"

"OK."

"I think I'm gonna go home," I said. I stood up and pulled on my jean jacket.

"What's the matter with you, pussy?" Kim asked.

"I just don't feel like going."

"Well, Bobby and Tony are up there. You guys can watch me kick that girl Laura's ass," Kim said.

"Why? I thought we liked her," Gretchen said.

"I did, until I found out asshole-Bobby made out with her."

"I thought you guys broke up and were seeing other people and all," I said.

"We are—I mean, we kinda are. We're still kinda dating and not really talking again. And I told Laura, you know, that Bobby and I had stopped talking again, and she was like, 'Well, you guys are meant to be. It'll work out'—and then Bobby the douche-bag goes and tells me he felt her up in the back of his van."

"I think you two ought to just leave each other alone, once and for all," Gretchen said with a nod, slipping on her black boots.

"I would if he didn't know how to fuck, but shit. I mean, you know, Bobby is like a total fucking retard, but when it comes to fucking . . . well, I dunno. Hey, Tony Degan was asking about you again."

I sat back down on the floor, waiting to listen. I started going through Gretchen's record collection. I wanted to hear what Kim had to say, to well, see what my chances were, maybe.

"He was asking about me?" Gretchen asked in a whisper.

"Yeah, he was. He said he wanted to 'see' you again. What do you think that means?"

"I dunno."

"You were totally making out with him the other night, in the parking lot and all. And I thought you were, like, all junior-high babysitter—'I hate boys, I'm gonna save my virginity for Glenn Danzig or Ian MacKaye'—and shit."

I felt my heart become small and shriveled like a baby bird left to burn alone out in the sun. I turned and stared at Gretchen who was blushing. She looked so fucking cute blushing it made me want to punch a wall.

"I dunno. Tony, he's real quiet, you know? He's very gentle. You couldn't tell by looking at him, but he's like a little kid. He told me he sometimes cooks for his mom when she's tired, you know? Well, I dunno, I dunno."

"What? What is it? He's totally hot."

"I dunno. I mean, he's really, well, he's all into White Power. That's kind of fucked up."

"So, you're not black, are you? What the fuck do you care?"

"No, I dunno, I mean . . ."

"What the fuck then? I mean, he's cute, and he's cool, and he said he's way into you. I mean, Jesus, Gretchen, I'll jump his bones if you don't, douche-bag."

"I guess. It guess it just kind of scares me."

"Jesus, Gretchen, remember when you were real fat? Remember when you used to sit inside and do homework on the weekends? Do you? Because I do. You were like a total dork. Now you look good, and you got some hot guy that's totally into you and you're acting like a total douche-bag. What's the fucking problem?"

"No problem," Gretchen said quietly.

"Good. Listen, if that girl Laura's there, I'm gonna stomp her fat ass. Tell me who Bobby roots for." Kim turned and stared at me. "You coming, Brian?"

"Nope," I said. I grabbed my mix-tape and slipped it into my front pocket, pouting.

"Well, see you later. Let's go already."

After that, I went by Rod's house. I didn't even go up and knock. I just stood there and walked along the side of the house and listened and somebody, maybe Rod's dad, was playing some loud, rowdy jazz music and the trumpet was freaking out and then it got very quiet and I decided I ought to do something. I didn't know what I should do, but I knew I had to do something. All I had was the shitty mix-tape I had secretly made for Gretchen, so I placed it beside his window, the red curtains lit from behind, and knocked twice, running before he could see who had left it.

After school the next day I took the bus over to where Jessica, Gretchen's sister, worked at the Yogurt Palace and said, "I think I'm in love with your sister."

"Duh."

"No, I mean it."

"Like I said, duh."

"I want to make her a mix-tape and I need to know her favorite song. So what's her favorite all-time song?" I asked.

Jessica looked me over, squinted her eyes, and then frowned.

"I don't think she likes you," she said, leaning over the counter to pat my hand.

"I know that already. But, well, I want to ask her to Homecoming. And, well, what can I do about it?"

"Oh, Brian," she said, patting my hand again. "You really don't have a clue, do you?"

"I guess not," I said.

"The only thing you can do is give up now," she said, pulling her hand back.

That night, I went back by Rod's to ask for his help.

"What? What do you want?" he asked, standing on his front porch, frowning at me solemnly.

"I need your help, Rod."

"What is it? You're not high right now, are you?"

"No, that's not it, man," I said.

"Well, then?"

"I need the perfect song, man."

"What?"

"The perfect song: I need the perfect song, Rod."

If I could woo Gretchen with the right song, if we could go park over by the cemetery and I could shut off the lights and pop in the right cassette, then maybe, well then maybe I'd have a chance. But Rod wasn't having any luck thinking of the right song either. We were sitting Indian-style in the middle of his room with all kinds of records and cassette tapes spread out all around us.

"How about 'Come Sail Away'?" he asked me.

"No way, retard, that's like a prom kind of song."

"How about 'Surrender'?" he asked.

"Too rocking. It needs to be more mellow."

"How about, well, something like Elton John?" he asked again.

"He's a fag. I can't put on any fag music with this girl."

"I don't know then," Rod said. "It's hopeless."

"Come on, man, don't say that. You're the only one who knows this kind of shit."

"I don't even know why I'm trying. You tried to steal from me."

"See, Rod, when you say shit like that it makes you sound like a puss. I was going to take that record to do this, but you wouldn't help, remember?"

"But I mean, you don't even talk to me at school," he said. "That makes me feel like a nerd."

"Jesus Christ, Rod, you are a nerd. You sit alone at that one table in the corner. You wear that red sweater all the time. You just kind of mope around, man."

"I don't want to help you with this anymore," he said.

"*I don't want to help you with this anymore*," I repeated, mocking him. "Fine, but when you're like eighteen and still like hanging out in your room and you haven't gotten any pussy yet, don't come crying to me, OK? I'm just trying to help you."

"Sure," he said.

"Rod, I don't want you to be a nerd either, man. I wouldn't mind hanging out with you at school, but you're just so fucking droopy."

"I don't try to be droopy."

"But you are. Listen, Rod, this is a one-in-a-million shot here. You got to help me with this song."

"Like when you tried to steal my dad's record?"

"Holy Christ, why do you keep bringing that up?" I asked.

"It is like our favorite record of all time. I just want you to know that."

"You are so faggy. How old are you, man? You talk like a little fucking kid."

"Oh, because I'm not cool and I don't swear for the sake of it? Well, oh, fucking this and, oh, dildo that."

"I knew I shouldn't have wasted my time with you," I said and got up to leave. He put out his hand, waving me to stay.

"Wait a minute, just wait a minute. How about an instrumental?" he asked.

"What?"

"It'd make you seem kind of cool. Like a theme song, with no words; you know, like you were in a movie or something."

"An instrumental?" I asked again.

"Yeah."

"Well, like what did you have in mind?"

thirty

At the Haunted Trails in the far corner of the parking lot, we were sitting inside Bobby's van—Tony Degan and Bobby B. and me—and we were splitting a 40. Aerosmith was on the stereo with "Sweet Emotion," and I was waiting to meet Gretchen up there because I had the new-improved Rod-version mix-tape in my pocket and was waiting for the right time to give it to her, and she wasn't up there yet, and Bobby had asked if I wanted to chill in his van. The song Rod and I had picked out was "Sleepwalk," this '50s kind of song by Santo and Johnny, and I kept thinking about it as Tony Degan started talking to me.

"You're pretty quiet, huh, Brian Oswald?"

"I guess," I said.

"Where do you live?"

"Evergreen Park," I said.

"Yeah, me too," he said. "Have you been seeing any niggers around lately?"

"Nope."

"I have. Hanging out, up at the park," he said.

"Huh," I said.

"Black people, man, they live like fucking animals."

"Yeah?" Bobby asked.

"They live like fucking animals and the next thing you know, they're living right next to you. Just the other night there were three of them up at the Evergreen Park, playing basketball like they owned the fucking place, jumping around, tearing down the nets. I ain't having any of that shit. This is our fucking neighborhood. My dad didn't work his ass off his whole life so a bunch of niggers could move in and start selling their fucking crack and having fucking babies and breaking into my fucking house at night. Just a week ago someone stole my little brother's bike. My fucking dad had to pay for that; he didn't get no government hand-out. So I've had enough of this shit. I'm going up to the park later tonight and if some of those niggers are hanging out there, I'm gonna take a tire iron to their big nigger heads and convince them they'd better fucking leave. And to stay the fuck out of Evergreen."

"What about the cops?" Bobby asked, squinting his eyes.

"The cops don't want them over there either. I know I got them on my side, but I know their fucking hands are tied. So it's up to you and me. OK?"

"OK," Bobby said.

"What about you, Brian?"

"I don't think so, Tony."

I started to open the van's sliding door and Tony pulled himself out too and when I climbed out, I turned and bumped into Gretchen. She had been leaning against a Chevy El Camino that was parked too close. I smiled and wondered if she had been there the whole time waiting. Before I could say anything, Tony Degan was smiling at her and she was smiling back and I felt the weight of the mix-tape in my pocket begin to vanish, totally disappear, just like that.

"Hi," I said.

"Hey," she said, still looking at Tony.

"Hello there," Tony said with a slightly dopey grin.

"Were you in there with some girl?" Gretchen asked him, half-smiling, half-frowning.

"I don't hang with girls," Tony said. "Girls will make you crazy," he laughed. "I guess that's how you say hello to somebody, though, huh?"

"Hello."

"Hello. You came up here to see me?" Tony asked with a wink, then slowly, very gently, he went to take her hand. Gretchen went stiff as soon as he did. He held her hand and smiled, running his finger over her silver rings. I felt sick to my stomach watching it, but I didn't want to walk away. For some sick reason, I wanted to watch it all happen.

"No, I didn't. Well, I came with Kim. She's looking for that Laura girl again. Apparently, Laura called her a transvestite."

"Laura already took off. She's got eyes on Bobby, bad."

"Kim knows. She said she's gonna stomp that girl's ass if she sees her around again."

"Yeah? You girls are pretty tough, huh?" he laughed.

"I dunno. Kim is. Me, I just tag along."

"You feel like taking off? Going for a ride in Bobby's van?" Tony asked her, and I could feel the dumb heat of it burning my face. I was just going to stand here and watch it happen. I wasn't going to say a fucking thing. Why? Because what did it matter? What did any of it matter?

"Who, me?" Gretchen asked with a big smile.

"Yeah, you. You feel like heading out somewhere?"

"I dunno." She looked down at her boots.

"Oh, you're playing hard to get, huh? Well, what if we go get something to eat, just you and me? How would that be?" He laced his fingers in hers and gave her hand a squeeze.

"Like at a real restaurant? With seats and everything?" she asked.

"Like what?"

"I dunno. Duke's?"

"The drive-in? They don't got any seats," he said with a smile.

"That's OK."

"Well, then, it's OK by me. I've only got ten bucks so don't go ordering no lobster or anything."

"OK."

"OK. Stay right here while I get Bobby's keys." Tony let go of her hand and strode off, back toward the corner of the parking lot where Bobby B. was smoking.

"OK, Tony," she sighed, nodding, standing obliviously beside me. The mix-tape disintegrated in my front shirt pocket. "OK, Tony."

thirty-one

Bad-ass songs about the Devil to play while stabbing somebody like, I dunno, Tony fucking Degan maybe, as you offer his soul up to fucking Satan for all eternity:

1. **Twist of Cain** by Danzig
2. **Black Magic** by Slayer
3. **Jesus Saves** by Slayer
4. **Number of the Beast** by Iron Maiden
5. **Shout at the Devil** by Mötley Crüe
6. **Helter Skelter** by the Beatles
7. **Children of the Beast** by Mötley Crüe
8. **South of Heaven** by Slayer
9. **Jump in the Fire** by Metallica
10. **Mr. Crowley** by Ozzy
11. **Soul on Fire** by Danzig
12. **Behind the Crooked Cross** by Slayer
13. **The Anti-Christ** again by fucking Slayer

thirty-two

OK, for fun sometimes, Gretchen and Kim would have these conversations while I was sitting there in the backseat and it was like they would just do whatever they could to fuck with me. We would drive around after school, killing time before Kim had to go to work, and they would sit up front and I would sit in the back and they would have their own fucking conversations and make fun of how lame I was and I would just sit there and fucking take it. Why? Because, well, you know why already.

"Hey, Brian, do you know if your hand is bigger than your face, that means you'll get cancer?" And I'd put my hand up to measure my face and—*BAM!*—Kim would make me smack myself.

Or:

"Hey, Brian, what's a dikkfur?" Kim would ask.

"I dunno," I'd say. "What's a dikkfur?"

"What's a dick for? What are you, retarded?" and she'd laugh.

Or outright stupid insults like:

"Hey, Brian," Kim would ask. "Did you hear they're making these machines in Germany you can have sex with. These wanking machines?"

"So?"

"So, there you go. You can finally get laid," she'd laugh. "Get it? Because you are a fairy-virgin. And you would need a machine to get laid." She punched my leg hard and started snorting and laughing.

"Why don't you go blow, slut?" I asked.

"So anyway," Kim said, turning around again, facing Gretchen. "I heard somebody was out doing something nasty with somebody in somebody else's van."

"What?" Gretchen asked.

"I heard somebody was out doing something nasty with some-body in somebody else's van."

"I dunno," Gretchen whispered.

"Well, Bobby said he gave Tony Degan the keys and then the two of you just disappeared. So, what do you got to say for yourself?"

"Nothing. I dunno."

"You're turning into a big fucking slut."

"No. Nobody . . . well, nobody looks at me the way he does."

"What?"

"Nobody else looks at me like that. Like he's going to . . . I dunno, tear my clothes off or something."

"Well, you should go hang out at the fucking Aladdin's Castle sometime, you know, the arcade in the mall? I was supposed to meet Bobby there and he was late as fucking usual and so I was the only girl in there and you would have thought I was Heather Locklear or something—fucking geeks."

"He didn't even say anything to me. He just looked at me, you know? He looked me over like they do in movies. Then he came over and put his hand on my face, like this." Gretchen placed the palm of her hand gently against the side of Kim's face. "And then he said, 'Do you want to go do something?' and I said, 'OK.'"

"Well, you better watch out. You know. Maybe he's just trying to use you for your sweet little pussy."

Gretchen sat up in the hard plastic seat, nervous. "Why? Why'd you say that?"

"What?"

"What you just said? Why'd you say that?"

"What? I didn't say anything. I was fucking around," Kim said.

"What you said, about him using me? How come you said that?"

"I dunno. I was just saying; I was just fucking around."

"What? That he has to be using me because he actually likes me? Is that it?"

"No, I just meant how he, well, you know, tried to get you to . . ."

"You don't know what it's like, Kim. You don't."

"Oh, fuck. Here we go again." Kim pushed her seat back and rolled her eyes.

"No, fuck you. You never were fat. You don't know what it's like. Boys won't even talk to me unless, you know, I happen to be with you,

you know, so they can find out if you're single or not and try to fuck you or whatever. You don't even know. You've never felt ugly a day in your life. You get very fucking lonely."

"What the fuck? I know what it's like. Boys are afraid of me!"

"Well, that's just because you want them to be. I mean, you like it when boys are scared of you. I mean, I didn't fucking ask to be born a size 12, you know. Fuck it. It doesn't even matter. It's always gonna be like this, even in like a hundred years. People don't like ugly people, you know. It's like the last real prejudice."

"Yeah, that and being fucking white."

"I dunno. You know what I mean," Gretchen said.

"Boys are all fucking jerks. All they want is to fuck you up anyway. You know that guy Mike, from the mall, with the mohawk? He won't return my calls now."

"Because he jizzed on your skirt?" Gretchen asked.

"How the fuck should I know. I mean, fuck, he's not even cool. He's like a dweeb, you know? He's not even punk rock, he just dresses like it. I mean, he's like into comic books and shit like that. I mean, the only good thing about him is that he's got a car. So that's, like, the trade-off."

"Bobby has a van," Gretchen said.

"But Bobby is a fucking asshole. I mean, he fucking told that girl Laura that she is his 'ideal woman.' Can you even believe that shit? I was the first girl to ever give him fucking head."

"Well, she must have given him head too."

"Sometimes I wish there was no such thing as fucking boys, for real. Fucking assholes. Except you, Brian," she said, and then, "No, no, including you too."

"Remember in junior high when we told everyone we were from outer space? From Planet Nav-o-nod?" Gretchen asked.

"Because Nav-o-nod was Jon Donovan's last name backwards," Kim said.

"I was so in love with Jon Donovan."

"Me too. Now he drives an El Camino—douche-bag."

Both girls groaned, making stinky faces. I laughed too, remembering Jon Donovan, who was tall and handsome with this massive blond head of exquisitely styled hair, like a game-show host.

"What was your name?" Gretchen asked.

"Xanadu. Like the Olivia Newton John song."

"See, that's what gave us away. When you told Mrs. Pinchi that at the beginning of seventh grade, she couldn't take us seriously."

"Yeah, well, what the hell, I tried. What was your name again? I forget."

"I was Queen Spellbinder," Gretchen said with a smile.

"That doesn't even make sense."

"I know. That's why it was so awesome."

"I guess."

"Remember when we had Brian scared shitless?"

I sat up and leaned my head forward. "What? What did you say about me?"

"Remember when we told you we had no men on our planet and we were gonna breed with you so we could continue our earth race?" Gretchen asked.

"Dude, you ran out of her bedroom and fell down the front stairs. I thought you were going to fucking puke," Kim said.

"Yeah," I said. "That was really fucking great."

"Hey Brian," Kim asked. "Are you still a fucking virgin?"

"He's always gonna be a virgin, even if he loses his virginity," Gretchen answered for me.

"Are you sure you're not, you know, a faggot?" Kim asked.

"I'm not a faggot," I said.

"He's not a faggot," Gretchen answered again. "He just has this 'I'm going to live in my mom's basement and work as a janitor for the rest of my life' kind of thing going on."

"Shit, once I caught Brian making kissy faces at me," Kim said. "Do you remember that?" she asked me.

"What! When?" I asked.

"A couple of summers ago, like in eighth grade, when we had the tent up in Gretchen's backyard. Remember when we had the math team sleepover?" she turned to Gretchen and smiled, "and your mom made us popcorn and hot dogs and your dad tried telling us a ghost story and his fly was totally undone?"

"Yeah," Gretchen said with a smile.

"Well, I woke up in the middle of the night and I saw Brian staring at me and he was pretending to kiss me."

"That didn't happen," I said.

"What did you say to him?" Gretchen asked.

"I said, 'Stop being gross, you fucker.'"

"What did he say?" Gretchen asked.

"He said he was just practicing. He said I was gonna come to my senses and that I'd want to make out with him someday."

"That never fucking happened," I said again. It was quiet for a minute and then Gretchen spoke up.

"I wish we didn't ever have to grow up. Yuck."

"Me too. But shit, then I think of Bobby and his dick it makes me never want to be a kid again."

"I guess. Maybe it's just easier for you. Don't you wish you were a kid again, just sometimes?"

"No, being a kid sucked. I want to be on my own as soon as possible. You should too. I mean, you gotta grow up sometime, right? Listen, before you drop me off, can I borrow your geometry homework?"

"Yeah, I'm done with it." Kim reached into Gretchen's bag, fumbled around, and dug her geometry homework out.

"I'll get it back to you in the morning, OK?" Kim asked.

"OK."

We pulled up in front of the Chicago Ridge Mall, right by the entrance to the food court where Kim worked at the Orange Julius, and Kim got out. "See you," she said to Gretchen, then turned to me and pressed her hefty chest against the car window. "Bye, lover," she said, huffy, breathy, laughing, as she spat a loogie and disappeared behind the thick glass doors.

"Are you going to come up front?" Gretchen asked.

"Not if you keep making fun of me," I said.

"Well, then stay back there, homo," she said and took off, laughing.

thirty-three

In the afternoon, Gretchen and I would still drive by Stacy Bensen's. I dunno why. To kill time, maybe, or because Gretchen was still feeling guilty for busting up her face, to torture her—who knows, really. It was about three-thirty, right after school, and, well, after cruising past three or four times Gretchen actually parked the car and got out. I followed, not knowing what the hell she was doing. Gretchen walked on up to the cement front porch and rang the doorbell and I looked at her, wondering, and asked, "What the heck are you doing?" and Gretchen just shrugged, blowing some hair out of her face.

Like that, Stacy answered the door, still wearing her school uniform which fit her long body perfectly, and she had on a pink sweatshirt, her blond hair done up in a ponytail. She was drinking a Diet Coke, leaning against the door, and if her eyes weren't still so very black and blue and her nose still covered with the white gauze bandage, she might've seemed hot, maybe. She was smoking, exhaling from the corner of her mouth with flair, and I thought I could see it there—that look, as busted-up as her face was, that sense that no matter what, she would always be better than us, maybe.

"Yeah?" Stacy asked. "Brian Oswald? What do you people want?"

"Is this really where you live?" Gretchen asked, peeking in at the huge silver and mirrored front room. I thought her question was kind of weird considering how many times we had already been there.

"Yeah," Stacy said, exhaling.

"It's pretty," Gretchen said.

"Yeah, it is," I said, and decided that would be it for me trying to speak to Stacy Bensen.

"Yeah. I guess it's OK," she said. "I saw you two drive by yesterday. What do you want?"

"I dunno. We just came by to see how you were feeling."

"My face still feels like shit. I think you gave me a deviated septum."

"Yeah, well, sorry about that," Gretchen whispered, nodding. "So. So are you really fucking pregnant?"

Stacy looked at Gretchen, then at me, and blew out a mouthfull of smoke. "Why do you care?"

"I dunno," Gretchen said, shrugging her shoulders. "I thought, I dunno, maybe we could do something for you."

"Well, I'm not pregnant. I got my period yesterday," Stacy said, letting out a breath. She took another drag on her smoke and nodded to herself.

"Oh," Gretchen said, nodding back. "Well, that's good, huh?"

"Yeah. Now Mark Dayton can go back to fucking whoever else he wants."

"Mark Dayton? That kid from Marist? He was the guy?" Gretchen asked.

"Yeah. You know him?"

"I guess," Gretchen said. "He's a fucker."

"He really is," Stacy said.

The two girls looked at each other—Stacy with her arms crossed, Gretchen nodding—in a way that was like, *Maybe you're OK, maybe.*

"So were you the ones who did that with the animals?" Stacy Bensen asked.

"The animals?" Gretchen asked.

"The lawn animals, having sex."

"Yeah. That was us," Gretchen said.

"How come?"

"I dunno," she whispered. "To cheer you up, I guess."

"It didn't cheer me up. It freaked me out."

"Sorry about that," Gretchen said.

"Yeah. It was pretty funny, though."

"Yeah."

"Well, thanks for coming by, I guess."

"Yeah." On the porch, we all stood for a moment, the faraway sound of laughter from a sitcom on the TV rising. *Was it* Charles in Charge? *Was she watching TV? She's just as lonely as us*, I thought suddenly.

"Do you guys want to come in or something?" Stacy asked, holding the side of her bandaged nose. There were tiny red flecks of blood along the edge.

"I dunno. Can I bum a smoke?" Gretchen asked.

Stacy nodded, dug into her sweatshirt pocket, and handed Gretchen the pack. Gretchen fumbled nervously for a cigarette, placed it in her mouth, noticed it was a menthol, asked, "Is this menthol?" to which Stacy nodded, but Gretchen lit it anyway.

"Does Brian want one?" Stacy asked.

"No, he doesn't smoke," Gretchen said.

"Nope," I said. "My pipes are clean," I said, and then definitely decided there would be no more talking for me.

"So," Gretchen whispered, nodding again.

"So," Stacy whispered back. "So. So you ever been to a tanning salon?"

"Who me?" Gretchen asked. "Nah."

"I got a tanning bed in the basement. You guys want to look at it?"

"I dunno. Not really," Gretchen said with a shrug.

"Well, do you guys want to help me make cookies? I promised my little brother I'd make him some."

"Yeah, I dunno. But thanks for asking. We gotta be going, Brian's got to be home."

"OK," she said.

"OK."

"So see you around, though."

"Yeah, see you around," Gretchen said, starting down the steps. As soon as we heard the door shut, Gretchen turned and grabbed the first blue bunny from the garden, put it up right behind a garden gnome like it was humping it, and then ran to her car, started it up, and began honking. Stacy Bensen came to the door, holding her nose, and nodded, looking at the poor rabbit and gnome, just standing there. I could not tell whether she was laughing or crying.

After that, we drove over to Marist High School's football field where Gretchen said Stacy Bensen's boyfriend would probably be practicing. All the sport-os and jocks had their red practice football uniforms on and were doing drills and throwing passes and smacking each other's asses after every fucking play. Gretchen and I sat in the Escort listening to it idle hard, and cranked up "Wasted" by Black Flag when it came on.

"So what are we doing here?" I asked, finally.

"We're gonna fuck that guy up."

"Are you gonna run him down or something?" I asked.

"No. I dunno. Do you got any ideas?"

"No."

"We could throw something at him and then drive off."

"Like what?"

"How about a brick?"

"I don't know about that. How about some sloppy food, like chili?"

"No, no, I got it," she said. "How about a bag of shit?"

"Where are you gonna get a bag of shit?"

"I dunno," she said. "Do you need to take a crap?"

"Nope," I said, shaking my head.

"How about a bag of piss? Do you have to pee at all?"

"I could pee," I said. "I could definitely pee. Where do we get a bag?"

We drove over to the Jewel on 103rd, bought the largest size of Ziplock bag we could find, and doubled back, parking in front of the football field in exactly the same spot. I thought if I did all this Gretchen would think I was kind of bad-ass—you know, unconcerned with getting busted and all—and I was fine with it until we were there in the Marist High School parking lot and she said, "OK, go pee."

"Right here?"

"Yeah, I don't care."

"I'm not going to pee in front of you."

"Why not?" she asked.

"Fuck you, why not," I said.

"Then do it behind one of these cars."

"Fine."

I hopped out of the car, taking one of the big plastic bags with me. I slumped down behind someone's red convertible and unzipped my pants, took out my dong, and started peeing into the bag. It was hot and it stunk and I scrunched my nose as I smelled it, laughing. Gretchen was in the car, watching it all in the rearview mirror. I finished peeing, filling the bag up halfway, then zipped it up quick. I carried the bag of piss, all hot and steamy inside, back to the car and started sitting down again.

"Dude, you're not getting in this car with that," she said, slamming down the lock with her hand. I stood there, holding the bag of piss, shaking my head.

"Dude," I said. "I don't even want to be doing this shit. You made me do it, now open the door."

"Look, look, football practice is ending," she said, pointing across the field. The entire football team was in a large huddle, all of them with their helmets off, their short hair mussed, their handsome faces glistening with sweat.

"Do you know who the guy is?" I asked.

"I know him," she said.

"So how are we going to do this?"

"We'll pull up to him and you open the bag and toss it at him."

"I have to toss it?" I asked.

"I have to drive," she said.

"Fine, fuck you, whatever, open the door," I said.

Gretchen popped up the lock of the car door and I sat down, holding the bag away from my body.

"That smells," she said.

"Yeah, it does."

"It's bright yellow!" she shouted, holding her nose and laughing. "Why is it so yellow?"

"I dunno. I take vitamins in the morning, maybe that's it."

"Jesus, put it in the backseat or something."

I nodded and put the bag down by my feet.

"Now what?" I asked.

"Now, we wait," she said, and backed the Escort toward the front of the parking lot, where a long, narrow cement path led from the field-house to where the students parked their cars. We waited, listening to the same songs which had been playing over and over again since her last mix-tape got stuck in the tape player, the monotony of it comforting, familiar, something you could always count on. After twenty minutes or so, a brown metal door opened and five or six football types clambered out, laughing, snorting, high-fiving each other, nodding.

"OK, tell me when," I said.

"He's blond," she said, "and he's got this shit-eating grin."

"How do you know him?"

"He fucked Kim, when she was a cheerleader," Gretchen whispered, and at once I knew this had more to do with that than with poor old Stacy Bensen. I looked back to where the football players were marching out—whistling, he-hawing—and then Gretchen leaned over and pointed, grabbing my shoulder hard. "That's him. That's fucking him, all right."

I swallowed hard and grabbed the bag of piss at my feet.

This guy, Mark Dayton, didn't look like such a bad guy, except that he was tall, blond, and good-looking—the kind of guy girls wet their fucking pants over all the time. His face was wet and shiny, and he had a soft white towel around his shoulders, still drying his hair as he talked over important jock stuff with some other football-type, the two of them nodding seriously, maybe mumbling, *"32-29-36, hike?"* then, *"Fumble, pass, first down?"*

I unlocked the car door, grabbed the door handle with my left hand, held the pee bag with my right, and waited, waited, waited until Mark Dayton was like three feet from the Escort. Then I flung open the car door, shouted, "Hey, fucker!" and whipped the bag of pee at Mark Dayton's chest. It flew end over end at him, smacking him directly on his neck, then fell at his feet, still closed, not even broken—just this hot, clear bag of pee lying there unopened at his feet. I felt the hot stupidity of the situation smack me in the head, suddenly remembering, *I forgot to open it. I forgot to open the fucking thing.*

"What the fuck?" the thick-necked dude beside Mark Dayton asked, throwing down his gym bag and charging toward the car, but Gretchen had already hit the gas. I was slow closing the door and it nicked the back end of someone's Blazer before we pulled away, spinning out of the parking lot like a scene from a car-chase-type movie.

"Sorry," I said after a while. "I guess I forgot to open the bag."

"You're just an idiot," was all she said back.

thirty-four

OK, I had some beers with Mr. D. Like I said, I went by to see Gretchen and there was like only five days left before Homecoming, and I decided I would finally, finally, finally ask her. Mr. D. answered the door and said, "Hey, Brian, how you doing, champ?" and he had a can of the Beast—Milwaukee's Best, my dad's favorite beer—in his hand and I think he might have been drinking for a while because he was still wearing his, "Kiss the Cook" apron and smiling a little too much and winking at me, I guess. I asked, "Is, um, Gretchen home?" shrugging my shoulders, staring down at my feet.

"Brian, all the girls are gone for the night. Jess is at work and Gretch is out with Kim," which I knew was straight-up bullshit because Kim was working at Orange Julius, which must have meant Gretchen was either out hanging alone at Haunted Trails waiting to choke down Tony Degan's member, or doing whatever she had decided to with him, pinned underneath his gorilla-type cro-mag hands already.

"Oh, that's cool," I said. "I'll call her later."

"You can hang out here, if you want to wait 'til she gets back."

"Yeah, I dunno, Mr. D. I might just head home."

"Oh, come on, pal, why don't you come on in and we'll have a beer. How's that sound, champ?"

OK, now, nowhere, in the short history of my life, had any adult ever asked me to have a fucking beer with them. It was so random and weird that I didn't know what else to say but, well, yes.

I nodded and followed him inside and we went to the kitchen and he fished another Beast out of the fridge and handed it to me, just like that, as if it was something we just did, the two of us, always drinking together.

"Wait a minute—you want it in a glass?" he asked.

"No, the can's cool," I said, feeling more weird and uncomfortable than ever. I followed him over to the kitchen table and we sat down, him across from me, as he started patting down this thinning hair and smiling strangely at me.

"So it's just us. Just the men," he sighed. "Just the men. The bachelors," he said.

"Yep," I said.

"Hey, how long have you known Gretchen?" he asked, kind of surprised by his own question.

"Since junior high," I said.

"Sure, sure, you were on the math team together, weren't you?"

"Yep."

"Go math team!" he hooted. "Those were the days, huh?"

"I guess."

"You guys were unstoppable, huh? All out victory!"

"Yep," I said.

"Whatever happened to that Chinese kid on the team?"

"Greg? He was Filipino," I said.

"That kid. He was a great kid. Whatever happened to him?"

"Oh, you know, he's going to high school," I said, taking a swig of the beer.

"Yeah, high school," Mr. D. said. "Hey, you remember that time you guys made it to the semifinals and we all drove down to Springfield?"

"Yep."

"And Mrs. D. made all you guys T-shirts, the ones that said, 'Math Team Semifinal Champs,' but you didn't win, but you all wore the T-shirts anyway?"

"Yeah, that was kinda funny."

"Yep," Mr. D. said, "that was kind of funny. Remember, we stopped at that truck stop and that little girl—who was the little girl?"

"Andrea?"

"Andrea wouldn't get back in the car because she felt so bad for losing."

"Yeah," I said. "She was a weird kid."

"Well, it was her parents," Mr. D. said. "They had very high expectations for her, you know? All we ever wanted was for you guys to do your best, right?"

"Right."

"That poor girl, well, she was, what, in seventh grade?" Mr. D. asked.

"Seventh, yep," I said.

"And her parents must have laid a lot of pressure on her to make her feel like that."

"Yep," I said.

"Well," he smiled, nodding, "Mrs. D. calmed her down and, even though Andrea was in seventh grade, she got her to sit in her lap, and we went home and all you kids were so nice about it. You never told anyone about that, did you, Brian?"

I had never told anyone about that day. I didn't know why, only I didn't. "Nope," I said. "I never told."

"I didn't know that day was going to be one of my best memories," he said, still smiling and nodding. "You never know. That's the trick, Brian. You never know which times are going to be important until later."

"Yeah," I said, feeling more weird each fucking minute. "I guess."

"That's why you shouldn't worry. You should just be happy when you can."

"That sounds good, Mr. D.," I said. "Listen, I think I'm gonna head home. I'll call Gretchen later."

"Brian?" Mr. D. whispered, raising his head.

"Yeah?"

"You're a good kid. In case nobody ever tells you that," he said, and I almost started fucking crying right then.

thirty-five

The truth, then: I was very in love with Gretchen and wanted to ask her to Homecoming, but I was a pussy and embarrassed about being in love with her because she was fat, and also because, well, I knew she didn't even like me. Not only that, but she was also bigger than me, physically, and also because deep down in the only honest part of my heart, I knew two things: one, she was still very hung-up on Tony Degan; and two, she could, without any trouble, truly kick my ass in like five seconds flat.

So the truth of the matter was this: Homecoming was like two days away and I thought if I took Gretchen maybe I would regret it. I had had a bad enough high school experience as it was and, well, you know, did not exactly fit in and all, and I was afraid that Gretchen might do something at the dance, you know, like break Amy Schaffer's arm. I'm not joking—I mean, she had done that kind of shit already, for real.

OK, as we were driving around in the Escort a few days later, I told Gretchen about not having anyone to ask to Homecoming. "I probably won't even go now," I said, hoping she'd say something back, like *No, no, ask me*, but instead she said:

"Homecoming is like the most chauvinistic night of all time. It's like, 'Look, I bought you a corsage and now you should go down on me.'"

I nodded, though that wasn't exactly what I had been thinking. It was quiet for a couple of minutes, us just driving, and then Gretchen sighed and looked over at me. "I got to tell you something," she said.

"What?" I asked. She turned down the Clash or whatever it was on the radio and immediately I could see she was starting to cry, and then she tried to smile and said, "I let Tony Degan dry-hump me the other night."

"What?"

"I let Tony Degan dry-hump me. Two days ago. In the backseat," she said, glancing over her shoulder. "Right in front of his house."

"Jesus, Gretchen, he's like thirty," I said.

"He's twenty-six," she said, and I could tell she wasn't sad as much as she was angry. "The thing was, it wasn't even bad," she whispered. "Not that I'd know, considering he was the first guy to ever dry-hump me."

I nodded, because *what could I say?* Here I felt terrible for her and mad as hell myself because, well, I mean, here I was walking around with an erection every ten minutes and all she had to do was ask.

"Let's get something to eat," she said. "I'll buy."

And so we headed over toward Haunted Trails. As soon as we pulled into the parking lot, I could see all the punks and stoners hanging out by their cars, some good-looking ones, some pieces of shit, Ford Escorts and El Caminos and a few station wagons that looked all the same except they had different punk stickers like Operation Ivy or The Specials on them.

I got out of the car to go get three hot dogs from the snack shop, and as I was walking back with the food I heard Gretchen shout, "Douche-bag!" and when I looked over, she was already running—and for a big girl, she could move pretty fast—and there, there was Tony Degan with his shaggy blond hair and sleeveless T-shirt which said, *I'm with Stupid* and he had this girl we knew, Erica Lane, this skank, straddled around his middle as they crawled out of the back of Bobby B.'s purple wizard van, laughing and kissing and pinching each other very happily, and then, well, then Gretchen came flying out of nowhere and before anyone could stop it, she was pummeling Erica Lane's head against the hood of the van, and Tony was trying to break it up but laughing at the same time, and I thought about going up and taking a swing at Tony, but I knew I never would, and so I helped pull Gretchen off and she shoved me and I spilled the hot dogs on my shirt.

Gretchen walked back to the Escort and started it up and I said, "Why do you got to act like a fucking dude all the time?" and she looked at me and said, "Fuck you, you fucking sissy," and she started crying, and I felt like crying too, and then she threw the car into gear and took off.

I had to take three buses to get home that day and I had mustard all over my shirt.

I was a teenage teen
march 1991

"Finished with my woman
'cause she couldn't love me with my mind"
—*"Paranoid"*
Ozzy Osbourne, Black Sabbath

"For whom the bell tolls,
Time marches on"
—*"For Whom the Bell Tolls"*
James Hetfield, borrowing from John Donne, maybe?
Metallica

one

In our history class, we had to do a twenty-minute oral report on An Event That Changed America so we picked the Boston Strangler—it was Mike's idea, mostly, as my history partner. Mike was a stoner or a head or a burnout—as my super-anorexic sister called him—and, like me, he was very into metal and slasher movies. He also smoked a lot of grass. Mike had this hair, this really long reddish hair, which he tucked into his dress-shirt collar in the back and tied up with a rubber band at the end. There were a couple dudes like him who had tried to grow their hair long, but sooner or later they got busted and had to cut it all off. That's how it was in Catholic high school. You could even argue that if you looked at paintings of Jesus he had long hair, but they weren't gonna hear it. It was all dress shirt, dress pants, dress shoes, ties, proper grooming. Proper grooming meant being clean-shaven, no mustaches or beards, and short hair. But somehow, like a fucking miracle, Mike had been able to escape Bro. Cardy, the drill-instructor-like dean of discipline, long enough that if he got caught now, all would be fucking lost. Bro. Cardy would either hit him up with so many detentions or cut his hair off in his office, right there, right then.

So when Ms. Aiken, our new super-fine history teacher who replaced Bro. Flanagan when he needed throat surgery, wrote the assignment on the blackboard, Final Project: An Event That Changed America, Mike and I looked at each other and nodded. He pulled out a piece of notebook paper, drew a quick picture of a muscular man strangling some other comic book–figure person with a huge rope— it was bigger than the both of them—and over their heads, nodding and winking, he scratched out a five-pointed pentagram. He showed it to me and I nodded at it for some reason. Why? Because he was like my friend and I thought his drawings were pretty amazing. I mean, Mike was the only dude I hung out with at the time.

Oh yeah, by then, I had tried to forget all about Gretchen. If she called for me, I wouldn't talk to her for long and if she asked to go hang out, I told her I was busy.

I had been hanging out pretty much every day with Mike. After school, we would just sit around his basement and listen to a lot of old metal records, like early Sabbath with Ozzy, Alice Cooper, KISS. Also, like I said, he was very into serial killers. He had pictures and books and movies all about Charles Manson and John Wayne Gacy. We would talk about serial killers and watch slasher movies and some-times he'd try to teach me how to play Dungeons and Dragons, which I still didn't understand. Mike also knew a lot of girls, all kinds of them. Girls seemed to really like him for some reason—mostly because he got them high, I think, but also because he had this easy-going way with them, like they just didn't make him nervous; like he didn't care if they liked him or not, which made them like him even more. So he would have all kinds of girls down in his basement and then he'd invite me over and we would put on some stoner records, like Pink Floyd's *The Wall*, and then they would smoke dope—I didn't really smoke dope, I would just try to get high secondhand—and then the girls would get all giggly and sometimes, sometimes, if I was lucky, I would end up making out with one of them. Mike was like the best friend I had ever had for inviting me over like that, though later he said it all just was part of his plan. He said girls were more comfortable coming over together than alone and that he always needed a second man, which I was more than happy to be, like I said.

The whole hanging out thing and finally meeting girls led me to make a very important decision. As an early birthday present, I told my folks I wanted contacts instead of my plastic-rimmed glasses. I appealed to my dad, simply saying, "You know, for girls," and he took me to the eye doctor himself. Getting contacts had practically changed me. That and not hanging out with Gretchen anymore. I didn't feel like such a total loser all the time, and because of Mike, I could at least talk to the girls I liked.

"All right, guys, Dave Dupree and Alex? What historical event are you thinking of?" Ms. Aiken asked, hot like always, her blond hair in a bob, her short white skirt, and her see-through blouse perfectly cupping her severe rack.

"You know," Dave Dupree mumbled, scratching his enormous forehead. Dave was an huge kid, up around 300 pounds already; he was smart but like a human juggernaut. He would kind of tremble, visibly, whenever Ms. Aiken asked him anything. "You know, probably all that Revolutionary War stuff."

"OK, good. Try to keep it specific," Ms. Aiken said with a smile. She turned to Mike and me and winked. "Mike Madden and Brian Oswald? What do you think, guys?"

"We've got some ideas, Ms. Aiken," Mike said, still nodding. "Real good ones we don't want to say until we've had time to, you know, debate them."

"Good," she said, turning quick to catch Billy Lowery staring at her beautiful, marshmallowly delicious ass. "Let's break up into history partners and discuss for ten minutes and then I will ask you to make a decision. Then if you're good, we'll play History Jeopardy."

I fucking loved this woman so bad it was almost incomprehensible to me. I mean, one, she was a teacher; but two, she was so hot and so genuinely nice. I had a total boner throughout the whole fucking sixth period. Seriously. I mean, Ms. Aiken, she was like twenty-four, just a few years older, and short and blond and hot and flirty, and like she made it all like a game, you know, with goofy names like History Partners, that was her thing, and like History Jeopardy. She even had this lunch one day where we ate foods from different people's nationalities—you know, it was fucking crazy burritos and pasta and corned beef and everything. Like Mike's hair, though, I thought it was only a matter of time before the evil Holy Brothers caught wind of her wacky shit and canned her quick. Not before I begged her to let me go at it with her, you know, or that's what I hoped, sincerely.

Ms. Aiken strolled over beside Mike and my desks, which were side by side. She looked down at Mike's drawing of someone being strangled and rolled her eyes, unable to keep herself from laughing.

"You two," she said. "They ought to let you take art classes."

Mike was too dumb to be able to take art and even if he could, he wouldn't. Like anyone smart, he would have taken study hall instead of an elective, unlike me, the dumbass who took band instead. On his own, though, Mike drew hundreds and hundreds of weird Greek monsters all over his class notebooks, in the middle of his notes, dragons and Minotaurs and horse-men and Titans all stabbing each other with huge swords and menacing curved knives.

"That's a pretty good drawing. Does it have anything to do with your project?" Ms. Aiken asked.

"Yes, ma'am," Mike said. "We were thinking about, you know, doing something on serial killers, maybe."

"Serial killers? Any one in particular?"

"We don't know. We didn't really discuss it yet," he said.

"Brian, what do you think about doing your project on serial killers?"

"I like it," I said.

"What is it with you guys and gore?" she asked, referring to our last project as History Partners, which was supposed to have been a visual representation of an Historic American Event, which for us was a very bloody and graphic depiction of two soldiers from the Civil War, one from the South and one from the North, cutting each other into tiny pieces. Besides all the blood and entrails, Ms. Aiken said we captured the emotion of the dire conflict. So, you know, we scored.

"I dunno," Mike said. "It's like life, you know, it's the stuff no one wants to talk about, dying and all. Like Bro. Flanagan getting his throat cut open," Mike said, miming himself stabbing his own neck. "That is the real stuff."

"Well, I have high expectations for you two, based on your last project," Ms. Aiken said, with her beautiful little sparkling smile. "I hope it is just as honest."

"Cool," I said, borrowing a phrase from Mike.

Ms. Aiken began to turn, to move on to the next pair of desks, but stopped and raised one single dark eyebrow, reaching out her small hand to the back of Mike's neck. I felt my mouth drop open. I saw Mike close his eyes, grit his teeth, and mutter *fuck* under his breath. Ms. Aiken, so gently, so easily, caressed the back of his head, pressing her small white fingers into his bushy hair.

"That's awful long," she whispered, blinking at him.

"Yes, ma'am," Mike said, still squinting. Ms. Aiken leaned down beside us and smiled.

"It's OK," she whispered. "I think it's good that you pick how you look. It helps build identity, you know."

"Yeah?" Mike said, confused and in total wonderment, I guess.

"And, well, my boyfriend has long hair," she said and without one more word, turned and started asking questions to the next group. Mike's eyes bugged out as he stared at me and smiled.

"Dude," he said. "One day, I'm going to make that woman mine."

"Get in line," I said.

"So, what should we do?" Mike asked, darkening the points of the pentagram. In a moment, the five star points had become a goat-head, with two horns rising up, its ears jutting out, and a long narrow face and chin—the band Venom's symbol.

"I dunno, what do you think?" I asked.

"Dude, what about that fucking movie?" he said.

Mike and I had just watched this movie about the Boston Strangler, with Tony Curtis and Peter Fonda, I think. It was all about the case and how people in America were totally freaking out. I had no idea how it might qualify as An Event That Changed America.

Ms. Aiken stepped lightly to the front of the classroom, clapping her hands together once, which meant *shut the heck up*.

"OK, guys, who has decided? Who'll volunteer to offer their ideas first?" she asked and like that, Mike just raised his hand like a lightning bolt firing into the air.

"Yes, Mike, what do you guys have?"

"We are going to do it on the Boston Strangler, how does that sound, Miss A.?" he said in one hurried, excited breath.

Ms. Aiken nodded and smiled warmly at us. "So why do you think the Boston Strangler is an appropriate Event That Changed America, guys?" she asked.

I thought we were busted right there, but Mike, just being Mike, all laid back, said, "It has greatly affected our sense of trust and comfort and, um, belonging," and Ms. Aiken just nodded, impressed with us, I guess. She gave us a check mark in her assignment book, and her giving us the big OK was only our first mistake.

two

At the same exact time, Mrs. Madden, Mike's mom, got her divorce finalized. She finally lost it, and one day while we were in her kitchen, Mike smoking over the sink, me inking *OZZY* on the knuckles of both of my hands with a magic marker, Mrs. Madden stopped, looked at us, set down the basket of laundry, pulled her hair, took a deep breath, and said to Mike and me:

"That's it. I'm giving up on the both of you as human beings."

"What?" Mike asked, squinting dumbly.

"Fine. If you want to be anti-social, fine. If you all want to grow up without any prospects for the future, it doesn't bother me in the least."

"What are you talking about, Mom?" Mike asked, shaking his head. Mrs. Madden stood before us, let go of her hair, took a deep breath, and smiled, but kind of meanly. She was a very skinny lady, tall, with poofy blond hair. She wore slacks a lot and smoked more than Mike, I think. She made me kind of nervous when she talked to me because she seemed to want answers to questions I didn't even know about. Like once when Mike was making out with some girl in his room and I was down playing pool on their pool table by myself, she stared at me for a minute and then said, "What do you think you're gonna end up doing with your life?" And without thinking I said, "I'm gonna be in a band, probably," and she let out a quick, sharp laugh and then shook her head and asked, "Really?" And I just shrugged my shoulders and went back to playing pool and didn't ever know if she saw me hit the eight ball in by accident on the very next shot.

Mrs. Madden opened her purse and fumbled for her Virginia Slims, lit one, and pointed it at Mike, then at me.

"You two are no longer my problem," she said.

"Really?" Mike asked.

"Really," she said. "I've got this piece of paper from your father saying my marriage has been undone. So you," she said, pointing her cigarette at Mike, "and you," she said, pointing it at me, "don't even exist to me."

"Cool," Mike said. "What does that mean?"

"That means," Mrs. Madden said, gently tugging on Mike's long red hair, "you two are no longer my responsibility. I am giving up on trying to fix men," she said, kind of laughing to herself.

"So we can do what we want?" Mike asked, grinning wildly.

"You can do whatever you want," she replied, nodding.

"We can smoke in the basement?"

"You already do," she said.

"We can smoke dope down there?"

"I don't care," she said. "As long as you don't try and drive later."

"Cool," Mike said. "We can have chicks over?"

"I don't care," she said again. "But no going all the way. If either of you guys gets a girl pregnant in my house, you'll be out on your ass." She said that looking at me, and I wasn't even her kid.

"Can we hang out as late as we want?" he asked again. "No curfew and all?"

"I don't care what you do. You two are no longer on my radar," and she gave Mike's hair one more tug and disappeared downstairs to do the laundry.

"This is fucking incredible," Mike said.

"It really is," I agreed.

"I mean incredible," he said, his eyes glassy with possibility. "I will have to call and thank my dad."

"What do we do now?" I asked.

"We have a fucking party. No, no, an orgy. Do you know any girls that will be in an orgy?" he asked me.

"Nope," I said.

"Too bad."

"Well, what first?" I asked.

"I am going down to sit on the couch in the basement and smoke the biggest bowl ever."

"I will join you," I said, and we went downstairs singing, making trumpet sounds like the advance of kings, following the wood stairs to the unfinished cement basement, one long gray concrete rectangle, past the hallway that was stacked full of boxes and junk and old clothing. Their basement had a pretty decent used pool table in the center of the room and two secondhand sofas pressed against the side wall beside an old rabbit-eared TV. Mike had put a calendar up of the Jägermeister girls, these buxom blond chicks from a liquor ad, and an Ozzy poster from the *Tribute* record on the opposite wall. Because Mike's room was in one corner of the basement, barely sectioned off by thin wood paneling and two-by-fours, the entire basement smelled like his cigarettes—everything: the sofas, the felt of the pool table, the black curtains covering the small glass block basement windows which hardly let in any light anyway.

Mike crept into his room, dug under his bed for an empty shaving cream can he had made into a place to stash his dope, pulled out a small plastic sandwich bag full of dry green weed, and sat down on his bed to pick out the seeds. He did it quick, in a flash, and was already packing the bowl by the time I had completely made up my mind to smoke it with him.

"OK," he said, nodding, holding the pipe in front of his mouth. "It's easy. You just light it, wait until it glows, right? Then suck it in as slow as you can, don't like try to swallow it down, just like, like, breath it in." He found his blue plastic lighter and lit the weed inside the bowl, which crackled and gave off a thick, earthy smell. I had smelled it before and it always reminded me of Jessica, Gretchen's sister—her jacket mostly, this corduroy furry-collared thing—Jessica was the only person besides Mike who I knew smoked a lot of dope. Mike held the lighter over the bowl for a minute, killed the flame, then slowly sucked in a breath, squinting his eyes closed again. He tightened his lips and then smiled, still with his eyes closed, then began to speak, still holding the smoke in.

"OK," he hissed. "Then you hold it like this," and he coughed a little and let out a great cloud of bluish smoke. "No problem," he said, nodding.

He handed me the bowl and the lighter and I put it to my mouth and said, "No problem," and did what he told me. I felt the tar kind of taste burning the back of my throat and mouth and tongue, then deeper, down, down, down, into my lungs, and I held the smoke there as long as I could before I shot it all out of my mouth, smiling the way he had. Somehow I started coughing, my eyes ballooning up with tears. Mike pat my back and laughed.

"Cough to get off," he said, taking the bowl back. I didn't feel much different. My eyes were still watering and my throat felt raw and scratchy. Mike took another tug on the bowl and passed it back to me. I took another hit, trying not to cough this time, but it happened anyway, Mike laughing harder this time, my eyes feeling like a thousand pounds as I blinked the tears out of them, laughing at myself. I felt my ears kind of open up then, like they had been clogged, and my tongue felt hot and large and heavy. Mike got up and put on some Black Sabbath and all of a sudden it started to really hit me. The song, which I knew well, "War Pigs," sounded different, broken into a hundred parts like a symphony, each instrument separate and multiplied, Ozzy's voice warmer somehow, like he was someone I knew singing in the room with me. Mike sat back down on the bed and patted my back.

"You fucked up?"

"I think so," I said. "I think I am," I said again. "This is OK," I said. "It really is."

"Do you want me to call some girls?" Mike asked, winking.

"OK," I said. "Thanks, Mike, for everything." Mike nodded, pat my back again, picked up the phone and dialed, then said:

"Amanda? It's Mike. You'll never believe what happened," and Amanda, a blonde hair spray junkie, and her friend, Katie O., who had a lot of acne and so wore tons of pancake makeup but was otherwise pretty cute, were over there in like ten seconds.

OK, the bad part happened when Mike came home from school two days later and noticed his mom had taken out all the telephones in the house. All the phones were gone. He asked her what was up and she just shrugged her shoulders and walked away. The next day when we walked into his house, some dude from the phone company was there and he was putting in an actual pay phone, I mean, right on the fucking kitchen wall, like Mike's kitchen was a bus stop or something. Mike and I stared at it and he said, "That is seriously fucked up," and the poor phone guy just shrugged his shoulders and said, "Sorry," and went back to connecting the phone. Mike shook his head and went to open the fridge to grab an after-school snack of frozen pizza and Jewel-brand pop, but get this: When he pulled on the refrigerator door, it wouldn't give. He pulled and pulled and then looked down and there was a lock. There was a goddamn lock on the fridge.

"This is incredible," Mike said, covering his face. "She is fucking insane."

"That," I said, pointing at the small golden lock, "is the scariest thing I have ever seen," because before the divorce got signed or whatever and before Mrs. Madden completely flipped out, you could go over to Mike's and dig around in his fridge for like anything, usually frozen pizza and Jewel-brand soda pop, and we would eat it there, over the sink standing up, without plates, so we didn't have to wash them, but nope, none of that now.

"What the fuck is she thinking?" he asked, shaking his head.

"I have no idea," I said, because I didn't, and I started thinking about my mom and dad—who, after like six months, was still sleeping on the couch in the basement—and what strange tortures might be in store for me.

"Mom!" Mike howled. "What in the fuck is all this?"

Mrs. Madden appeared from her bedroom, in a baby-blue terry-cloth robe, blue towel holding her hair up above her head, blinking coyly. "Yes, neighbor?"

"What is all this shit?" he shouted, shaking his hands.

"All this shit is my shit," she said with a smile, then edged a Virginia Slim from the pack on the counter.

I stepped back and started taking it all in.

"If you want to use the phone, you're going to have to get a job to pay for it. Same with food."

"Wow," I mumbled out loud.

"Holy shit," Mike said. "You've lost it."

"Not at all," she said. "This is the most sane I've felt in nineteen years."

"Well, what about Molly and Petey?" he asked.

"Everyone is going have to pay their way," she answered, nodding, then turned and disappeared back into her bedroom.

"Seriously," Mike said, "this is crazy."

It was crazy. Mike and his little brother Petey, who was only twelve, well, they had to buy their own groceries or pay their mom for meals. The first thing Mike did was go and sell all the records he hadn't listened to in a while, to avoid having to get a job. He thought his mom would at least come around on the food deal, but she didn't. Seriously. Mike's older sister Molly, who had a big round face, the way I liked a girl's face—kind of mean and smart-mouthed, you know the kind, the kind of girl who looks at you like you aren't nothing, and then makes out with you just because she's bored—well, Molly, who was two years older than me and Mike, nineteen and in junior college, well, she came home from work at this bar, O'Reilly's, saw the pay phones and the lock on the fridge and took off two days later with the tour manager from the band REO Speedwagon—who was very big in our neighborhood because one of the guys, the drummer I think, went to our high school, Brother Rice—and headed out on the road.

That was another blow. Molly leaving just about killed Mike, being his older sister and all. She had always bought beer for us and would tell us what girls like you to do and how to get them to at least consider having sex with you by saying stuff like, "I feel like you're the only one I can say personal stuff to."

Now he had no food, no phone, no beer, no older sister to help him through. Sure, he could smoke dope in his basement, but the price of it was hardly worth it, you know? So in a matter of hours it went from the greatest situation in the world to the worst, just like that.

It got real bad for Mike. One night, a few weeks after Mrs. Madden had said she was giving up on us, we had two girls down in the basement, two girls who Mike had met at the grocery store while he had been shopping. All he bought were cans and cans of Chef Boyardee to eat. The girls were definitely Catholic high school girls— from Queen of Peace, which was in a Hispanic neighborhood— because they were as clean as any girls I'd ever seen; not just their soft brown hair, but the way they talked and smoked like very polite foreign movie stars, and even the way they crossed and uncrossed their legs. Well, we passed around the bowl and the girls got high and then I put on "I Can't Fight This Feeling Anymore," which was a song by REO Speedwagon and a good one to set the mood, because Mike had used it before. I was on one couch with one girl, and Mike was in his bedroom. Then I had my hand up this girl's shirt and was feeling her up over the bra and she had her eyes closed, and her name was Teresa, so pretty, but I thought it was weird that she kept her eyes closed, like if she had her eyes closed she wasn't going to have to go

to confession next Saturday or whatever Catholic girls feel they have
to do. Well Mike, he just walked out of his bedroom suddenly and said,
"What the fuck is this shit you're listening to?"

And I said, "What?" sitting up, pulling my hand back.

And then he said, "Don't you got any goddamn consideration for
my feelings, man? I asked you not to play this record anymore."

And I said, "I don't get it, it's a good record," and he said, "Turn
that goddamn thing off unless you want to go in the backyard to do
your dry-humping." Which I did not, because I knew Mike's secret: A
girl on a couch is a lot more likely to just lie there and let you do what
you want than if you were, say, in the backseat of a car or under her
back porch. By then, I had made out with like ten girls, but I still didn't
know what went on in their heads, if they just looked up at the ceiling
and counted the tiles or if they were thinking about their homework
assignments or imagining I was somebody special like Scott Baio, but
like Mike said, if you can get them on the couch you are halfway there,
my friend, or so I have seen.

"Fuck, it's no big deal," I said. I stood up and lifted off the record
arm and put on Cream with Eric Clapton instead, but the mood was
ruined already. When I went to undo Teresa's bra, she stopped me and
asked, "Is there a bathroom around here?" and I nodded and pointed
up the stairs and she sat up there for like a half hour until her friend
came out and the two of them left, not coming back down to say
goodbye or thanks or anything.

three

I fell in love with a girl named Dorie. She was Mike's neighbor and the moment I met her, I was so into her it was not even funny. Most girls I didn't really fall for at first, like Gretchen, who had been my friend for so long that it probably would have never worked out, and, well, I was not one of those kind of guys who was very particular with girls. Mike told me to take what I could get, so I did. There were tons and tons of mostly decent-looking girls who wanted some non-descript, renegade, loner-type to de-virginize them so they could have it over and done with and so they never had to see the doofus again. That was where I liked to think I came in, though it hadn't happened like that exactly for me yet. Monica Dallas: over the bra. Kelly Madley: down her pants. Kathy Konoplowski: not totally de-virginized, but close.

OK, so the first time I met Dorie it was a Friday night and about a month since Mike's mom had gone crazy. Mike had to finally go out and get a job, at DiBartola's Pizza, which was this take-out place by his house, which meant he was not home from work until after eleven most nights. So that night, I had to sneak out of my house through my bedroom window, which was ground level, and ride my bike over, then walk down the basement steps. "Moonlight Drive" by the Doors was playing loud; I could hear it even when I was outside. When I came down, like that, there she was: this tall girl just sitting on the sofa beside Mike, smoking a roach, and she had on this Iron Maiden "Somewhere in Time" T-shirt, which must have been black once but was now gray and soft from being worn so often. Dorie was tall and skinny and had long greasy brown hair that was cut in bangs. Fuck. No girl had bangs that I knew, they all wore their fucking hair in ponytails. I mean, fuck. Also, she had this love bite, you know, on her neck; one bright red mark at the base of her throat. Which to me meant she must have fooled around, I dunno. She was sitting down there in Mike's basement and cussing out this other dude we knew, Larry with the superbad acne, and she was yelling at him for him spilling his beer on her shoe and Larry, quiet as he was because of his uncontrollable pimples, just nodded and apologized, wiping it up off the tip of her black boot. Then, by mistake, Larry with the superbad acne looked up and smiled and simply said, "Sorry, dude."

"Do I look like a dude to you, you fuckface?" she asked.

Fuckface? I thought to myself. Who even uses the word "fuckface"?

The girl of your dreams, my heart said.

Immediately, and I know this is weird, I had this kind of vision, this daydream: I imagined Dorie standing up from the sofa, smoothing down her brown hair, and then unzipping her dirty blue jeans and, well, I know this is strange, but, well, I imagined there'd be like this golden crown that would appear, this magical golden crown would just appear as she unzipped her pants, like a flower blossoming, and then that would be it for me. I came down the steps, flashed Mike the devil sign, said hi to Larry with the superbad acne, and took a seat directly across from where Dorie was sitting.

"Hi," she said, just waving her hand very quickly. "I'm Dorie."

"Dorie?" I asked.

"That's right," she said, rolling her eyes.

"She's my neighbor," Mike said, passing me the roach. "Since we were kids."

"Cool," I said, taking a long hit.

"We used to set up the Slip 'N Slide between our front lawns when we were little," Mike said. "Those were the days," he added, nodding.

"Now I have to work all the fucking time," Dorie said, nodding. "No more Slip 'N Slide for me."

"Really? Where do you work?" I asked, blowing the smoke out without coughing.

"My dad's restaurant, Dockie's." I passed her the roach and for a moment our hands touched, oh so briefly.

"The fish place? On Kedzie?" I asked. "How long have you been working there?"

"Since I was a kid. I'm the night manager."

"The night manager? You're like a kid."

"I'm seventeen," she said.

"Well, how can you be the night manager?" I asked.

"My dad needed help, you know, he had back surgery and there's nobody else, so I go there at night and help him. Plus," she said, "this guy Ken, the cook, he usually gets me high."

"Is he the guy that fucking mauled your neck?" Mike asked, being all brotherly and everything.

She looked down and then lifted one eyebrow and said, "None of your business."

"How old is this dude?" Mike asked again.

"Fuck off," she said, "twenty-five."

I looked at her and realized I was so in love with her it was not even funny. I wanted to ask her right there if she would maybe think about being my girlfriend and she could wait until we were married before ever doing it with me, but instead I asked:

"So you like Iron Maiden?"

"Their older stuff, when they talked about elves and sorcery and stuff. 'Wasted Years,' that's a good song, though."

I was very fucking impressed. I looked at her and decided to ask her the hardest question I knew to ask a girl ever, which was:

"Hey, Dorie, what was the first record you ever bought?"

"Honestly?" she answered.

"Yeah," I said.

"New Kids on the Block."

"Really?"

"Really." Which to me meant she was not a liar, and not worried about being cool, because New Kids on the Block was like the first album for every girl I knew, it was just a matter of whether they admitted it or not. I was completely and totally shocked.

"Those guys were fucking hot," Dorie said.

"Yeah," I said, agreeing for some reason. "Once I recorded one of their videos off MTV and tried to learn how to dance from it."

"No shit?" Mike asked.

"Yeah," I said, kind of blushing. "I did it to try and impress this girl."

"I think that is hot," she said, grinning. "I wish some dude would learn how to dance like the New Kids on the Block for me."

"I still could if you want me to," I said.

"I'll have to think about that," she countered, smiling a very small smile at me.

"You let me know," I said.

"I will," she said, and then it was just us—it was only us—talking. She was staring at me and asked, "Didn't you used to wear glasses?"

"I got contacts."

"I used to see you at the mall all the time, at Aladdin's Castle," she said.

"Really?"

"I worked next door, at the airbrush T-shirt place."

"Wow," I said. "I went in there once and got a T-shirt made."

"What did it say?"

"'Reckless Youth,'" I said. "That was the name of a band I was trying to start."

"That's not a bad name."

"I know," I said. "That's why I got a T-shirt made. So no one could steal it."

"That's a good idea."

"I know. I have like three others, all with different names, in case, you know, I ever get a band together."

Dorie smiled and squinted, pointing her cigarette at me but not saying anything. I pointed back with my finger. Things were happening, but then Dorie said:

"Well, I think I've gotta split."

"Really?" Mike said.

"Yeah, I've got to work all day tomorrow."

"That's too bad," I said, my heart pounding up in my ears.

"Yeah," she said.

When she stood, I saw how tall she really was. Her small breasts poked against the front of her Iron Maiden T as she pulled it down. "Nice meeting you," she smiled, awkwardly. She started up the stairs, her long legs stretched out beneath her as she climbed.

I panicked and stood up, saying, "I think I forgot to lock up my bike."

"What?" Mike asked.

"I think I forgot to lock up my bike," I said. "Hey," I called out. "I'll walk out with you."

Mike looked at me and smiled, winking. I hurried and walked

behind her, watching her sweet ass as it swayed, and we got outside and I fumbled for a cigarette, offering her one nervously.

I asked her, "Hey, you got a boyfriend or something?" and she said:

"No. Not really. Why?" And I said:

"I dunno. You know, what about your neck?" and she said:

"That was just some asshole that mauled me," and I said:

"Somebody I know?" and she said:

"Shit, I don't even know his name," and it was like I fell in love with her right there, maybe.

four

Mike's mom and dad were definitely getting split and the paperwork had definitely been signed and his dad made it obvious by going out and buying a brand-new red convertible Cadillac with all the extras: leather seats, big beautiful chrome bumpers, automatic sun roof. Mike and I were at the mall killing time with this new cop-killer game at the arcade and then we were outside waiting for the bus, throwing rocks at the seagulls, and we saw his dad cruising by with some blonde in this red convertible and they were both laughing like they had known each other their whole lives. Mike's dad, who was tall and balding, with a dark ring of hair around his ears, had a flashy '70s yellow silk shirt on. He saw us and pulled over and said, "Get in, dudes, I'll drop you off." I looked at Mike's dad and then at the bimbo who was like twenty-eight, tops, in some low-cut red deal that showed her fake tits. Mike's face got all red and he said, "Mom's supposed to pick me up," which was a total lie, and his dad nodded and said, "See you later, dudes," and pulled away.

Seeing his dad take off in this brand-new car with this girl Mike didn't even know made me feel weird and uncomfortable and lonely, and so I asked Mike, "Hey, man, are you all right?" And he just frowned and said, "Jesus Christ. This is not how I imagined my junior year going at all," and I said, "Yeah. Shit," and then just to say something, I said, "Maybe we should stop by the library and see about this Boston Strangler dude," and he said, "Maybe," but we just stood there, not saying anything else, waiting for the bus, not even laughing when a group of junior high kids showed up and they were all wearing these stupid fucking Color Me Badd T-shirts.

five

Because it is time, I will teach you how to really make out, said Mike later on, when we were back in the basement. *Here's some things you should know by now:*

Rule #1. Like always, get her on a couch or a bed. Something happens to girls when they are on a couch or bed, they just give it up easier or whatever! Clean up your room first and put away dirty magazines where a girl will not look, like inside a *Sports Illustrated* is good! If you are at my house, which you usually are, clean up the place where you plan on making out! Empty the ashtray and stick the rest of the shit under the couch. When you are about to make your move and she sees how clean it is, she will immediately know what you are expecting, because it will be like a secret message you are sending her, and this will make her happy. She will understand that you have cleaned for her, so if she does not go for it and you spent time cleaning, dump her quick, dude!

Rule #2. Always have some music playing because some girls get freaked out by the sounds you make when you are making it with them. Also, make it a long song, friend: anything from *The Wall*, like "Wish You Were Here," or "Stairway to Heaven," or anything from the Doors, like "Riders on the Storm"—something you don't have to change every two minutes! My personal favorite: "Planet Caravan" by Black Sabbath. It is a good song to get stoned to, which brings us to:

Rule #3. Smoke them out. Yes, if you don't have any smoke, then you can try and drink with them, but this is tricky because some girls will fall asleep! I have had it happen to me, dude. I have. A drunk girl is sloppy, too, and I dunno, I would much rather nail a girl who was high than drunk.

If a girl has to get drunk before she messes around, dump her quick!

Rule #4. Be cool with the girl. Don't be a jerk earlier in the evening and then go expecting something! Take her somewhere to eat if you can, maybe close to your house, but don't eat something nasty! No onions! Be willing to pay if she is very hot or at least offer to pay and if she says no, cool. If she says yes, she is the kind of girl who expects things like that all the time and who can afford that? Dump her quick!

Rule #5. Try out this scenario I invented: Tell her your parents are going through a rough divorce, which they are, and that you don't know who to talk to about it, which you don't, and you just need somebody to share your thoughts with and get her comfortable and tell her you just want to hold her. Then make out with her hard. If she says she's not interested, fake-cry and see if she lets up about it. If she doesn't, tell her you are moving soon and want to share this with her. If she still doesn't go for it, you should dump her quick, because this woman is heartless!

Rule #6. Also, have a van or car to go pick up the girl. This impresses them and makes them think you are upwardly mobile and decent! Clean the van or car out before you pick her up. Have decent music playing when she gets in the car. You can make a mix-tape for making out and pop that in. If she gets in your ride and starts bitching about how old it is, or the weird gasoline smell, you know what to do. There are hundreds of other girls out there—dump her quick.

Rule #7. Brush your teeth before you go to pick her up, or if she is coming over, brush right before she rings the doorbell! Ask a girl and they will tell you it makes a difference!

Rule #8. Try out this other move I invented. Actually, I did not really invent it, this crazy Filipino chick Denise, who I used to fool around with before she moved, did it to me. Take a magic marker and write her name on your hand. That's it. Don't talk about it, don't say anything, just watch what it does for you. She will see it and think about it all night and even if she doesn't totally like you, she will see how much you like her without you having to say anything. If a girl doesn't go for that, my friend, dump her quick.

six

Up in the sky, there were fireworks. But I wasn't looking at them. I was lying on my back beside Dorie, watching her smile, the shape of her chin, everything. Mike's older sister, Molly, had sent him an assortment of bottle rockets, roman candles, and M-80s from Indiana where she had visited on tour with REO Speedwagon, which we found out was not even made up of its original members anymore.

It was like the first warm day of spring, somewhere in the beginning of April, just some Saturday night. Mike and me and Dorie and her very quiet friend Erin McDougal, who Mike had had a crush on since they went to public grade school together—a nice-looking Irish Catholic girl, a blonde with not much of a chest—were all lying in Mike's backyard and he was lighting off fireworks, shooting a dozen bottle rockets in the air all at the same time, igniting them with the end of his cigarette as he lay on his back, nodding and smoking.

"Fourth of July is my favorite holiday," Dorie said.

"It's not fourth of July, stupid," I said. "It's only April."

"I don't care," she said, smiling back at me. And then that was it: She took my hand and started holding it and I felt my breath leave. Now, I had fooled around with a bunch of girls by then, I mean, I had pretty much done it, without doing it, if you know what I mean. If you don't know what I mean, I mean frenching, finger-banging, and dry-humping; I had even kissed Kara Burton on her cooter and that was about all I was going to do down there for now. But when Dorie leaned over and took my hand, well, I dunno, it felt better than fooling around, I guess. In a moment, she leaned her head over and put it on my chest and without moving I could smell her hair, which smelled very different than all the other girls I had had the chance to smell. Dorie's hair didn't smell all flowery and fancy and fruity, like fucked-up strawberries and kiwi, all weird and phony. It was very clean-smelling, just like plain soap; just very simple, natural, even a little oily.

"When I was a kid my brother would give me those snakes, you know, the stupid little black things that grow and get all puffy," she said, and I nodded, remembering those things, the dumbest kind of fireworks ever, which were exactly the ones I pawned off on my little sister, "and I'd sit in my mom's lap and my dad would make like a big show of it and everything."

"I burned my finger when I was kid," I said. "On a sparkler."

"A sparkler?" she laughed. "That's not even like a real firework."

"I know, it was real stupid," I said. "I tried to hold the sparkler in my teeth because that's what my older cousin was doing and I got scared and grabbed it and burned my finger. I still got a scar on that finger." I held my finger up to her face and pointed it out, frowning. "See, it looks like a little ghost."

Dorie sat up and stared at my finger. She blinked, squinting at it. "It does look like a ghost," she said. And then, without any warning, she went and kissed my finger on the spot, and I almost felt like crying because I had not expected it and when she did it my whole heart felt as big as my chest. She closed her eyes and laid her head back on my shoulder. In the meantime, Mike had taken the rest of the fireworks— like thirty more bottle rockets, four roman candles, a bag full of M-80s, and some bright silver sparklers—and had stuck them all over him: in between his collar, up the sleeves of his dirty denim jacket, in all his pockets—even the small triangular ones—his pants, back and front. Then, like a retard, the ends of the fireworks sticking out, their fuses dangerously dangling, he put on a bug-eyed look and started waving his cigarette around.

"Look out for Firework Man," he began to mumble, like a robot, like a theme song—"Firework Man!"—and he started chasing poor Erin McDougal around the backyard, his arms outstretched, stiff like a monster, igniting the sparklers in his front pockets. Erin McDougal squealed out of pure delight, the first sound she had made all night, as he grabbed her around the waist. He pulled the sparklers from his jacket and waved them about Erin's face. "Firework Man has put you under his control!" he shouted. "You are under his control!" And she squealed again, giggling, covering her face with her hands. Mike leaned forward, backing poor Erin against a fence, and then he let out a loud shout.

"Fuck," he mumbled, shaking his hand. "I think I just burnt off a finger." He threw down the sparklers and began sucking on his finger, and he said, "That hurts like a bitch." Erin became all concerned and sweet and motherly, holding his hand, kissing it, the two of them laughing. He looked at me and winked and said, "I think I should go inside and wash this," and Erin nodded and, still hanging on him, followed him inside, Mike taking the time to turn to me and wink once more with his stoner-type smile.

At that, Dorie sat up, kind of fixed her hair, and said, "Do you want to sit on the picnic table with me?" and I said, "OK," and I followed her over to the red, wooden one-piece picnic table/bench. I sat beside her, holding my breath, and finally after she turned and looked bug-eyed at me as if she was asking me a question like, *Well, here we are* or *What are you waiting for*? I leaned over and kissed her as soft as I could, touching her hair with my hands. It was a very good kiss. Maybe the best. Because she wouldn't stop kissing. Once we started, she refused to stop. If I backed away to swallow, she would attack me, slipping her tongue into my mouth or going to bite my ear.

"Wow, you're a really good kisser," I said, all out of breath.

"You," she whispered. "You," like she caught me at something. We started going at it again, her kind of growling and pinning me down against the picnic table, and then she stopped and said, "Oh shit, what time is it?" and I turned and looked at my calculator watch and said, "Twelve-thirty," and she said, "Oh shit. I've got to be at work in the morning," and she got up and wiped her mouth and then leapt at me again, kissing for round three.

We walked around the side of Mike's house, stopping twice more to kiss again, and then we were at her front steps and she kissed me on the nose, just once, and I said, "Can I call you? Is that cool?" and she said, "OK," and then she hopped up her steps, stopped, ran back down, kissed me once more, open-mouthed, and said, "I can't help it if I like to make out," with a big smile, then ran up her front steps and disappeared indoors.

After that, I rode my bike home in a daze. I didn't even remember riding home. I had no idea how I got there. Somehow I was in bed already and I couldn't stop myself from smiling about, well, everything.

seven

Like I said, Mrs. Madden, who was very thin and tall and blond with short poofy hair, who might have been hot if she hadn't been so nervous and twitchy and, well, crazy all the goddamn time, well, she made it obvious that the divorce went through by wearing the same see-through yellow nightgown all day, which began to get dirty quick. Also, she had started smoking a lot more, borrowing cigarettes from Mike, which she did not do before. And drinking. Canadian Club whiskey. We were down in the basement smoking dope and it was late and I was going to sneak home and I came up and Mrs. Madden was sitting on the floor in the front room, smoking and drinking a bottle of Canadian Club and watching *Mary Tyler Moore* reruns. I thought about it as I was riding my bike home. When I got there, my dad was crashed out on the couch and upstairs I could hear my mom sewing, the sewing machine going at like two in the morning. I thought, somewhere, someone's parents had to be happy about something.

So here's a secret: When I was feeling bad about my folks and weird about my dad and how it seemed pretty inevitable now that at some point he would be leaving, because he had been sleeping on the sofa for a while now and it didn't seem like they were working anything out—in fact, it seemed things were getting worse because my dad was now doing his own laundry—well, when I started feeling down, I would go rent a horror movie. It was usually something old and black-and-white, like *The Wolf Man*, and was always from the video store by my house. I'd end up going like every other week. The overweight guy, with his greasy carryout food fingers, would roll his eyes and mutter, "Lon Chaney Jr.? He doesn't even earn the name. Did you ever see *Phantom of the Opera*, with his father? Now that's a classic horror movie."

I would just shake my head and bring the video home and watch it downstairs alone, and my older brother, Tim, would come down into the basement—he'd be wearing, like, sweatpants and a baseball hat or some other sorta jock gear—and he'd ask what I was doing and why I didn't go outside ever, and I'd say leave me alone already and he'd say, "You're turning into a real mutant fag." Then my little sister, Alice, would come down and she'd be pouty, like always, because she was a freshman and thought if she became a cheerleader or whatever she could be somebody, but she wasn't a cheerleader and the whole high school melodrama thing was getting to her, and I dunno. She'd say, "I want to watch TV," and I'd say, "Too bad," and if she tried to take the remote control away, I'd get her in a half-nelson and then push her on her head. I didn't really talk to either one of them. They both seemed like strangers I sometimes shared meals with, I guess.

When it would quiet down, I'd go back to watching the tape and Lon Chaney Jr. would be running barefoot along the marsh, sick with guilt about what he was about to become, and there in the distance, in the shadow of the trees, was some poor British lady, and I would sit there and nod, because that was how I was usually feeling about everything: very confused and very lustful and very angry. Soon my mom would come home from work and she would be frustrated and she would start yelling about why no one else ever cooked dinner, and it was during one of those times, watching Lon Chaney Jr. on one of his rampages, that I decided I needed to get a job and stay the hell away from my house for as long as I could, maybe.

eight

The Yogurt Palace in the mini-mall on Pulaski is where I went. Like I said, I needed a job to get out of my house and also, I had decided I would try and start saving up for a car or a van. In fact, I had recently seen a van with a spider on the side of it, the kind of vehicle I thought a girl like Dorie might like a guy to have. So I went into the Yogurt Palace after school one day and I saw Jessica was there working, and decided to see what she could do for me. She had been working there for like three years and was like the assistant manager already. She was behind the counter and had on her pink apron and pink painter's cap. When she saw me, right away she started shaking her head.

"What do you want, Brian Oswald?" she asked, leaning against the counter and frowning. I just shrugged my shoulders and went up and said:

"I would like an application for employment, please."

"What? Is this a fucking joke? Did Gretchen put you up to this?"

"I would like an application for employment, please."

"Get fucked," she said, flipping me off.

"No. Please, Jessica, I need a job."

"Why?"

"I need to get out of my fucking house," I said. "My mom is always home, fucking crying."

"Yeah?" she asked, looking at me funny, kind of considering it, maybe.

"And," I said, "and I'm saving up for a van. I'm a good worker. And I got a lot of free time, you know?"

"Well, can you work nights?" she asked.

"I can work anytime," I said. "Nights, weekends, whenever you need me."

"Really?" she said, nodding. "Well, when can you start?"
And it was just that easy.

So the van I had seen, the one I decided to start saving up for, had a black widow on it, right on the side. The van was black and the spider was black and outlined with yellow with white spiderwebs around it. I saw it parked in front of this dude's house about two blocks away from Mike's. I almost wrecked my bicycle when I saw the *FOR SALE* sign on the dash. I guess I needed a van because, like Mike always said, guys who had vans always got the most trim, after the guys who could grow mustaches. Jeb Derrick had a mustache, a blond one, and girls were always sitting in his lap in the parking lot of Haunted Trails. Like I said, for some reason I couldn't grow a mustache to save my life. But I knew two other guys—real nobodies at school—who got hot vans and, within weeks, they were going out with foxes, and if they weren't foxes they were at least girls with big knockers. I would settle for an ugly girl if she noticed what song was playing on the cassette player if we were out cruising or parked somewhere. But most girls didn't seem to notice shit like that, at least the girls that went by Mike's. I dunno. Those kind of girls seemed too worried about their hair, maybe. I dunno. I thought that if some girl I was with had bad acne but said, "Is this Black Sabbath with Ozzy?" I would close my eyes and think of someone pretty and kiss her gratefully. Dorie, well, Dorie knew the difference between old Black Sabbath and the newer Sabbath stuff with Ronnie James Dio, which completely sucked. It was one of the reasons I liked her so much. She was tall and pretty and not afraid to listen to music that rocked.

As I learned in the week I worked there, the Yogurt Palace had thirty-three flavors, not thirty-one like Baskin Robbins, though I could not tell you what the other two flavors were, except that Superman ice cream wasn't nothing but vanilla with red, yellow, and blue food coloring in it. Because it was all free—to keep you, as an employee, from stealing—I could create all kinds of crazy ice cream experiments, like pineapple, chocolate, cherry, and rum shakes; and seven scoops of Irish cream parfaits, which after getting high by the garbage dumpster made me glad there was a counter to lean against. Also, there were always tons of thin, body-conscious divorced women in leotards and

ponytails who would come in after working at the Jazzercize studio to try
our nonfat soft-serve yogurt. Even better than that, there was no boss
because the boss had been diagnosed with MS and his son Caffey let
the goofy teenagers like Jessica D. run the joint. It was such a fine job I
didn't ever think about stealing because I truly wondered what the hell I
was gonna do when/if I got caught, which I knew I would because, like
all kids, I would be too stupid not to.

The bad-ass part of the job was on Friday night. Friday night was
my first night working alone at the Yogurt Palace, because Jess
wanted to go out partying, and I had been working there for a week
already, so it was OK with me because, well, there was a dual cassette
player in the back for the store radio, and so I did this thing where I
tried to create the most perfect rock'n'roll mix, one unbelievable song
after the next, like "Surrender" by Cheap Trick going into "Too Young
to Fall in Love" by Mötley Crüe, one after the other all night, as if I was
being judged by somebody like Ed McMahon, or like there was a live
audience there or something. In the middle of waiting on a customer,
I dove into the back room where the stereo was and started up the
next song before the first one was over, kind of bleeding it into the
second—"Paradise City" by Guns n' Roses going into "Revolution" by
the Beatles. No one noticed but me probably that Friday night; not the
marrieds and their runny-nosed kids who you knew were gonna drop
their single scoops before you handed them their ice cream; not the
lonely housewives in yellow sweatpants who were obviously filling the
gaps in their hearts with triple scoops of mocha fudge sundaes; not
even the other teens, on dates, awkward and wondering if they had
enough to cover the bill. I did this thing at ten then, when I had to
close: I swept and mopped to "Wild Horses" by the Rolling Stones.
That was going to be like my Friday night thing, you know.

Also, the job had given me plenty of time to develop these long
fantasies where I'd be behind the counter of the Yogurt Palace and
Dorie would come in and "Beth" by KISS would be playing and her
brown hair would be blowing and she'd unzip her jeans and the golden
crown would rise on up and we'd go in the back and have some sex and
I never worried if I was good or not, because it was always only a dream.
So what I really wanted at that time was Dorie, and not just the van or
to be out of my house. But the van did have a spider on it and fuck you
if you say I already mentioned it, because it was just that bad-ass.

The other dude I had to work with on Saturday nights, Tom, was no good. On the first Saturday night we worked together, an empty, boring night with no customers the entire evening, Tom looked at me, kind of checking me out, staring at me up and down, and asked, "Bro', can you keep a secret?"

Tom looked like a regular kid: medium height, medium build, mild case of acne, gray tattered baseball hat always turned around backwards on his blond head. He had a goofy way of talking, kind of like ghetto, I guess, even though he was more pale than me. I don't think he was too sharp a kid. I mean, I think he would have been an OK guy if he hadn't been so dumb and greedy.

"Yo, can you keep a secret or not, dude?" he asked again.

"Yeah, I guess," I said.

"Check this," he said, pointing over to the cash register, "I got a system."

"A system?"

"A system," he said, nodding. "It's perfect."

"Really?"

"Check it," he said again. "When the people come in, I don't ring them up."

"So?"

"I mean, I take their money, you know, charge them or whatever, and then I pocket the money."

"Why the fuck do you do that?"

"What do you mean, why?" he asked. "To make money."

"Don't you get paid for working here?"

"Yeah, but that's shit. I go to my crib with cash money doing this."

"Well, that's cool, just don't do it when I'm around. I need this job."

"What, you don't think I need this job too?" he asked.

I kind of laughed and turned, going back to wiping down the glassy sneeze guards.

"I axed you a question," Tom said, stepping over beside me.

"You *axed* me a question?" I said, mocking him. "Where are you from anyway?"

"What the fuck do you care where I'm from," he muttered, giving me a tough look. "I come from Oak Lawn."

"Oak Lawn?" I asked, shaking my head. "Do you even have black people living there?"

"Yo," he said, holding his hand up in a weird gangster sign, "you need to give respect here. I don't take anyone's shit, see?"

"I'm sorry," I said, turning my head so I didn't laugh. "Good luck with your system."

That night when the only customers came in—two elderly women in matching blue head scarves who ordered the smallest scoops of mint chocolate chip we sold—Tom tried to do his "system" on them, asking for their money without ringing them in. I stood beside him, making up my mind not to let him fuck this up for me.

"Yo, Tom," I said as he reached out to take their money, a measly dollar-fifty, "you forgot to ring them in, bro."

He turned to me and glared, blinking, then turned to the ladies and said, "I'll ring them in after I take their money."

"Yo, Tom, why not ring them in now?" I asked.

"Don't you have tables to clean?" he asked, still holding their dollar and two quarters in his hand.

"No, I got them already. Here, let me do it," I said, and punched in two small cones. The cash register buzzed and bleeped and I took the money from Tom's hand, placing it in the appropriate bins.

"You're fucking dead, bitch," he said, whispering under his breath. All night I was waiting for him to come at me with a knife or a set of brass knuckles or a roll of quarters or a broom even, but he didn't do anything. We locked up, finished cleaning, and just as he was leaving, I said, "Sorry about that, Tom. I just don't want to get busted," and he nodded and stormed off to his car, a gold Cutlass Supreme with vanity license plates that said, "MR.SLICK."

I came in the next day early to work my shift and found out I had been fired. Tom had gone home and called Caffey, the boss' son, and told him he had caught me stealing, and also mentioned he knew about Jessica and Caffey fooling around, and that was it for me. The dreams of my staying the hell away from my house, the dreams of the van with the spider on it, the dreams of impressing Dorie, all gone, just like that.

I swore if I ever found out where that kid Tom lived, I'd put a hurt on him for lying and getting me fired, I swore to fucking God, sincerely.

nine

In the 7-Eleven parking lot, I kissed Dorie again. We were waiting for Mike to try and buy cigarettes and Dorie was standing by the dumpster which was littered with graffiti like EAT PUSSY and ME, 1988, and there was the big red-and-green 7-Eleven sign burning in the night and some mother was in the passenger seat of a long brown station wagon screaming at her kids and some guy in a white Air Conditioning/ Heating van had left it running with the radio on and Buddy Holly's "Every Day" was playing with its corny toy piano and Dorie was leaning against the red bricks of the 7-Eleven and she had her light-blue jean jacket on and blue jeans and a T-shirt that said *Spay and Neuter Your Pets*, and her brownish-red hair was looking very straight—her bangs just above her tiny eyebrows—and she was carving her name into the brick with a white stone, which wasn't really working, and she had been eating an orange popsicle and was singing along to Buddy Holly, and so when I finally kissed her for a second time, well, it tasted just like Orange Dream.

ten

At this time, I decided it would be cool to have lines shaved into my hair—you know, like Brian "The Boz" Bosworth from the Oklahoma Sooners—like where you have long hair in the back and the sides are short and there are lines like shaved into the side of your head in a cool pattern. I thought that might, you know, make it for me; might, you know, be my "thing," you know, who I could be: the guy with the shaved lines in his hair. I had seen Bosworth on TV months before, when my older brother Tim was watching some homo-erotic football game, and the dude's hair looked very cool. So I asked Mike to try it and he wouldn't do it. I mean, I even went to Osco Drug and bought a hair-trimmer kit for twenty bucks and there I was and no one would do it; I even asked Mrs. Madden and she said she'd do it for fifty bucks. It was like everything else: You get a good idea and people go out of their way to make it hard on you.

Like Mike's basement: It sounded like a great idea, but now his life was shit. He had to work at the lousy pizza place all the time, had to buy his own food, couldn't make telephone calls, hadn't seen his sister Molly in a month, and because of all that, he had started fucking up bad at school. He would just not study. He would not turn in his homework or do any assignments and he went from being a low-B/high-C student to being a hardcore flunker, just like that. There was nothing I could do, nothing I could say to cheer him up. He was smoking a lot of dope—before school and after and even sometimes in between classes—and he had bombed our last history test very, very bad, and the hot Ms. Aiken had asked to see him after class and she wanted to know what was going on with him and he just shook his head and got up and left. So, shit.

We were down in Mike's basement and he was pouting like usual, going through his depression thing, which I think all his dope-smoking didn't help at all, and Dorie finally came over because I had been calling her all day, and, well, I thought maybe she could get Mike out of bed. She came by with a book she had gotten from her school library about the Boston Strangler and one about American serial killers and I thought, *What an excellent girl*, and she was planning on helping us with the Final Project. But Mike, he was in such a fucking mood, he just kept playing "Changes" by Black Sabbath—which was a very weak song where there was like a piano, *a piano on a fucking Black Sabbath song*, and Ozzy kind of mumbled about going through changes—and all Mike did was lie on his bed, and it was the first time I really had looked at his room in a long time, with the bowls and one-hitters and dirty girlie magazines lying out in the open, and Dorie just shook her head and said, "Mike, your home life is definitely fucked," and he lifted his head up from the bed and said, "I totally know."

"Listen, man, we need to do this project," I said.

"Who gives a fuck about it?" he asked, moaning. "Everything else is fucked up."

"What about Erin McDougal?" I asked. "That's going good, right?"

"Fuck," he sighed. "It's only a matter of time before I fuck that up too."

"You need to snap out of it, man," I said. "Come on, let's go to the mall or something."

"Just leave me alone!" he shouted, burying his head under his pillows. I pulled on his bare foot, but he wasn't moving.

"Forget it," Dorie said, sad, "if he wants to be miserable, let him be miserable. I got to get to work anyway."

I followed her up the stairs and out into the backyard and asked her, "Dorie, would you still like me if I got my hair cut like Brian Bosworth?"

"Who?" she asked, lighting a cigarette.

"The guy from football with like lines cut into his hair? Like a design."

"I think it's going to look stupid," she said, shaking her head. "I like your hair the way it is. It's nice," and she patted it.

"Yeah, I guess," I said. "It was just kind of a dumb idea I had."

"Give me a kiss, I've gotta go," she said, checking her watch. She snapped open a tube of whitish lipstick and quickly redid her lips.

"You really gotta go?" I asked.

"Yeah, my ride's coming to pick me up."

"OK." I reached up and kissed her as hard as I could, sliding my tongue in and out of her mouth, holding her hands in my hands as she giggled and then growled, planting a big white lipstick kiss on my cheek. I walked her to the front of Mike's house and a super-fine black Firebird pulled up beside us, idling at the curb. The dude behind the wheel—some dick with mirrored sunglasses, a black headband, and a furry black mustache—honked twice, turning down Winger or some other bad-hair rock on his arena-rock-sized speakers. I stood beside Dorie, my mouth dropping open.

"Call me later," Dorie said, disappearing into the car. I watched them burn rubber as they pulled away and immediately, in my brain, I began to do some very poor mathematical calculations:

• I did not have cool hair, contrary to Dorie's comments. I did not have my own look at all.

• I did not have a job anymore, which meant no money coming in.

• At this rate, I could afford to take Dorie to a matinee, enjoy one cheap appetizer at Bennigan's, and take the bus back to an enchanted evening of romance and bliss watching Mike blaze up and then complain.

Like this, I was never going to get to do it with her if I couldn't get some money together, and, well, things did not look very good for me.

Until

Until

Until the events that transpired one afternoon at a fucking Dungeons and Dragons game changed everything.

eleven

OK, on Saturday afternoon these geeks that Mike knew, these nerdy Dungeons and Dragons kids, called him up out of the blue and asked if they could buy some dope off of him. It was a golden opportunity, because there were like five or six of them and each wanted to buy some. Why? I dunno, to prove they were all cool or something, maybe. The main geek was this kid Peter Tracy, who I knew from our high school. Mike had gone to public grammar school with him and had played D&D with him a couple of times, I guess, back in junior high, but they hadn't talked in years. So when the kid asked, "Can you bring it by tonight? It's important," Mike said, "We will be there," and hung up the phone quick.

The idea was to give them just a little pot, just enough to get them slightly stoned, and pack the rest with oregano, an old stoner trick. That way Mike was only selling a little of his stash and getting paid for like five times as much. It was simple and brilliant and easy. We hopped on a bus and ended up in Oak Lawn, off of 111th Street, down a row of apartment houses to a dead-end street. We walked around back as the head geek had instructed and knocked on the back door twice. The kid's mom, a very June Cleaver type, with the short brown bob and blue dress, white apron, and dishpan hands, answered the door, smiling. "Oh, hello there, boys," she beamed. "Come in, come in."

"Thanks," Mike said, patting down his hair.

"We haven't seen you in a long time, Michael. How are your parents?"

"Swell," he said. We walked in through the back kitchen door, smiling and nodding at Mrs. Tracy as she asked us to wipe our feet. You could tell she was one of those ladies right away. Like I said, she had perfectly bobbed brown hair, a blue and white frilly apron on, and a soapy mop in her hand. Mike and I apologized and wiped our feet on the mat, and she said, "The boys are in the front room in the middle of a game right now."

"Great," Mike said, rolling his eyes.

"Would you like to hang up your coats?" Mrs. Tracy asked.

"No, we're just stopping by quick," Mike said.

"Oh, but I insist," she said and made us take off our coats. I looked around the kitchen for a minute and saw how clean the countertops were, how spotless and perfect every surface was, how all of the geeks' jackets were hung by the back door, Mrs. Tracy's blue linen jacket, her red purse, all perfectly arranged on descending hooks, how everything in this house seemed to be singing; and I thought of Mike's kitchen, which was a fucking mess and had this diseased head of lettuce sitting in the sink for weeks, and my kitchen at home, which was never used for anything because no one wanted to be at home to eat. We walked down the hallway, past the goofy photos of Peter Tracy as a baby—dozens of them, because he was an only child—and you could almost tell he was going to grow up to be geeky: His head was huge, like eight times larger than the rest of his body, and he had a moody, arrogant kind of look as he regarded the camera coldly. We walked through the hall, then out into the front room where five or six ultra-nerds were doing their fucking role-playing, shouting and tossing their twelve-sided dice and what seemed to me like kind of mentally jerking each other off, maybe.

"My elf attacks the Evil Orc!" some red-haired doofus announced, rolling a handful of dice.

"My thief joins the fight!" some other wuss shouted, banging his hand on the wood kitchen table. *Good god,* I thought, *these kids are bigger pussies than I have ever been in my entire life.*

Peter Tracy was at the head of the table wearing a kind of black cloak—yes, a black fucking cloak—covering the top of his head, acting as Dungeon Master: the king geek who orchestrated the fucking game.

"Ah, but it is a trap," Peter said with a serpentine smile. "For this Orc is not an Orc at all, but a shape-shifting demon!"

All the geeks sucked in a breath, titillated and amazed, until one kid, who was chubby and sweaty, leaned in and said in a very dramatic, geek-type accent, "My conjurer casts a spell of detection! We will see how mighty a foe this shape-shifting demon is!"

"Ah, Gentlemen," Peter said, looking up, nodding in our direction. "It seems we have guests."

"Who are these dire strangers?" the fat kid asked, still with the full-on geek accent.

"Perhaps they are fellow travelers!" the red-haired kid shouted.

"Perhaps they are shape-shifting demons!" the fat kid replied.

"Right, whatever," Mike said, getting uptight. "We brought you the stuff, OK?"

"Ah, yes. But perhaps you'd like to awaken your character, Gaston the Ranger, first? A few rounds of a proper Orc-thrashing?" Peter asked Mike, pulling an empty seat up to the table.

"Yeah, I'm good," he said. "We've got other places to go, actually."

"So," Peter asked, whispering, "do you have it? All of it?"

"Yeah," Mike said. "But what do you need all this for?"

"Well, we all want to try it," Peter said.

"Well, there was a debate about how much it usually takes. Maybe you can answer that?" another kid, one with enormous glasses, asked, raising his hand.

"How much does it take? To get high? Huh," Mike said, nodding, looking down into the brown lunch bag. "This should be enough for each of you."

"Cool," the geek with the big glasses said, lowering his hand.

"Who do I pay?" Peter asked, opening a large gold metal treasure-type chest set in the middle of the table.

"Um, me, I guess," Mike said. Peter stood, counted out fifty dollars—ten dollars a kid—and placed it in Mike's palm.

"That, I believe, concludes our business, dear Ranger," Peter said, readjusting the cloak on his head. He slipped the brown bag full of a little weed and mostly oregano into the treasure chest and turned a lock, securing it with a very tiny golden key. "Now we must celebrate!" Peter announced, clapping his hands like a Medieval inn-keeper. "Mother!" he called into the other room. "Our chalices, please!"

In a moment, Mrs. Tracy returned, carrying a large silver tray full of collector *Star Wars* glasses, the kind I got when I was a kid, I think, from Burger King. I wasn't sure. Each of the geeks had his own specific one, apparently, and each was filled with what looked to be a different drink—the fat kid, milk in a Darth Vader glass; the red-haired kid, orange juice behind Princess Leia's face. Peter reached out and took the last glass, announcing, "And Chewbacca, old friend, I believe you are for me."

"Excelsior!" the geeks shouted in unison, holding their glasses high and saluting, toasting with their drinks.

"I'm sorry, boys, I didn't know you were coming over or I would have brought you something. Michael, I believe there's an *Empire Strikes Back* glass upstairs with your name on it."

"No, I'm good, Mrs. Tracy," he said. "But is it cool to use the washroom?"

"Well, of course, Michael. You remember where it is, dear?"

"Yes, ma'am," he said and got up and disappeared down the hallway.

I stood there, staring at the geeks at the table, and thought how close I had been to becoming like them: weird, unhappy, maladjusted, perpetual virgins. But then again, there was something kind of funny about them, kind of goofy, like they knew what they were doing was gay, but they didn't care. I mean, Peter Tracy had a fucking druid's robe on and he didn't care. There was something kind of, I dunno, brave about it, just not fucking caring what the whole rest of the world thought of you. And they all had each other; they were like their own little group, with their own little rules and way of talking and everything. In that way, it was kind of cool. I took a seat where Mike had been sitting and the kid with enormous glasses leaned over and asked, "Do you play RPGs?"

"Um, I don't know that means," I said.

"You know, Role-Playing Games? Do you play?"

"Not really," I said.

"That's too bad," he said, like he felt bad for me, his breath all hot and milky. "It's a great way to meet people."

"I bet," I said.

"Bruce brought his girlfriend last week." The kid with glasses pointed at a taller, quieter kid at the corner of the table, who smiled at me and nodded.

"You guys have girlfriends?" I asked.

"Well, just Bruce. But, well, that's what the . . . magic ingredients are for."

"The what?"

"The narcotics," the kid said, nodding toward the chest in the center of the table. "Tonight, Mr. and Mrs. Tracy are going out all night for a wedding. We're having a *party* here," he said snidely, as if I had never heard of a fucking party before.

"Good luck with that," I said.

"I'd invite you, but we don't want to throw off the male-female ratio. It's been coordinated perfectly."

"I bet," I said. I looked up and Mike came charging down the hall, waving at me.

"OK, let's go," he said, blinking at me furiously.

"OK, chill out," I said.

"No, we got to split now. I have things to do tonight, you know?"

"Relax," I said.

Mike grabbed me by the back of the shirt and shoved me down the hall toward the back door. "OK, relax, we're going." He grabbed his jacket, then my jacket and threw it at me, opened the door, waved to Mrs. Tracy who was busy scrubbing a pan or something, muttered, "See you, Mrs. Tracy," and pushed me down the back porch steps.

"What? What the fuck?" I asked. "Those dudes weren't so bad," I said, but Mike kept pushing me, dragging me by my jacket collar until we were halfway down the block. He stopped, started laughing, caught his breath and then lifted up the front of his T-shirt. There, wedged between his underwear and the front of his pants, was a red vinyl pocketbook, like a lady's kind of wallet.

"Dude, you lifted his mom's pocketbook?" I asked.

He nodded, coughing a little, and then winked.

"It was just sitting by the back door. I saw it when I went to the bathroom."

"How much is in there?" I asked. He flipped open the clasp and looked inside and his eyes went big and wide.

"It looks like about a hundred bucks or so. Plus the fifty."

"We are totally rich," I said.

"Well, I am," he said.

"Fuck off."

"Just kidding."

"What do you want to do with it?" I asked. He looked at me, wiped his nose, and said:

"Let's go to the mall. I got an idea."

OK, so we had $150 and all Saturday afternoon and here's what we came up with: Mike bought Erin McDougal one of those necklaces that is really two necklaces, like it is a silver heart that is split in two and the guy gets half and so does the girl, and he got it engraved and everything, so that was sixty fucking bucks right there. The engraving was an extra twenty-five, so that was actually eighty-five bucks spent just on one stupid gift, which, when it was all done, read, "Mike and Erin, So Sexy 1991," which didn't make a fucking bit of sense to me, but there was no hope of talking him out of it, so I just kept my mouth shut.

I went to the one store where they had crazy, goofy, crappy jewelry and scrunchies and sunglasses and other cheesy girl-gifts, The Canary and the Elephant, where I had once almost gotten my ear pierced back in junior high, but had chickened out.

"What are you going to get here? This place is all plastic jelly bracelets and shit."

"This," I said. "This is what I'm getting her." In the corner of the store were all these stuffed animals—teddy bears, puppies, bunnies, kittens, and baby tigers—and, like, candy and bracelets and glitter and crap, which they could all put inside this super-durable balloon, you know, like this present: this stuffed animal with like candy and shit, but inside a balloon. To me, it was fucking genius.

"Dude, you are going to get her a balloon?" Mike asked.

"It's like an animal inside a balloon."

"For sixty bucks?" Mike asked.

"It lasts for like a month."

"Dude, that is the dumbest idea ever."

"No, dude," I said. "Getting some girl you haven't even been dating for like more than three weeks a silver fucking engraved necklace is the dumbest idea ever."

"It's fucking classy," he said.

"No, it's not, man. It's gonna freak her out."

"How is it gonna freak her out?" he asked.

"It's like asking her to get married and shit. My thing, it's fun, you know? It's like goofy."

"Man, it sure is," he said.

"Um, clerk-girl," I said to the fifteen-year-old blond girl with too much makeup on, looking bored behind the counter. "I want an animal in a balloon. Can you help me with that?"

She snapped her gum and nodded at me.

"What animal?" she asked.

"I dunno. What animal, Mike?" I asked.

"Don't get a dog. Her dog got run over when we were kids and she took it bad."

"OK, no dogs," I said. "How about . . . how about a bear?" I said.

The girl behind the counter rolled her eyes. "That's what everybody gets," she said, grabbing a white teddy bear.

"All right then, all right, how about a tiger?"

"A tiger?" Mike asked.

"Yeah, I'm getting her a tiger. In a balloon. Just pay the girl her money," I said to Mike. He nodded and dug into his pocket for the rest of our loot.

"Why a fucking tiger?" he asked.

"I dunno," I said. "I just like tigers. It's funny, right? It's fun?" I asked the girl who was busy blowing up the gigantic red balloon. She looked over her shoulder and nodded, sad.

"I wouldn't turn it down," she said. "I wish to God someone would do something like this for me, for no reason. That's how you know you're dating a good guy. They do stuff like this for no reason," she said, and I elbowed Mike in the side, grinning.

Believe it or not, the "Mike and Erin, So Sexy 1991" engraved necklace went over like a fucking charm. Erin McDougal fucking loved it, I mean *loved* it. She jumped into his lap and made him help her put it on, and then did the same for him, the two of them wrestling on Mike's sofa, kissing, Erin McDougal giggling and saying, "It's so pretty, it's so pretty."

Well, I was up next and dug into the white paper bag and told Dorie to close her eyes, which she did, but then she began peeking so I had to stop, and she sighed and turned around on the sofa, and I pulled the big red balloon out and winked at Mike, who was shaking his head, and Erin McDougal was looking at me like I was crazy, maybe wondering, *What the hell in the world is that thing?* but I didn't care, because, well, I knew it was goofy. I knew it was kind of weird and dumb and I didn't care because that was me, I guess, and I really liked this girl and wanted to, like, be myself with her. So finally, I placed the big red balloon beside her and said, "OK," and she opened her eyes and looked at the balloon, then at me, then back at the balloon again.

"It's a tiger," I said. "In a balloon."

Dorie stared at it again and smiled, and I couldn't tell if she was faking it or not but then she leaned over and kissed me on the cheek and said, "I really like tigers."

"You do?" I asked.

"Yeah," she said. "I mean, I don't have a collection or anything but I really like them."

"Me too," I said and kissed her again. "It's not dumb, is it?"

"No, I really like it. It's funny," she said. "It's, like, you."

"I figured, well, you don't really wear jewelry, so, well," I said. "I didn't want to be all, 'Let's go steady,' or anything."

"I like it, I really like it," she said, throwing her arms around my neck.

"Well, good," I said. We leaned back on the couch, the tiger in the balloon sitting on Dorie's lap.

"Hey," she said.

"Yeah?"

"I've got a secret."

"Really?" I asked.

"Really." She leaned in close to me and put her lips beside my ear and said the words, the words which would change my life, indelibly. "No one's home at my house."

"Really," I said, sitting up, smiling.

"Really," she repeated, winking back.

"So?"

"So no one's home at my house," she said again and we got up and ran off, us, hand in hand.

twelve

I had never been in Dorie's room before, let alone the rest of her house or anything. I had stood on her front porch and that was about it. Dorie's room was all white and the carpet was red and it was all very clean and there were posters on the wall of David Bowie in drag and she had a heart-shaped pillow on her narrow bed, which kind of surprised me.

"So?" she said, kind of nervous. "This is it. This is my room. What do you think?"

"It's nice," I said.

"Yep."

"It is."

"So?" she said, kind of clapping her hands together.

"So," I said and we began making out again, this time falling together onto her bed. In a flash, Dorie had her brown shirt unbuttoned, had my sweater off, her shiny black boots kicked to the floor, my pants unbuckled, her jeans undone, her socks pulled off, her hair in my face, her mouth against my chin, her brown satin bra unclasped, my pants pulled down around my feet, her hands at the bottom of my T-shirt pulling it up over my head. The two of us dove quickly under her beige comforter as she waved her white cotton panties in the air, spinning them around and tossing them to the floor and laughing. I could feel her skin and it was so smooth and it smelled so good and she had goosebumps for some reason and I, kind of awkwardly, pulled off my underwear and kicked them off the side of the bed and then sat up, remembering, and dug into the back of my pants pocket for the rubber Mike had given me.

Cut to:

Mike in the Osco Drug parking lot, leaning against the motorized merry-go-round, lighting a cigarette, digging into the back pocket of his pants for his wallet, unfolding it, digging out a foil-wrapped condom, and saying, "You got to be cool about this shit. You don't wanna find out you got a kid, right?"

"Right," I said.

"So you got to change it like every few weeks," he said. "Or else."

"Or else," I said, repeating.

"So here," he said.

Cut to:

Mike, sitting on the brown sofa in his basement in his white skivvy underwear, rolling a joint, looking over his shoulder every so often toward his small, paneled-off room, shaking his head and smiling. Him saying, "I'm gonna need that rubber back," and winking, because Erin McDougal was in his bedroom waiting, and me unfolding my wallet to hand it to him and smiling.

Cut to:

Mike running like hell out of the Osco Drug, grabbing my arm as he runs, booking full speed across the parking lot, past the train tracks, over the fence, and into the cemetery, me hardly breathing, my heart up in my ears, and him digging under his jean jacket and tearing open a brand new box of condoms, handing a few to me, saying, "Ribbed," and out of breath, "you know, for her pleasure."

"Yeah," I said, hunched over, trying to breathe.

"This one," he said, planting one of the small foil circles in my hand. "I can tell this one is going to be lucky."

Cut to:

Yearbook photos of every girl I have ever met, thought of, or looked at: girls Mike introduced me to, girls like Gretchen who I was so sure I was in love with, girls I have never even spoken to, like the one who worked at Spencer's Gifts in the mall, girls, girls, all who had seemed so impossible, so out of reach.

Back to:

I looked over my shoulder at Dorie who was still laughing, kicking her feet up and down quick to make the sheet rise and fall like waves, mumbling, "Hurry up, I'm cold." I turned, opened the wrapper, climbed back under the covers, and said, "OK, you're gonna give me some pointers, right?"

"Duh," she said, rolling her eyes.

"It's, you know, my first time."

"Duh," she said, rolling her eyes again.

thirteen

In the basement, Dorie and Mike and I were doing the Ouija Board and trying to contact some spirits, right, and Mike said it was all bullshit anyway and went in his room to call Erin McDougal to, you know, make nice, and so it was just Dorie and I playing, our hands touching the small white plastic pointer, kind of moving it from side to side over the board with all the letters and numbers and words and everything, the two of us giggling and laughing, and I asked, "Did you ever get a spirit to contact you before?" because it was her Ouija Board, and she said, "Yeah, in junior high, me and Jenny Elwood used to do this all the time," and I said, "Are you sure you guys weren't just moving it yourselves?" and she said, "Duh, no," and we kept moving the pointer around and around until it kind of stopped by itself, kind of getting very hard to push, and then I didn't know if it was just Dorie pushing harder or what, but Dorie asked, "Are you a spirit trying to contact us?" and the pointer went to "yes" and so she said, "Are you a good spirit or a bad spirit?" and it spelled out "G-O-U-D," and Dorie said, "Maybe he is a little kid or something, you know, like he can't spell," and I said, "Yeah, maybe," and then she asked, "Are you a young kid?" and the pointer went right to "no," and Dorie asked, "How did you die?" and it began to spell out, "S-I-C-K," and Dorie and I kind of looked at each other, startled, and I began to try to resist pushing the pointer at all, and it was really moving, and so I said, "Does Dorie really, truly like me?" and Dorie looked up and smiled, kind of surprised I asked that, I guess, and like that, the pointer slowly slid over to "yes."

fourteen

At my locker before school even began, I was kneeling, picking through the random shit I had stuffed inside, looking for my Religion and Chemistry notebooks, kind of in a daze, thinking about nothing but Dorie—her hair, her hands, her face—and singing this song she always sung, "Changes" by David Bowie, and not really knowing the words but "Cha-cha-cha-changes, turn and face the . . ." I didn't know what he sang next so I just sang, "Turn and face the day," because it was like the beginning of the fucking school day, even though later I found out the line was, "Turn and face the strange," which would have worked too, had I known. I was down on my knees, shoving mounds of homework assignments, notebooks, failed tests, single random sheets of loose-leaf paper with my band names on them, and trying to retie my black tie at the same time, when out of the corner of my eye I saw John McDunnah, his big, square, blond face and oddly Herculean shape looming down the hallway toward me, and before I could register what was going on I felt the egg come down. I knew what it was right away, the feeling of it was exactly the same: the sharp strange sting of the eggshell against my scalp, the runny-sticky foul odor of it leaking down my neck, the yellowish globs on my white shirt and black pants, the clumpy whiteness growing hard in my hair. I looked him in the eyes as he was walking away and he was laughing his jungle-hyena laugh, nodding to his two pals, and all at once it made total sense. The first time had not been an accident, not really. He had picked me, known who I was at least, or what I looked like— which must have been like an easy fucking target or a wimp or a pussy or someone who he knew would never do anything back. Realizing that, well, that was what fucking hurt about the whole thing.

fifteen

In Dorie's room, I was lying in her bed after school, reading, and her mom was still at work (her mom was a receptionist at a hospital) and I had my shoes off and so did Dorie and I was reading this dumb book about serial killers for my history project and she began to slide her bare foot against mine and I pretended to ignore her and then she took off her shirt and started kissing my neck and I kept on reading and she started growling, which she did, and she was dry-humping me and unbuttoning my pants and I kept on reading, and then she had her hand down my pants and her fingers were on my crotch, inside my pants, and I started getting excited down there and not knowing what to do, and so I kept on reading, and I felt her hand grab the whole thing and Dorie shouted, "Hurry it up, Romeo, my mom will be home any second!" and she dug under her bed for a rubber and we started doing it and

As a boy, Pee Wee Gaskins saw a cobra kill a live rat at a carnival. In a confession he later wrote, this was the first time he felt violence's attraction. Later named America's meanest killer, Pee Wee spent most of his life in prison. In 1969, after getting released for the murder of an inmate, Pee Wee began killing at an unprecedented rate. He saw a difference between his "coastal kills," victims he found while driving around the roadways of America who he killed for pleasure, and the "serious murders," victims he killed for very specific reasons. His victims were usually found along the coastal highways, where every few weeks he would go to try and silence his terrible feelings of "not belonging."

the serial killer book fell off the bed and landed on the floor and scared the hell out of us both and I jumped out of the bed and we figured out it was just the book and we both started laughing, and it felt so good to be there and I said that to her before we started going at it again.

sixteen

We got busted pretty bad by Mrs. Madden, finally. I guess it was only a matter of time. Mike and I had devised this kind of chemical pressure explosive, perfect for blowing the hell out of mailboxes, and that was the thing that did us in. Some dude in Mike's gym class told him that if you took a two-liter plastic soda-pop bottle, put a big ball of tinfoil inside, poured in some mercuric acid—which is like some fucking metallic kind of acid you can get at any hardware store—then sealed the bottle top, the acid would eat away at the tinfoil and create like this tremendous gas that would cause the whole thing to blow.

We had to try it. We got like three soda-pop bottles and a roll of tinfoil, went to Osco and bought a little container of this acid stuff, and one night we just went outside, walked to the end of Mike's block, put the tinfoil in one of the bottles, poured in the acid, sealed the top, shoved it in a mailbox, and started running. In a few minutes, the bottle blew like a pressure bomb, knocking the little red wood mailbox right off its post, like three feet into the air, completely destroying the fucking thing. We blew up another one right away, crossing over to the other side of the street. This time we blew the hell out of a plastic barn-shaped mailbox, knocking it off its post, but not completely. It was still dangling by some kind of wire, I guess.

We were all set to do the last one when some angry neighbor-type individual came out, some big dude in a white T-shirt who grabbed Mike around the neck just before he could pour the mercuric acid in. He grabbed me by the back of my shirt and marched us over to Mike's, rang the doorbell, then knocked on the door hard until Mrs. Madden appeared. She was drunk off her ass, her eyes all red and glazed, looking very happy and stupid, all in her yellow nightgown, smoking, with a very amused face.

"Nahhh," she said, smiling. "These two aren't mine."

"Mrs. Madden, these kids just blew up two mailboxes and were going for a third."

"They're no longer my responsibility," she said. "If you want, you can take it up with that boy's father," and she pointed to Mike with the end of her lit cigarette.

"Mrs. Madden," the angry neighbor mumbled, clearing his throat, "I don't want to have to get the police involved, but . . ."

"You go ahead and get the police involved," Mrs. Madden shouted, "and you'll be wishing you hadn't!"

The angry neighbor rubbed his chin, taking a step back.

"What the heck do you mean by that?" he asked.

"I mean everyone has eyes, Mr. Hickman. Everyone . . ." she slurred, "has. Eyes. Understand?"

Mr. Hickman, the angry neighbor, shook his head, looked at Mrs. Madden, then at us, all up and down, and then he walked away, shaking his head. He stopped a few feet from the front porch and said, "It's no wonder they act like that."

"Tell it to the judge!" Mrs. Madden shouted, kicking the screen door open. "Tell it to the judge, you phony!"

Mike and I started to walk inside and Mrs. Madden laughed, snapping her drink up, some Canadian Club whiskey, heavy with ice, tossing her head back.

"You two," she said, closing the door. "You two don't live here anymore."

"What?" Mike said. "You can't do that."

"I can do whatever I want," she said. "I am the official homeowner."

"Mom," Mike said, holding his hands out. "You have to let me live here."

"I've done everything I could," she whispered. "This is all I can do."

"You're really fucking serious?" Mike asked, covering his face.

"Unless you're ready to live by my rules," she said, looking down at her poorly painted red toenails and frowning.

"Mom . . ." Mike whispered, and it seemed like he might start crying.

"I'm gonna take off," I said, heading for the front door.

"No, this affects you too, orphan boy," Mrs. Madden said, laughing at her own joke. "Where are your parents anyway? Don't they care where you're at every night of the week?"

"No," I said. "They got their own problems, I guess."

"Huh," she said, looking me up and down. "That's a good answer. Well," she added, taking a sip of her drink, the ice clinging together. "Michael, you know how I feel. I've had one asshole in my life and I'm not going to take the same from you and . . ." and then she stopped. Just in the middle of her sentence, just like that. Her eyes got wide and full of tears and she kind of bit her lip and looked at Mike and then at me and said, "I can't anymore. I'm sorry," and ran off into her bedroom, crying.

"I'm gonna go," I said, whispering. "What are you gonna do about her?"

"What can I do?" he asked. "Neither one of us is changing." He lit up a cigarette and exhaled through his nose. "I just think, fuck. It would be nice to be treated like a kid once in a fucking while."

seventeen

OK, the most haunted place in the Midwest was supposedly this old cemetery in the middle of a forest preserve called Bachelor's Grove, which was somewhere in the middle of the south suburbs. Mike had been told about the place by his older sister Molly when she was still around, and we had talked for months about going out there to see if there really were any ghosts or anything but we never did, because we had no way to get there, but Erin McDougal—you know, "Mike and Erin, So Sexy 1991"—had a car. So one night in the middle of the week, when Mike and Dorie weren't working, all four of us hopped in Erin McDougal's used Toyota Camry and drove out to 127th or wherever it was, parked on some tiny subdivision street, and hiked through the forest preserve in the pitch-black dark. Right away, Erin McDougal was squealing and giggling and holding Mike's shoulder, and Dorie stopped to make out with me every couple of feet. I've got to be honest, it was kind of fucking freaky, being out in the woods all alone in the middle of the night and everything, I dunno. Maybe I had watched too many fucking slasher movies, but all I kept thinking about was a guy in a fucking burlap-sack mask chasing us down with a chainsaw or something. Mike was the only one with a flashlight, and we found our way along a narrow trail, then to a second, larger one, and then there were the gates of the small little cemetery—green wire and kind of covered in branches and ivy. It was very quiet; only the sounds of the nearby highway and crickets and Erin McDougal's nervous giggling.

We crept through a hole in the fence, each of us walking around a little on our own, checking out all the super-old headstones, some like from 1850 and everything. Dorie jumped out from behind a tree, landing on my back, tackling me, and kissing me on the mouth, and then running off again. In a minute or two, we all sat around the largest headstone, FULTON, it read, and it was big and rectangular, and Mike lit up a cigarette.

It was dark, some blue night sky breaking through the branches overhead, as I felt for Dorie's hand. It was hard to see anything much but lightning bugs and brief flashes of cars from the highway. I could kind of make the shape out of Mike's head and Dorie's nose and Erin was a big dark blur. I looked out of the corner of my eye every so often, making sure no cop or weirdo sprung out at us. Dorie leaned in close to me and I could smell her hair and I thought I was the luckiest guy in the world just then.

"My dad," Mike said, "he told me him and his pals came out here once."

"Yeah?" I said.

"You know, when they were kids, teenagers, whatever. I asked him if he saw anything, and he wouldn't answer me."

"No shit?" asked Dorie.

"No shit," Mike said. "And I kept asking him and asking him and finally he said, 'If I tell you, you won't sleep for a week.'"

"Whoa," I said. "That's fucked up."

"Yeah," Mike said. "So I asked him, you know, to tell me what he saw."

"So?" Dorie asked.

"So, he told me. He said he and his buddies were sitting around, having drinks and everything, and then this man—this very tall man in a tall black hat, like Lincoln, you know—came out of nowhere, just like walked toward them, and my dad took off running."

"Jesus," I said. "Man, that's fucking freaky."

"Yeah," Mike said. "I know. Because you know my dad, he doesn't bullshit. I mean, he's not a pussy, you know."

"Shit," I said. "That's intense."

We all looked around, kind of holding our breath and listening.

"I don't want to die," Erin McDougal whispered, and then out of nowhere started crying, I mean really crying. It kind of freaked me out. I guess Erin's dad had emphysema and was like bedridden, you know, at home dying, and all the talk about ghosts and death and everything had upset her, you know. But having a girl start crying in a graveyard, well, that's weird fucking business. Mike hugged her and she folded into his lap and said, "I'm sorry, guys, I'm sorry. It's just my dad," and right away, I started thinking about my dad and, well, my mom, who I didn't think about a lot because, well, she was a lot harder to get along with, I guess, and what the hell would I do if one of them was dying or worse, died? And for a second, I thought about Gretchen, and her mom and her mom's funeral and, well, all of it and, I dunno, I felt more scared than if I had seen a ghost.

Dorie was pulling on my hand and we were running all of a sudden, just Dorie and me, and I asked, "Do you know where you're going, Dorie?" and she just said, "Shhhhh," and I said, "Dorie, seriously," and she just said, "Shhhhhhh" again, and it was just the two of us running in the dark because Mike had the flashlight and was still sitting in the cemetery, and we were running through the woods, just the two of us, and I didn't want to look behind me, I just wanted to keep running, holding Dorie's hand.

We got back to the car somehow and I was out of breath and Dorie grabbed me and started kissing me like crazy and I asked, "What? What was it?" and she started unbuttoning my pants and we hurried into the backseat of Erin McDougal's used Camry and it was one of the best nights of my entire life. Really.

eighteen

"The Boston Strangler Timeline"—which I dug out of the book Dorie gave me because Mike was either too depressed or too busy making kissy-faces with Erin McDougal so the history final project was all on me—didn't give me much to think about, really:

Jan. 4, 1964 — Miss Mary Sullivan, aged nineteen, the last of the eleven female victims, is found dead, presumed murdered in her apartment in the Beacon Hill neighborhood of Boston.

March 4, 1965 — Albert DeSalvo, factory worker, who is serving time for armed robbery and various sex offenses, confesses to the Boston Strangler's eleven murders and two others. However, he is never once charged for any of the murders.

Nov. 25, 1973 — DeSalvo is killed in prison by another inmate.

But then I dug this up:

As a boy, Albert DeSalvo bragged about being able to ejaculate five or six times a day. As an adult, his sexually frigid wife was a complete mismatch for his perpetual sexual aggressiveness. The Boston Strangler killed between the years of 1962 and 1964. The female victims were usually found dead in their own apartments, usually sexually assaulted, and often times bound with articles of their own clothing. What characterized the Boston Strangler's own mode of murder was that he left the naked bodies very carefully and sometimes provocatively posed with the tools of strangulation tied in decorative bows around the victims' necks.

How did that change America? I dunno. I was thinking maybe people having to, like, confront their sexual desires and, like, people being afraid, feeling unsafe, you know, that there were like these men, these people who were like animals with these raging sex drives, you know, because, to be honest, that's exactly how I felt sometimes. I felt fucking crazy like that, thinking about sex all the time and masturbating like crazy. I mean, sometimes it kind of scared me, really, like I was sick in the head or something, and like I was afraid maybe people could see what I was fantasizing about, see that I did not exactly fit in, because of all the filthy things I was thinking. OK, I also found this weirdo information out about serial killers, in general, from Dorie's other book:

Serial killers are usually white, heterosexual males, usually in their twenties and thirties, who are somehow sexually dysfunctional and have low self-esteem.

That sounded exactly like Mike or me. Also, I got this:

At a young age, serial killers may enjoy hurting and torturing animals, setting fires, and may be chronic bed-wetters. As young adults, many serial killers may have some type of brain damage and be addicted to alcohol and/or drugs. There is also a strong sense of alienation, of a lack of an immediate community.

Which again could be Mike, me, or even Dorie, I dunno. I think that was the point of it all. That it was like these serial killers didn't feel like they fit in—and maybe they didn't—and so they felt shameful about it, which made it all worse and, like, because these serial killers did not belong and were out killing people and everything, it probably made America more distrustful, you know, like people were more alienated then and everything. Like belonging, feeling a part of something, or like being with someone who really knew you, was like a very important thing, I guess, and maybe that's how it changed America—making everyone kind of distrustful or worried, which then just probably made people feel less connected and then the problem probably just kept getting worse until it was like our neighborhood where no one said anything to anybody. Maybe it was weird to think about those things, like serial killers and being alone and everything, I dunno. Maybe it was better not to know things like that. Maybe it was better to just go on believing everything was OK, even when really bad things were just about to happen.

ninteen

By mistake, I had taken Dorie's Iron Maiden shirt. Now when I think back on it, that's what did it. I freaked her out because I accidentally took her shirt and maybe it made her think we were getting serious, I dunno. We were in her room after school fooling around, and I was kissing each mole on her back, one after the other, kind of naming them, when her mom came home. We heard her mom jingle her keys and unlock the door and kind of shove it open. Then somehow she must have spilled her groceries, the sounds of cans and jars hitting the tile floor, as she muttered, "Damn, damn, damn."

I was out of that bed in like a second flat. I had my pants on, zipped, belted, my feet in my shoes, my socks stuffed in my pockets, but I couldn't find my white T-shirt. Dorie's mom coughed and swore again, dropping a few jars of something down the steps.

"My shirt," I said.

"Here," Dorie whispered, handing me her T-shirt, the gray Iron Maiden *Somewhere in Time* one, rolling her eyes at me. I pulled it over my head as Dorie opened the side window, slid open the screen, and gave me a quick shove through.

Two nights later, we were down in Mike's basement watching a rerun of *CHiPs,* Mike and me, and Dorie came down, looking sad, her eyes small and squinty. She took a seat beside me and sighed, poked me in the side, and said, "We got to talk."

"OK," I said, poking her back. "Talk."

"No, me and you."

"OK," I said. I grabbed my nylon jacket and followed her on up. It was cooler, even though it was like the middle of April, and kind of wet and rainy, still getting dark out.

"So," I said.

"So. I need my T-shirt back."

"What?" I asked. "OK, why?"

"Because you can't have it," she said.

"OK," I said, defensive now.

Dorie looked down, which, as tall as she was, happened to be just about eye-level with me. Then she started crying.

"Oh god," she said.

"Oh god, what?" I asked.

"Oh god, oh god, oh god," and like that she was really fucking crying. I went to take one of her hands, but she folded them under her arms, shaking her head. "Oh, god, oh, god, oh, god, I'm sorry."

"What for? You're freaking me out, Dorie."

"Oh god. OK. I have a boyfriend. I mean, I had one and I'm supposed to be getting back together with him. Oh god, I'm sorry."

"What? Who? Who the fuck is he?"

"Ken. His name is Ken."

"The dude with the car? From your work?"

"He doesn't work there anymore. He's going to trade school."

"Holy shit! Holy shit, I cannot believe this is actually fucking happening," I said, holding my hands over my face.

"I'm sorry, Brian. I am. I wanted to, I wanted to tell you before."

"Like when? When we were doing it?"

Dorie looked down, blushing, wiping her eyes with the backs of her hands. "It wasn't supposed to happen like this. He, he doesn't know about anything."

"Why the fuck are you still going out with him then?" I asked.

"I dunno," she said. Then she said the weirdest thing I ever heard a girl say: "He said he's going to marry me." And she just ran off, just like that. It was just that dumb and quick and random, exactly fucking like that.

Later, Mike and I were in the basement getting stoned and then Erin McDougal came over and when I saw them kiss, it actually made me a little sick. We were all sitting on the floor and I was trying to do the Ouija Board myself, asking it, "Does Dorie still like me?" and, "Will Dorie and I get back together?" but the fucking pointer kept sliding right over to "no," every fucking time.

twenty

About two days later Mike cut all his hair off, because Erin McDougal's dad died and we all had to go to the funeral. No one could believe he cut it all off, maybe not even Mike. When I saw him in school the day after he did it I could not stop myself from fucking laughing. I mean, I knew why he had done it, but when I saw the way he looked—his dark red hair no longer a straight wave running down to the top of his back, his hair now short and combed, parted down the middle like some prep from some suburban subdivision with a peaceful name like Park Forest or Orchard Hill or Spring Lane, some fucking pretty-boy with initials that were both the same, like John Justice or Gary Grant, when I saw the tops of his ears, which no one had seen in fucking years—I could not choke down my laugh. Without the long hair, he looked just like the rest of them. And the rest of them could suck it.

I mean, Mike cut his hair for a good reason. Like I said, he had been seeing Erin McDougal and they were doing it pretty regularly, you know, "Mike and Erin, So Sexy 1991." I mean, they were like serious. It happened overnight, you know? One night Mike and I were down his basement talking about who you'd screw, Wonder Woman or Lita Ford, and why, and then the next night, like magic, it seemed we had both found girls who were exactly as lonely as us. I mean, I had found somebody, but, well, Dorie had dumped me and now she had her real ex/current boyfriend, some dude named Ken who had a hot car and a job and everything, so that was it for me, I guess. But Mike and Erin McDougal were still very serious—"going out" or whatever you call it. I guess she was known as the girl with invisible parents. You know, because her mom worked nights and her dad was bedridden. Like I said, her dad had emphysema and was hooked up to all kinds of oxygen tanks and heart monitors and in an emergency the poor man could have not made it down the fucking stairs.

So Mike cut his hair because Erin's father had died, which was not a surprise to anyone, I guess. I had only seen the man once and then only for an instant, when Mike and I went over to Erin's house a few weeks before and I looked up the front staircase and saw a grayish man in a white robe crossing, with a walker and an IV on a wheeled trolley, into the bathroom, from where his bedroom must have been. He did not see me and I always had the feeling it was like seeing a very gentle kind of animal going about its work, like watching a very delicate bird building a nest, you know, or like preening its wings. Maybe looking up the staircase at him gave me the feeling that he was a citizen of some other place, you know, somewhere else; he was part of something older, something delicate, something beyond anything I had ever known, but which I was just beginning to grasp. Dorie had broken my heart, and now I was feeling and thinking things from sad, strange new angles.

The four of us—Mike, Larry with the superbad acne, me, and a kid named Eddie, who did not know Erin or her dad but who insisted that we help spring him from school—all got excused absences to go to the funeral, which meant we were done after third period. The funny thing was, this kid Eddie went with us not so much because he wanted to, but because at the last minute he realized that since he did not have to go back to school, he didn't have anything else to do.

The funeral service was at St. Cajetan's church with a priest and everything. All of Erin's big Irish family were there, and it was all very quick, very stilted, and very uncomfortable—for us anyway. At the end, as the bereaved began to leave and the pallbearers began to roll the coffin back toward the front doors of the church, Erin let out a cry. She was standing somewhere up front and Mike looked at me and he was terrified. None of us knew what to do. I gave Mike a tug and we made our way toward the front and Dorie—my Dorie—was already there, stroking Erin's hair and saying, "You'll get through this, you'll get through this," and I wondered, *How does she know?* Dorie was just a kid still, like the rest of us, tall and foul-mouthed or not. But somehow when you heard her say it and saw the way her brown eyes looked, her hand moving along Erin's soft blond hair, you knew she was right. *You'll get through this. You'll get through this.*

After the funeral service, we drove in the procession to the cemetery in Larry with the superbad acne's blue Celica station wagon, the one with the back window that had been replaced with a transparent piece of plastic. There were only two good things about the Celica, the first being that it belonged to Larry with the superbad acne. Apparently, he had worked all summer at the same place Mike did, DiBartola's Pizza, saving up for it. Larry with the superbad acne had to endure a forehead full of his now trademark zenith zits. He had missed his chance to score with Carolyn Stieber who, because of a birthmark above her right eye which she thought was unforgivable but which I thought was the most beautiful thing I had ever seen, made her the easiest of Catholic school girls. Worse than all that, Larry with the superbad acne had to listen to his boss, who was in a KISS cover band, describe all the women he nailed with interesting details like, "She could suck the chrome off a bumper," over and over again, just so he could own his own car.

The second good thing about the wagon: It had a working cassette player. Larry with the superbad acne slid in a mix-tape and the soft, sad dirge of "Fade to Black" by Metallica clicked on. No one said anything. It was like the soundtrack to your worst day on earth, and after seeing Erin crying like that, the song made you feel very awful, Metallica or not. Larry fast-forwarded the tape, then stopped, and a song came on, just like that.

"I got something to say!" *Dun-Dun!* "I killed your baby today!" *Dun-Dun!* "It doesn't matter much to me as long as it's dead!"

It was "Last Caress," a Misfits cover, a song I recognized from Gretchen playing the hell out of it, and it was very upbeat and even hopeful-sounding in some ways.

"Sweet lovely death, well, I'm waiting for your breath, one sweet death, one last caress."

In that moment, as Larry pulled the Celica in line with the rest of the automobiles, which were slowly forming a kind of motorcade, a terrible thought came over me: I am still alive.

I am still alive. Mike Madden, my good friend, bad haircut and all, is still alive. And Larry with the superbad acne, with this superbad acne and crappy car, and even this kid Eddie. We are all still alive.

One of the most tremendous feelings of joy swept over me, down my neck and hands and fingers, and my heart wanted to cry out, *We are the picture of youth! We have triumphed over this thing death! You are gone and you were brave and good and better than us in almost every way, but somehow, somehow we have found a secret passage! It is not the end! Dorie will not break my heart because we have found a way! We are still alive and the world is alive and we should all be singing!*

At that moment, the Celica pulled into the cemetery, and through the clanging of its severe metal gates, the terrible truth issued its response: *The world is one mad graveyard, in all kinds of fucked-up ways. But you are still alive.*

And that, that was how I felt for about a week or so after Dorie broke up with me.

twenty-one

OK, out of nowhere I decided to go by Gretchen's. I was feeling bad off and on—mostly bad all the time, I guess—and Mike was busy with Erin McDougal and she was kind of high-strung after her dad died and everything, where Mike had to watch everything he fucking said, and, well, I, I was feeling lonely again and so I went by Gretchen's house and saw the superbad Ford Escort sitting out front, and said to myself, *What the fuck*, and just went up and rang the doorbell.

Mr. D. answered and beamed at me, patting my shoulder and said, "Good god, man, where have you been?" and I nodded and laughed and he was wearing his *Kiss the Cook* apron and asked if I wanted to have a beer, and I said, "No, I'm cool," and he winked at me and pointed up the stairs, and I walked up there slowly, listening to the Descendents' "Christmas Vacation," which Gretchen had blaring, and when I knocked on her door no one answered, so I just walked in.

So Gretchen was lying in bed on her stomach, facing the wall, and she had her stereo going at full blast so I decided to sneak up on her and shout, "Mission command to patrol? Over?" Gretchen shot out of bed, hitting me with one of her school books as she cussed and caught her breath.

"Jesus Christ, Brian, you don't just walk in my room like that. Fuck, you're lucky I didn't kick you in the nuts. I thought you were some kind of teen-molesting pervert or something."

"Sorry. Sorry. I knocked, you know," I said, still laughing. "I, you know, haven't seen you in a while."

"I've been busy," Gretchen said, going back to her homework. Her hair was now kind of whitish-blond, I mean, most of the pink had washed out.

"Yeah, me too. I've been kind of busy, I guess," I said, looking down at my feet nervously. "Well, I just came by to see how you were doing."

"Like I said, I've been busy," she said, kind of mean.

"Yeah, well, that's cool. How's Tony?" I asked, kind of looking down at my feet.

"Fine, I guess," she said.

"Are you still, you know, seeing him?"

"Yeah, I guess," she said. "When he bothers to call me."

"Sure. OK. Well, yeah, well, that's it. I was just, you know, saying hi."

"OK," she said sarcastically. "Hi."

"OK."

I stopped at the door and turned, then smiled. Making a V with the first two fingers of my hand, I brought them up to my face like a mask and smiled. "All hail Planet Nav-o-nod!" I said.

"What the fuck was that?" she asked.

"You know, when we were in junior high: Planet Nav-o-nod and all."

"Right." Gretchen did the same hand gesture and smiled back. "Hail Planet Nav-o-nod," she said.

I started walking out the door, stopped, and said:

"Hey, Gretchen, are you doing anything right now?"

"My fucking homework," she said, sighing.

"Oh." I stood there a moment more and didn't say anything.

"Why?" she asked.

"I dunno," I said. "Feel like taking a ride?" She looked up and for some reason I felt like I was going to cry, and I thought, *If she says fuck off, I'll never talk to her again, this will be it, because then she is not and was not really ever my friend,* and she kind of smiled at me sadly and said:

"I heard that Dorie girl dumped you." And I said:

"Yeah. She did."

"OK," she said, "just let me get dressed," and I went into the hall and closed the door, feeling like she had just saved me from something, maybe.

twenty-two

OK, I had decided finally, *fuck it, I will cut my hair myself.*

I was down in Mike's basement waiting for Dorie to come by and pick up her fucking Iron Maiden T-shirt, and I just decided, *Fuck it, why am I sitting around like a fool?* and so I got out the clippers I had bought, took off the plastic quarter-inch guard, plugged them in, and turned them on. I sat in front of a weird poster/mirror/painting Mike had won at a carnival which depicted Randy Rhoads, Ozzy's old guitarist, now passed on, in the middle of a blazing solo, his polka-dot flying-V guitar sizzling with fire and electricity. I placed the clippers beside my head and was just about to begin when Dorie came in, kind of pounding down the stairs. She looked around and said, "Where's Mike?" and I pointed toward the small wood-paneled bedroom where he was on the phone, doing his daily after-school kissy-face routine with Erin McDougal.

Dorie looked at me, squinted, and said, "Did you bring it?" I nodded, putting down the clippers, lifting the T-shirt out of my backpack, and holding it out to her. My mom had washed it and folded it, thinking it was mine, and somehow it still smelled exactly like Dorie. I handed it to her and she took it and said:

"Thanks for washing it."

"No problem. My mom did it."

"Are you OK with everything?" she asked.

"Am I OK with everything?" I whispered. "No. What do you think? Am I OK with everything?" I mumbled again to myself.

"It's not easy for me either," she said, looking down at her feet. She was so tall and so pretty and her bangs perfectly framed her face.

"So forget it," I said. "Let's say we're still going out."

Dorie just stood there, kind of half-smiling, then shook her head.

"We were never going out. I was supposed to be going out with *him*."

"What, is he waiting for you outside?" I asked.

"No, he's picking me up."

"When?"

"I dunno, ten minutes."

"Why ten minutes?" I asked.

"Because that's how long I told him."

"But why did you tell your boyfriend ten minutes if you live next door?"

"I don't understand," Dorie said.

"Why did you say ten minutes if you were just coming to pick up the stupid shirt?" I asked.

"I dunno," she said. "I just did."

"It doesn't take ten minutes to pick up a shirt, does it?"

"I dunno," she said, starting to cry maybe.

"So why did you say ten minutes?"

"I wanted to talk to you and make sure you were OK."

"You wanted to make sure I was OK? That doesn't take ten minutes."

"Well, that was it. I wanted to make sure we were still friends," she said.

"Oh, we're still friends," I said smartly.

"Why are you trying to make this hard on me?" she asked.

"Why are you trying to make this hard on *me*?" I said, starting to cry a little too.

"I don't know what I'm supposed to do," she said. "Really. I like you and I like Ken and he's been my boyfriend for like a year and so I think I should be with him."

"Great," I said. "Great for Ken."

"Great," she said, wiping her eyes.

"So why did you tell him ten minutes?" I asked once more.

"Why do you keep asking that?"

"Because I think you wanted to come here and not go with him."

"What?"

"I don't think you want to be with him. You want to be with me, but you're chicken."

"I have to go," she said and turned, starting up the stairs.

"Dorie, wait," I said.

"What?"

"Just wait."

"Why?"

"Please," I said, and she looked at me and shook her head and ran on up. I just stood there for a while, staring at the spot where she had been on the stairs, and all I felt like doing was crying, and then Mike came and put his hand on my shoulder and said, "Sorry, man," staring at the same spot as me.

"Mike," I said, turning to him, "I need you to do something for me."

"Yeah, what is it?"

"I need you to do me a favor."

"Sure, man, what do you want?"

"I need you to help me put lines in my hair."

"What? Dude, that's gonna be dumb."

"Seriously," I said. "I need you to cut lines in my hair."

"Why?" he asked.

"Because that's what friends do, Mike."

"It's going to look stupid," he said.

"I don't care."

"I don't care either," he said. "I'll fucking try."

I went over to the pool table and handed him the clippers and took a seat in a metal folding chair.

And then he did it all in like five minutes, right there in his basement, with my hair on the floor by the two mismatched sofas, and me almost crying for some reason, and it looked bad-ass when he was done with it: three straight lines across, above my ears on each side. I stared in the hand mirror Mike had stolen from his mom and I said, "If you want, I'll give you a couple of bucks." And he said, "Just make sure you remember I did this for you the next time I need to borrow some money." And I said, "I won't forget it, man," and I looked in the mirror again and one of the lines was kind of crooked on the left side but that was OK with me, maybe.

At school the next day, people freaked out. I went to my first class, Religion, where Bro. Dorbus refused to look at me, and by my second class, Bro. Hanlan, my Chemistry teacher, just frowned, looking at my hair and shaking his head and said, "I don't know if that hair is appropriate personal appearance," and I said, "But it's short," and he said, "That might not be the point," and right after second period I was called down to Mr. Gregor, the soft-hearted guidance counselor with a black comb-over and mustache who explained everything in terms of some metaphorical football game I could never follow. He looked at me and then asked, "Is everything OK with the home team?"

"Everything's swell," I said, even though, like I said, my mom and dad hadn't slept together in the same bed in months. "Everything's swell, man," I repeated. Mr. Gregor nodded, made some notes in my file, and let me go. When I strode out of the counselor's office, smiling, the fluorescent hallway lights bounced radiation off my head in the spots where the narrow lines were cut bare. Some freshman stared at me, kind of laughing, and I shot him a dirty look and he seemed pretty scared. I was on my way to my third class when Bro. Cardy, the villainous Dean of Discipline, stopped me in the hallway. He was wearing his standard black ordained-brother uniform with the small white collar, his white hair short and cropped in a military 'do, and his two meaty arms were folded in front of his chest as he regarded me, shaking his head.

"Nope, no sir," he said, eyeballing me. "That hair is not gonna pass."

"But it's short, Bro'," I said.

"It looks like it might be gang-related," he said.

"It's not gang-related. It's like the football player, Brian Bosworth."

"Football season has been over for months."

"But I just got this haircut now," I said.

"Sorry, young man. You can either get rid of those lines somehow or I can shave your entire head in my office myself, right now."

I stared at this dick, this self-righteous authority figure with his big arms crossed in front of my face, and thought of how bad I had wanted that fucking haircut, how I thought it would change me, save everything, but how I had ended up losing Dorie to some guy who already had her anyway, how I hadn't even had the haircut for one fucking day and already there was trouble, because a haircut wasn't ever going to save me or make me someone I wasn't, and besides that, I was feeling low and awful already, so when he said, "Sorry, young man. You can either get rid of those lines somehow or I can shave your entire head in my office myself, right now," I just nodded and said:

"Let's go shave it then," and that's what happened to all my hair. Just like that. All of it gone. Just like that.

twenty-three

In the end, we opted to do a skit for our Final History Project, because Mike thought it was the best way to disguise that we didn't do any real research or anything. It went like this: Mike was the detective telling the class about historical facts, reading from his poorly written yellow note cards in his slightly stoned voice, "So this is a skit about not belonging, right. It, um, is meant to show you how terrified our nation was of itself, you know, and like how distrustful, and also, how it was like a turning point, you know? Like people not trusting other people, some people feeling like not part of other people. How like it was like our nation growing up, you know, facing some real bad things, but then like that is part of it, you know, bad things and being alive is part of like being in America, maybe, which people didn't really think about much. So it was like America learning there is bad things out there and that is part of America and like still trying to be like happy and trustful anyway. OK. Right. So the year is 1962, Albert DeSalvo works at a rubber press during the day; at night he tracks his quarry all over the city of Boston."

So I was the Boston Strangler and I had a stocking cap on because he had one on in the book Dorie got me, and Ms. Aiken—the lovely Ms. Aiken, the only one who believed in us in the whole world, maybe, which was probably a mistake—well, she was the victim, and she was sitting at the head of class, filing her nails and pretending to chew gum and doing whatever victims do before they get strangled, and right there I decided to do something different. Instead of going to strangle Ms. Aiken, who was looking bored, and lovely, man, really lovely, well, I crept up the side of the classroom and strangled this twerp, Frankie Manning, and the kid started screaming, but I covered his mouth and Mike saw what I was doing and shouted, "See! The

Boston Strangler has struck! No one can tell where he will commit his evil deeds next!" and he ran beside Frankie and said, "Another victim of this unpredictable killer who is impossible to predict!" and by then I had strangled Blaine Reed, who, because he was a theater fag, got the drift and fell out of his seat, playing dead, and Ms. Aiken started shouting, "OK, guys, that's enough, that's enough," but I didn't stop until I had my hands around Ms. Aiken's neck, and it was long and soft, and I thought I could feel her breathing, oh God, I could actually feel her breathing, and there, there were two brown freckles popping out of the top of her shirt and I wanted to try and kiss her more than anything in the world, and she could tell, probably, because she looked up at me and blinked, but like a high school girl, with all her eyelashes—which was something she never did, because if she was one thing, it was classy—and so I decided not to murder her, and thought, *Fuck it*, and instead, well, I just ran out of the room and took off the stocking cap and sprinted with my bare head down the hallway, and then I hung out in the cafeteria the rest of the day and didn't get busted because the lunch ladies there knew I was cool.

the album that saved my life
may 1991

"Shoplifters of the world, unite and take over . . ."
—*"Shoplifters of the World"*
Morrissey, The Smiths

"Punk ain't no religious cult.
Punk means thinking for yourself"
—*"Nazi Punks Fuck Off"*
Jello Biafra, The Dead Kennedys

"I ain't no goddamn sonovabitch.
You better think about it, baby"
—*"Where Eagles Dare"*
Glenn Danzig, The Misfits

one

The Album That Saved My Life was *Walk Among Us* by the Misfits. It was thirteen amazing songs with B-movie horror titles that seemed to howl about the very weird disintegration of my own life:

1. 20 Eyes
2. I Turned into a Martian
3. All Hell Breaks Loose
4. Vampira
5. Nike A Go Go
6. Hatebreeders
7. Mommy Can I Go Out and Kill Tonight [Live]
8. Night of the Living Dead
9. Skulls
10. Violent World
11. Devil's Whorehouse
12. Astro Zombies
13. Braineaters

At that time I was feeling exactly like each song title, as out of place on this earth as a fucking teenager from Mars. I was so angry all

the time and looking for a fight, any kind of fight, because I felt so seriously furious for some reason—well, mostly because of my folks
always arguing and fucking Catholic school trying to constantly brain-
wash me and Dorie breaking my heart like that, and, well, every song
on that record seemed to be about me feeling just like that: "Prime
directive: exterminate the whole human race." Recently, Gretchen had
made a tape of *Walk Among Us* for me and, like two days later, I went
and took a bus to the mall to buy another one of their records, *Legacy
of Brutality*. It was just as good. "Hybrid Moments," "She," "Some
Kinda Hate," and the greatest anthem of all, "Where Eagles Dare,"
where a young and skinny Glenn Danzig shouted, "*I ain't no goddamn
sonovabitch,*" which I would mutter to myself all the time, walking
alone to school, cruising down the hallway, eyeballing Catholic girls,
eating dinner with my zombie family, shaving my head with the elec-
tric clippers over the bathroom sink. That record, that one, *Walk
Among Us,* meant everything to me.

OK, I was at the mall, walking past the food court toward the
Aladdin's Castle video-game arcade and killing time until Gretchen
came by to pick me up, because, well, I was avoiding being at my
house as much as possible since things there were getting much
worse, with my dad not coming home for a couple days at a time and
my mom becoming more and more crazy until finally, during dinner
one night, she smashed a plate over my fucking head and so, well, I
decided to spend my Saturdays at the mall and hang out there until
Kim got off of work, at which time Gretchen would come pick the both
of us up and we would all drive around together, complaining. Good
old Mike Madden, who had been my best pal for months, had disappeared, totally. It was all him and Erin McDougal now, *Mike and Erin,
So Sexy 1991*, and when they weren't having sex, they were busy
fighting. I hadn't seen him in weeks. I mean, school was just about over
and it was warm out and girls were everywhere—in the mall, walking
down the street—they were like very lovely, strange-looking flowers,
and he was practically fucking married to Erin McDougal already.

OK, I had kind of started really listening to punk, at least the
Misfits anyway, which happened right after I got my head shaved and
Mike and I had stopped hanging out, and that day I was at the mall,
flying solo, and I had on my black hoodie, a Misfits "Crimson Ghost"

T-shirt, and my dad's black combat boots. I was done with metal and hard rock, I guess. Why? Because all the kids who were still into metal kind of seemed, well, ignorant to me. All the metal songs were about either fucking girls or worshipping the devil, which was fine and good, but, well, it was all a joke to me now. Without Mike around getting me to listen to Ozzy, I had decided the Misfits would be my band. Why? Well:

1. They didn't take themselves too seriously. I mean, they sung about old monster movies, but they were cool, kind of gruesome and a little cryptic without being like the wanker new metal bands, who were fake Satanic in order to sell fucking records. They were angry like metal, but kind of fun too, I guess.

2. Their music was the fucking best, kind of like pop from the '50s but loud, angry, full of references to the Devil and demons and dead celebrities like Marilyn Monroe and John Kennedy, which made you want to sing along. To me this was a big deal: They had songs you could sing along to. Who the fuck can sing along to Ronnie James Dio? Not even Ronnie James Dio.

3. Also, the Misfits had a fucking song, "Braineaters," in which the chorus was: "Brains for dinner, brains for lunch, brains for breakfast, brains for brunch." I could not think of anything better than that.

OK, so I had three Misfits T-shirts which were in heavy fucking rotation; that day's was the Crimson Ghost, a white ghost-skull face, which glowed in the dark. I still had my head shaved and I had a Band-Aid above my eye where a piece of the plate my mom had hit me with had cut me badly.

I was just passing the Orange Julius where Kim worked, and she rolled her eyes and held up her watch, tapping it, pretending to check to see if it was still working. I walked beside the rows and rows of plastic blue and yellow tables and chairs, over toward the Chinese Wok food counter, and just then these four dirty-looking metal kids started laughing at me as I walked past. They were your typical stoners, one with a black baseball hat that read "F.T.W."—which stood for Fuck the World—long brown hair running down his back, some other taller kid in like a black duster climbing like a cloak down to his ankles, a bigger-looking dude with long blond hair in a ponytail who looked stoned, and some other shorter kid with fuzzier, curlier long hair who was wearing a Deicide T-shirt. I kept on walking until the one with the F.T.W baseball hat mouthed the word "faggot" at me, laughing and elbowing his buddies.

I had never really been in a brawl or fistfight before. I mean, in grade school I had, kind of shoving fights mostly. Because I had been so short and tiny, I was like an instant target and everything— especially with my big glasses—all the way up into eighth grade, where high schoolers would, you know, take my stocking cap and toss it back and forth, laughing, then, getting bored, they'd throw it onto the roof of a house, and, well, I guess I never really did anything about it other than cuss them out. But I guess I wasn't a fucking grade-school kid anymore, you know? I had put on some weight and grown about a foot in the last year and shaved my head, and these dicks, well, they were like these little metal twerps, the kind of kids I knew because, well, I had been just like them. So when I saw him, the kid in the F.T.W. ball cap, laugh and mouth the word "faggot," I stopped, turned around, walked over to their table where they were finishing up their Burger King or whatever, and just stuck my fucking finger in his moth- erfucking face, not saying anything, just holding my finger there, grinning, until the kid in the baseball hat kind of leaned back, freaked out, I guess, and was all like, "What? What the fuck?" and I didn't say anything, I just sat there pointing at him, holding my finger out and nodding. The kid was young, maybe only thirteen, and he had a kind of budding mustache on the top of his lip which wasn't really coming in, he just probably had never shaved it and was maybe hoping it would be enough to kind of hide his age, also to make him look cool, more mature, I guess. He had a wicked bad case of acne and a mono- brow and an upside-down cross earring in his right ear. He was a kid, you know; he could have been me, four years before, fucking ignorant and dumb, scared of not being cool, scared of not fitting in. He really could have been me. That was what I started thinking. And I didn't like the idea of being made fun of by someone I used to be, some kid who was scared and who wanted to be something, anything, anything but himself. The thing of it was, I was really fucking angry, I was really fucking angry about a lot of things: about my mom and dad, about what happened with Dorie, I was angry Mike had kind of ditched me, and I dunno, I was really feeling very fucking angry, feeling really fucking bad, and didn't have shit to lose anymore. So, well, I just kept staring at this kid, holding my finger in his face, nodding, and he kept looking up at me, scared now, seeing I was bigger than him and kind of angry, kind of pissed-off already, and I wasn't saying anything and, well, he looked like he might start crying and was whispering, "What? What the fuck do you want, man? I'm sorry, OK, I'm fucking sorry," and so then I just turned and marched off, not looking back, the sounds of the mall hot in my ears, kids complaining, dance music from the record store blaring, the sounds of announcements on the loud-speakers. I kind of felt good and kind of felt like crying, my legs were all shaky and my heart was beating fast. I decided not to go to the video arcade, I would just walk around until I calmed down, and finally I ended up sitting on this carpet-covered mall bench, holding my hands on my knees to steady them.

I sat there for a while, watching the people come and go, looking to see if the four metal kids would walk by. They didn't. I sat there for a while, counting my change, and then two punk girls, one very short and one kind of chubby, with their punk guy friend who was skinny and young-looking, all of them with bright, dyed hair, the spiked chokers, the plaid skirts, the dude in a Dead Kennedys T, well, they all walked up to me, smiling.

"Here's a flyer," the short girl said. She was very tiny, almost like a little kid, with blondish brown hair that had been dyed blue, but kind of poorly. She was wearing a leather jacket and looked all dolled up, with tons of glittery eye shadow and black mascara and everything. She handed me a small yellow photocopied slip of paper. "Do you like 7 Seconds?" she asked.

"I dunno," I said.

"They're cool," she said. "They're playing at the Cubby Bear like in a few weeks."

"Where's that?" I asked.

"Downtown. Not downtown, but by the ballpark," the guy said, nodding at me.

"Cool," I said.

"They do a cover of '99 Red Balloons,'" the short girl said, nodding excitedly.

"That's cool," I said.

"You like the Misfits?" the guy asked. He was taller than me, but kind of skinny, his head shaved up to the top where his hair was like spiked with four different colors.

"Yeah," I said.

"*Earth A.D.* is amazing, huh?"

I nodded, not saying anything, because I did not actually, technically own any of their records except *Legacy of Brutality*. Everything else was on tapes and I did not think I had ever even heard of *Earth A.D.,* which was kind of silly considering how I had decided the Misfits would be my band and everything.

"You into the East Bay sound at all?" the punk kid asked.

"I dunno, some of it is good," I lied, having no idea what he was talking about.

"Well, Operation Ivy, I mean, they don't count, you know. They're more like ska."

"Yeah," I said, having no idea what he was saying.

"The Dead Kennedys kick all their asses," the chubbier girl said. "Jello Biafra is like a fucking genius."

"I don't know them," I said.

"You don't?" the chubby girl asked. "They are like intelligent, you know, they sing about the government and God and everything."

"That sounds cool," I said.

"Hey, maybe if you come to the 7 Seconds show, I'll make you a tape," the short girl said with a smile.

"Wow, that would be excellent," I said, still feeling like I was kind of pretending or something.

"Hey, I really like your boots," the chubby girl said. "Where did you get them?"

"Yeah, me too," the short girl said. "They look, like, original."

"They're my dad's," I said.

"Wow," the chubby one said. "He lets you wear them?"

"Yeah, he doesn't know I took them."

"Cool," the short girl said.

"Yeah," I said.

"Well, maybe we'll see you later," the short girl said. "I'm Katie, by the way."

"Hi," I said. "Brian," I added, kind of shaking her hand weakly. "OK, well, maybe I'll see you there." She waved goodbye and the three of them walked off, laughing and joking, and I thought of how I had never really been to a punk show before other than in people's basements and maybe that might be cool to check out, and I would have to ask Gretchen to see if she would go with me, maybe, and if she said yes, I'd even offer to pay for the gas, because I dunno, it seemed very important to me suddenly.

two

OK, overnight I had become punk rock. I mean, I was only listening to the Misfits and, well, also now the Ramones, and I had started wearing my dad's combat boots all the time, even to school, and no one seemed to notice, and I was sitting in the back of my class—first period, Religion—where Bro. Dorbus just kept yammering and yammering about the value of abstinence, and by mistake I closed my eyes and yawned. Well Bro. Dorbus, who was fairly young, a tall man in shiny gray glasses, grabbed an eraser from the chalkboard and whipped it at my fucking head, hitting me square in the mouth. I started coughing, swallowing yellowish dust, my lips stinging, and he came up and hovered over me and said, "This isn't your bedroom, Mr. Oswald, is it?" like the fucking thought had just occurred to the fucking prick, and without thinking—honestly, without hesitation—I just looked up and said, "Masturbate me," which was from the Misfits song "Bullet," in which Glenn Danzig sang, "All the people in the party, masturbate me." I had no idea what it really meant, but I liked that he said it and so, well, that got me sent straight to the Dean of Discipline.

    OK, so I was sitting in the narrow blue hallway outside the Dean's office and this kid I knew from my Chemistry class, Nick, this tall, skinny guy with a shaved head, slunk down the hall and took a seat beside me, holding the same blue detention note in his hand. He was wearing a pair of those cheap X-ray glasses, the kind you get in the back of a comic book. He took the X-ray specs off, folded them up, put them into his front shirt pocket, and then looked around the office. There was a gold pen lying on the corner of the receptionist's desk. He nodded, noticing the receptionist wasn't around, and grabbed the pen, slipping it up his sleeve. I kind of smiled, looking at him. He had a long face and pointy ears like a bat and he was smiling a kind of crazy fake smile, staring straight ahead. Then he kind of looked me over, rubbed his nose, caught sight of my Fiend Club button which was pinned to my belt, and nodded. "Misfits?" he asked me, pointing at the small black-and-white Crimson Ghost button, the only button I owned.

Even sitting down he was real tall, taller than I had noticed before, and he was wearing combat boots too. His head was shaved very short all along the sides up to the middle where he had a few long strands of hair which hung down in his face. It was a Devil-lock, how Glenn Danzig wore his hair. I hadn't ever noticed it on him before.

"They're my favorite band," I said, nodding and meaning it.

"Me too," he said, smiling. He pointed to the same button under the collar of his dress shirt.

"Cool," I said.

"Yeah," he said.

"Well, are you like into the East Bay sound at all?" I asked, being nervous, trying to remember what the one kid in the mall had asked me. "Like, um, Operation Ivy?"

"Yeah, they're cool," he said, nodding. "It's like ska but more punk."

"Yeah, I like them but I don't have any of their stuff," I said.

"It's pretty cool. I got most of it on vinyl."

"Cool," I said.

"Yeah," he said, "Cool."

"So you going to that 7 Seconds show?" I asked—again, trying to think of whatever those punk kids in the mall had said to me.

"Yeah, I dunno. I'd like to, but I don't know if I have enough cash."

"Yeah, that's cool," I said. "I heard it was supposed to be good."

"Yeah, their last record was fucking great."

"Yeah," I said, lying, having no idea. "It was pretty good."

"You skate at all?"

"Skate? You mean skateboard?"

He nodded.

"Yeah, I'm OK."

"Cool," he said. "Maybe we can skate somewhere sometime."

"Yeah," I said. "That'd be cool."

"Well, I got to get to class. You know, take it easy," he said, and then he crinkled up the detention slip and just started walking off.

"You're just gonna walk away?"

"Yeah. I just got thrown out of Spanish so I wouldn't have to, like, take this test."

"Cool."

"Later."

"Later," I said and stood up, crinkling up my own blue slip of paper. Something made me start smiling for some reason. I was like this whole new person, not just because of my hair and clothes and not just because of the music I was listening to—people around me were treating me different, some people just coming up and talking to me for no reason. It was kind of fucking weird, you know, how I hadn't ever noticed it before, that it was all about how you fucking looked. I started to walk away when Bro. Cardy's office door opened and he waved me in, nodding, "What a surprise, Mr. Oswald, come in, come in."

Bro. Cardy grabbed me by the shoulder and shoved me past his desk into the small chair. "Why do you keep being sent here?" he asked, taking a seat and folding his long gray hands together atop his desk. His face looked plain and old like a statue sitting in the sunlight there, a white face atop a dark slate uniform. "What is the problem this time?"

I said what I had to say, which was, "We are 138," from the song "We are 138" by the Misfits again, and I didn't know what 138 we were, but I still said it—"We are 138"—and that was just about the moment Bro. Cardy sighed very heavily and wrote me two Saturday detentions, signing them and handing them to me, shaking his old head and frowning.

As I was walking down the hallway at school a few hours later, I caught sight of Rod, who I hadn't seen in months because he was in all honors classes now, having decided maybe it was safer with all nerds around him all day. He looked skinnier, more nervous than ever, his eyes darting around the hall for possible attack from any corner. He was walking down the hall and had his head down, peering out of the sides of his eyes, and I stopped him and asked, "Rod, what's up?" and he shook his head.

"Did you hear about prom?" he asked.

I rolled my eyes. I had been thinking about it all week, specifically who the hell I was going to take. I didn't know anybody. I mean, there was Gretchen, but, well, that seemed kind of out of the question, and, well, Dorie, who I had tried calling a few times but would never answer, so it seemed like here was this momentous occasion again, you know, and, well, there was still nobody for me.

"No, what's up with it?" I asked.

"You're never gonna believe this, man. But they're talking about having separate proms this year."

"Separate proms? What do you mean? One for juniors and one for seniors? That's how they always do it, dude."

"No, man, no. Separate senior proms: one for white kids and one for blacks."

"What? You got to be kidding me. It's fucking 1991—who has separate proms? You got to be fucking joking."

"No. That dude Marcus, the one with the afro on the basketball team, he just made me sign a petition."

"Why are they gonna have separate proms?" I asked.

"Well, the student council kids, the seniors, can't agree on the songs, you know, the theme song. It's fucked up."

I thought if the pasty-white suburban student council kids couldn't agree on something, what hope was there for the rest of us? Fucking Christ Jesus.

"It doesn't matter. We're juniors," I said.

"I dunno, I was thinking of maybe going," he said. "If I could."

"To the black senior prom?" I asked, and I could see the answer was killing him, his soft black lips turned down. His eyes got very small, and I thought for a moment of all the kids who ever fucked with Rod, not one of them had been white because, even in that messed-up school, you know, no white jock was stupid enough to fuck with a black kid, tiny and faggy as he might be.

"Yeah, I guess," he said. "Maybe you could come too."

"To the black senior prom? What the hell are you talking about? I wouldn't fit in with them either."

He sighed and then nodded and we walked off in separate directions down the hall.

By the end of the day it was all over Brother Rice. Apparently, the story was this: The fucking seniors on student council, which was made up of all geeky, wanna-be politician-types, ran the senior prom. They picked the DJ, the menu, decided on what the theme song would be. So apparently the student council kids, who were almost all white,

decided the theme song would be "Wonderful Tonight," the fucking
Eric Clapton song, which had been the fucking senior prom theme like
every fucking year. Well, a few of the other kids, seniors too, two black
dudes and one Hispanic kid, suggested another song, "Make it Last
Forever," which was a black R&B hit. The two opposing parties
brought in their songs, played them for the student council, and the
black kids were of course out-numbered and out-voted. The black
kids tried to appeal, but the white kids weren't having it, and so the
black seniors said, *Fuck it. We'll have our own prom*, and that was
what they planned to do, I guess.

Bill Summers told me all about it after school, standing at his
locker, which was right next to mine. He was the junior class represen-
tative to the student council, a prep—so white it hurt—in a blue shirt
and blue tie, blond hair cut perfectly. After he told me about it all, he
looked at me and said, "Isn't that fucking stupid?" and I said, "I think
it's fucking stupid," but I didn't know exactly why.

I wasn't sure if I thought it was stupid that the white kids would
pick some song that had been the theme like eight hundred times
already, or if it was stupid that the black kids were so pissed that they
were going to go do their own thing, or if it was stupid that the mod-
erator, Mr. Helman, couldn't think of some other fucking solution. The
more I thought about it the more angry and confused I felt. I mean, the
white kids had followed the rules. They brought their song in and
everyone voted. The black kids had lost, fair and square, so maybe
they were just being fucking babies. Or maybe not, I wasn't sure. I
mean, maybe, since the student council kids were all mostly white, the
black kids never even had a chance in the first place. I mean, once I
thought about it, like if there were all black kids on the fucking
student council and one year, one fucking year, I wanted the song to
be "Sweet Child o' Mine," and I knew no matter what there was
nothing, not a goddamn thing, I could do to see that happen, I dunno,
maybe I would be pissed too. And if that shit happened to me all the
time, I mean day after day, with everything—like if every song on the
radio was rap or every person in every fucking movie was black, if the
whole fucking world was black and staring at me and there wasn't a
goddamn thing I could do about it to make it fair, even—well then
maybe, maybe, I'd be fucking sick of it after all and say, *Fuck it. Fuck
it. The senior prom only happens once and I want it to mean something*

to me, and so maybe, maybe, I would want to go out and do my own thing. It still seemed really fucking wrong and sad to me, though, like, well, like all those preppy student council kids had, well, just given up on something.

I said, "Later," to Bill Summers and decided since I was a junior and the junior prom was still going on fine and it was only the senior prom that was going to be split up, it was not really my fucking problem anyway, because, well, fuck that school.

three

Like always, I met Gretchen and Kim in the parking lot after school. I got out fifteen minutes earlier than them so I would wait, lying on the hood of the Ford Escort, staring at all the hot Catholic girls in their soft, white, see-through blouses and super-fine flannel skirts as they walked past, while I winked at them, kind of growling. It was hot outside, the very beginning of May, and I had taken off my dress shirt and was sitting in a dirty white T, lying on the hood of the Escort, waiting, the sun beating with white speckles and fuzzy circles onto my bald, shaved head.

OK. Junior prom was indeed coming up quick, and shit, I wanted to go. Why? Because, well, I hadn't gone to any high school dances yet and after this one there were like only two left for me in my whole high school career ever, and, well, I guess I wanted to prove to myself and everyone else, I guess, that I wasn't still a dumb quiet kid and a loser. But since I didn't know any other girls, really—I mean, Dorie would not take my calls and that girl Esme was dating the drummer for Jim's band, The Morlocks!—I thought about asking Gretchen, but, seriously, just as a friend. To be totally honest, I had no interest in her like that anymore.

OK, so that is a total fucking lie. I think, to be really honest, I wanted her very, very bad again, because I knew she had lost her virginity, which gave her a kind of, well, adult quality I found really fucking hot. I had tried to act like it wasn't true, but it was. I liked her more than ever.

Finally, Gretchen and Kim came out of the side school entrance, Gretchen with a load of books, Kim fooling around and pretending to be limping when she noticed I was watching. I couldn't take my eyes off of Gretchen. In her plaid gray skirt and white knee-socks and white blouse, with two small yellow barrettes in her hair, she looked really, really lovely.

"Hey," I said, sitting up, kicking my feet off the hood.

"Hey," Gretchen said, lighting up a cigarette. She offered me one and I waved it away.

"Hey, Brian," Kim said, grabbing my arm. "How have you been? Wow, have you been working out?"

"Fuck off."

"Are you sure?" she asked, squeezing my arm. "Look, look at these muscles."

We all got in the Escort as Gretchen started it up. Kim and Gretchen put on their sunglasses, big black plastic jobs you get at like carnivals or something. I put my dress shirt over my head, blocking out the sun.

"Hey, Brian, Gretchen and I were talking and we were wondering if you've ever screwed a girl in the ass?"

"Fuck off."

"But see, Gretchen and I have never been screwed in the ass and we were wondering if you would do it to us? One after the other or at the same time? Which one works for you?"

"*Brains for dinner, brains for lunch*," I mumbled, which was also from one of my favorite Misfits songs, "Braineaters."

"What? What does that even mean?" Kim asked, giggling, turning back to me.

"Well, you can go try and figure it out," I said.

"Just leave him alone. If you keep talking about sex, he's gonna get an erection back there," Gretchen said, and it was as if I hadn't gone anywhere the last couple of months, as if I had never stopped hanging out with them, and somehow almost everything was back to normal for me.

"So are you going to junior prom, Brian?" Kim asked.

"Yeah, I dunno. I didn't ask anybody yet," I said. "I mean, I'd like to go with someone I like know, you know? But it doesn't look good right now."

"Why the fuck do you wanna go?" Kim asked.

"You know, because it's fucking normal. I feel like I missed out on like everything, you know, all that normal high school shit. It's like a once-in-a-lifetime thing and all."

"That's bullshit," Gretchen said. "All those kids, all those kids that go are assholes. They're the kids who used to pick on you. And now you want to party with them and spend like hundreds of dollars to get dressed up and everything? It's a fucking waste."

"Fuck," I said. "I just want to have a nice time. I just want to go for myself, you know. I think it would be a lot of fun."

"Well, good luck," she said, looking at me, rolling her eyes.

"Good luck to you," I said back, nodding.

"What for?"

"Well, maybe Tony will take you."

"Fuck off," she said.

"No, like the two of you can go and he can be like Prom King. You can tell them he's like your dad."

At that moment, Gretchen pulled the car over in the middle of fucking 95th Street, cars honking and swerving as she threw the transmission into fucking park. "OK, that's it. Get out."

"What?" I said, laughing.

"You think you're like some bad-ass now or something. You got all this attitude now so you think you can, like, talk mean to me?"

"No," I said. "I was just joking around. You two fuck with me all the time." Gretchen shook her head and then threw the car into gear and started driving again. In a moment, she turned back to me and frowned.

"I still wouldn't go to prom," she said. "Even if he was a junior. Even if he asked me."

"OK," I said, because I had heard her say it, though we both knew she was lying.

In a moment, we pulled up to the mall and Kim got out and Gretchen and me were driving around together again, just Gretchen and me, and she asked, "Do you want me to take you home?" and I said, "Not really, I can drive around for a while," and she said, "Well, I'm meeting up with Tony," and I said, "Well then, I guess take my ass home," and we were heading over to my house and listening to the Ramones and I just wanted to blurt it all out and say, *You're like my best friend in the whole evil universe and I want you to go with me, just go with me to this stupid fucking thing,* but I didn't say a damn word. I didn't say anything.

We pulled up in front of my crummy fucking house and I said,

"Later," and climbed out and watched her drive away, thinking how badly I wanted to ask her to go with me, knowing she'd laugh and say no, because it wouldn't seem "cool" or because she was so in love with Tony Degan, and also knowing I could never ask her because of how much I actually liked her, and then she was pulling away and the Escort was just a funny dot and I thought, *Maybe things haven't changed at all. Maybe nothing in the world's changed for me.*

four

We got these rubber Halloween masks and started wearing them all the time. It was Nick's idea, mostly. We would put them on, the Wolfman and Frankenstein, and ride around on our skateboards, breaking into parked cars in the mall parking lot. In order to silently save the world, we'd remove the bad cassette tapes from ordinary people's brainwashed lives.

Like I said, it was all Nick's idea, mostly. It started out simple enough: He had asked, after school one day. Nick, the kid from the Dean's office, was leaning against my locker, his dress shirt off and tied around his waist, an Independent black and red and white T-shirt on, black backpack slung over one shoulder, shiny white skateboard resting behind his head. "You ready or what?" he asked me.

"For what?"

"Let's go tear shit up," he said.

"Um, I didn't bring my board," I said, lying. He looked at me like I was slightly crazy, kind of tilting his head.

"You didn't bring your board?"

"No, I forgot it," I said. "You know how it is."

"What kind of board did you say you had anyway?" he asked, squinting, kind of sizing me up again.

"I dunno," I said, kind of dumb and embarrassed. "What kind do you have?"

"Dude, do you know how to skate or not?" he asked, staring at me like I was very fucking funny, his eyes wide and his mouth parted a little.

"Not really, I guess," I said.

"Fuck," he said, nodding and smiling. "It's very fucking easy. Let me bring you a board tomorrow, OK?" and like that, he did.

On the skateboard there had once been an old school Tony Hawk drawing, in red and gold and black, this cool hawk skull screened on the deck's bottom, but now it was almost completely covered in magic marker that read, "I love Jennifer Bradley" and "JENNY" and "I love JENNY," which was the reason the deck had been out of commission, because apparently Nick was no longer in love with Jenny. The board did have brand-new trucks, wide Spitfire wheels—good for learning, Nick said—and grip tape that was cut in the blackish gray silhouette shape of a ghost.

"It's easy. Just stay on the board and, like, don't try anything funny," he said, and we walked out into the parking lot, leaving our shit in our lockers. I put one foot on the board and started to push off and fell on my ass right away.

"I think I broke my ass," I said.

Nick skated over and slid to a stop over me, shaking his head. "You better get used to that feeling quick," he said. "Check this out." He lifted his black field pants leg and showed me a huge red, white, and pink scar shaped like a strange insect covering his entire shin. "I got that shit two days after my first board."

"What happened?" I asked.

"It was the first time I got hit by a car," he said, proudly.

"First time?"

He nodded and smiled, lifting both of his sleeves, then his shirt, pointing to all the different scars and bruises. "This is from a pickup truck. This is from a 1985 Corvette. This is from my mom's minivan when she backed over my ass."

"Shit," I said. "Well, when was the last time a car hit you?"

"I ran into the back end of a Plymouth this morning."

On the skateboard, I was total shit. I mean, after a couple of days I could stay on the board most of the time, but I could not go over cracks in the fucking sidewalk or major bumps without kicking through them, having to push forward over them with my right foot. I could not go down or up curbs. I could not stop without almost fucking wiping out. But I could stay on the fucking board itself for a long time, I guess. Nick tried for like four hours one day to teach me how to fucking ollie— you know, kick the nose of the board up just enough to clear a curb— but I couldn't do it for the fucking life of me. I liked being on the board, I liked how I felt. I mean, I could get around from one point to another for the most part, I was just not very good at it. Which was OK, because it didn't seem to bother Nick, I guess.

OK, very quick, Nick and I were like skating almost every day after school, all over the fucking south side where skating was not cool at all, from the bus stop to Chicago Ridge Mall, mostly. We'd skate around the enormous parking lot and I'd practice my ollies onto the lower curbs and I still couldn't get enough fucking air to clear them and Nick would kind of skate around by himself, trying different tricks, rail slides, frontsides, shit I didn't even know the names for. Sometimes other skater kids would show up and they would kind of show off, you know, for each other, rail-sliding off the lower bike racks and trying to fucking jump on the stone benches. Mostly, I just watched them.

What we really started doing was this: We'd skate up to the mall, cruise around for a while, wait until the parking lot started filling up, and then we'd skate very carefully in between the parked cars, looking for people who had left their car doors open, which, believe it or not, was like tons of people, and then we'd kind of like help ourselves to what was inside. It was mostly nickel-and-dime stuff: an engraved silver cigarette lighter that said *Stubby*, a nudie girl cardboard air-freshener that was hanging on a rearview mirror which Nick wore around his neck all afternoon, a dime bag of very, very seedy weed which we tried to smoke but which was like totally cashed. And then we hit the fucking jackpot of all time. In the backseat of some blue Chevy minivan, full of toys and games and kids' jackets and shoes, there were all these rubber Halloween masks, one of the Wolfman and one of Frankenstein, and a few others like a monkey and a hobo which we didn't bother to take. Because I had found the minivan unlocked, I got to pick first, so of course I took the fucking Wolfman. We put them on and began to skate around, laughing like fucking crazy.

It became our thing, then, you know, riding around in the Chicago Ridge Mall parking lot on skateboards wearing these stupid Halloween masks after school like every day; the Wolfman and Frankenstein darting between parked cars, scaring the fuck out of the shoppers, popping out from behind vans and trucks and making monster sounds. It was pretty fucking funny to us. The fat-ass security guards were not amused, however. They would watch us skate around for a while, them standing under the rainbow-color canopies smoking or mumbling into their walkie-talkies, then two or three of them would come charging at us from out of one of the entrances, a chubby blur of blue, and we'd laugh and howl at them, making spooky sounds, skating to the other side of the mall before they even had a chance to nab us. It made it more fun, I guess, having them chase after us. It gave us something to look forward to, maybe. Once, Nick and I were sitting on our skateboards, him trying to light a fart with a Malibu Beach lighter he had just stolen, and we were both laughing and not paying attention, and from around the front end of a parked white Mustang convertible, this security guard came hauling ass toward us, making a grab for Nick. He got ahold of his shirt, a white Ramones T with their American Eagle In-the-Ramones-We-Trust logo, and Nick just jerked the shirt off over his head and started skating off, the top part of him naked as he laughed and snorted, pulling down the rubber Frankenstein mask while we made our getaway. "I really liked that fucking shirt," was all he ever said about the whole thing.

OK, Nick got together his own fucking agenda at the time, though. Going into people's cars was not just minor theft for him. For him, it was very serious business because he was like on this important crusade. It went like this: We'd skate around, wearing our masks, trying the different car doors. When we found one that was unlocked, we'd check around, make sure there weren't any fatty security guards standing by the mall's entrance watching us as they smoked, no busy-body suburban housewives glancing over arms of wrapped packages or curious, bug-eyed kids peeping at us, crying about the toy they didn't get, then one of us would open the driver's side door, because we figured that was less suspicious, and usually Nick would kind of peek around, checking in the ashtray, glove compartment, under the seat. If there was no loot, he'd begin looking through the cassette tapes—not to steal, but to fucking evaluate. So like most of the time these shoppers had like Crystal Gayle or Kenny Loggins or New Kids on the Block or George Michael and shit, and, well, Nick would take all the fucking tapes, I mean all of them, out of the car and fling them underneath the rows and rows of nearby station wagons and mini-vans. Expelled. Removed. Never to be heard from ever again. It was serious fucking business to him.

"Do you know the only shit they play on the radio is paid to be on there, so you don't have a fucking choice about what you hear?

It's all these fucking businesses," he'd say, and then whip a copy of the *Dirty Dancing* soundtrack underneath the wheels of whatever vehicle was closest. "Who the fuck wants to hear Patrick Swayze sing anyway? Poor corporate slaves," he'd whisper, sad, shaking his head. "D.I.Y., right?"

"Right," I'd say, having no idea what D.I.Y. meant.

"Our work here is done. These people will find a way to thank us someday."

As you can guess, not much was spared. If once in a million years someone actually did have something decent—the Beatles or Buddy Holly or something—Nick would just end up taking it anyway. It gave us something to do, you know, something we thought was positive and worthwhile, even though it was minimally criminal. We seriously thought what we were doing would somehow save the world because it was so easy to understand that bad music actually made people bad. We were the lucky ones; we had it all figured out. We had somehow managed to avoid being brainwashed by reckless corporations and it was our right—our destiny—to help by eliminating every bad cassette in the mall parking lot, tape by tape, car by car, day after day.

five

After school a few days later, I skated to the bus stop and took the bus to the record store on 95th to buy the only other Misfits record I didn't own by this point, *Earth A.D.* I had saved up enough for it by not really eating anything for lunch all week. I had been living on sugar packets and other condiments spread on pieces of garlic bread, which only cost ten cents. So I was walking up the small concrete steps to the narrow corner record store door and these four or five dudes in black and green bomber jackets—straightedge kids, I could tell right away, big X's on their shirts and jackets, some with band T-shirts like Minor Threat and D.R.I. and Life Sentence—shoved past me. The last one out, the shortest of the group, with a bald head barely covered in a bent-up gray dock-workers cap, his long, narrow skull-face jutting over a white T, stuck out his hand, blocking the door as I tried to go past. I stopped and looked across his arm over to his face. He kind of squinted at me, looking me down, taking a sip from a red straw jutting out of an enormous fountain drink.

"Who do you run with?" the short, skull-faced guy asked me.

"What?" I asked, leaning in closer to hear him.

"Who do you run with?" he asked again, looking over his shoulder at his chums and then turning back to squint at me again. "Who's your fucking crew?"

"What?" I asked again.

"Are you a fucking skin or not?"

"No," I said, patting the shaved top of my head.

"Well, then fuck you," he said, and flicked his plastic straw at me. It hit me in the forehead, wet with his spit, and then dropped to my feet. I just shrugged, trying to smile, feeling dumb for doing it. "Punk's dead," he said, nodding at me. "You're fucking next." He pointed his thumb in the air and then turned it down—meaning me, I was going down, I guess. His pals nodded and they all just ambled off, shoving each other and laughing. I just stood there on the record store steps and stared, having no fucking idea what bad business had just happened upon me.

six

OK, I was going to go to this punk show, my first ever, I guess, and I had my dad's beautiful black combat boots on, these nice twenty-hole lace-ups, and it was like eight at night, and I started up the stairs and I was taking them by twos because I didn't want my dad to have time to say anything to stop me, and also I didn't want him to see my fucking feet. But I guess I wasn't quick enough and he said, "Hold on a minute, pal," and I stopped and started back down, and my dad sighed and pulled himself off the couch, staring at me like I was totally fucking crazy, his eyes big and wild, his mouth parted, shaking his head, looking at my feet.

"Are those my jump boots?" he asked. He was still in his blue factory uniform, his glasses foggy and crooked on his face.

"Um, yeah. I think so."

"You have exactly ten seconds to take those off before I pull them off of you." I was standing a few steps up from him and we were just about eye to eye. He was still a little taller than me and I just stood there and looked down, not moving.

"I served in those fucking things," he muttered. "So you can take off those boots or I can take them off of you," he said again.

"I'll take good care of them," I said.

"Ten," he said, taking a step forward. "Nine. Eight. Seven."

"I'll make sure they're fine," I said.

"Six. Five. Four."

"Dad."

"Three. Two."

"OK," I said.

"Take them off."

"OK," I said. "OK," I whispered, sitting down on the stairs, beginning the tremendous procedure of unlacing them.

My dad turned and took a seat back on the couch, watching to make sure I was actually taking them off, and right then, all I could think to save myself from crying was, *"I ain't no goddamn sonovabitch,"* from the Misfits song, "Where Eagles Dare."

seven

After about an hour of fucking begging and after getting my boots fucking taken off my feet, I convinced Gretchen to go with me to the first punk show I would ever attend, 7 Seconds. It was one of the most amazing nights of my life, even though we only saw one song and even though some shit started there between some straightedge kids and some punk kids. It didn't matter though. It was not so much the best night because of the band, right? They were good and loud and kind of funny, and the only song we heard was the cover the little punk girl had mentioned, "99 Red Balloons," which was like a German hit from the '80s about nuclear war—I remembered the original video with the weird foreign-looking lady and the balloons and everything, and I guess growing up I had always been kind of freaked out about nuclear war and the song was so happy and poppy that I never even knew it was about that until much later—but when 7 Seconds went into the song, and when the singer, Kevin Seconds, announced "99 Red Balloons," the whole place went fucking crazy. I guess that was the reason it was like the best, you know? The kids there, or maybe just the feeling of it all, belonging to something like that, maybe.

The Cubby Bear was like a kind of sports bar right across from Wrigley Field ballpark, and it was in the middle of like a kind of yuppie part of town, but when we got to the show there was this huge line of dirty punk kids waiting out front and, I dunno, I got very excited. But we could not find a spot to park and we didn't have enough money to pay for parking and to buy tickets, and so after driving around for almost two hours, we finally found a place. We ran off and got in line and by the time we got in, the first two bands had played already and 7 Seconds was almost done with their set, and the place was totally fucking packed. It was all dark wood inside and the tables had been pushed out of the way and it was just lined with kids all punked-out to the max, with their dyed hair and black hoodies and plaid pants and skirts and buttons and patches and safety pins and black motorcycle jackets with band names like Screeching Weasel painted on back. There were a lot of the straightedge skinhead kids there too, most of them shaved bald, with their white T-shirts and black field pants, combat boots laced up high, and X's magic-markered on their hands, some even with X's on the top of their bald heads. Everyone was dancing; all of them shouting and moving in a kind of wide circle around the center of the room. It was unlike anything I'd ever seen, I guess.

So I knew the song "99 Red Balloons," I guess. I mean, like I said, I remembered it from being a kid, and when the singer said the name of the song, the place went fucking nuts, and then the bass player started the familiar bass line, but faster, really pounding it out, then the drums came in, first the high-hat, then the rest of the kit, and kids were going crazy—jumping around, shoving each other, dancing—and then the singer started at it, "Ninety-nine red balloons, floating in the summer sky," and eventually, when he got to the chorus, "Whoa-oh," everyone in the crowd sang along—everyone, even Gretchen and me—and I was jumping up and down and, I dunno, kind of feeling like I did when I used to sing in church, being part of something, you know, feeling like I belonged to something, and then it was the chorus again—"Whoa-oh"—and everybody repeated it with him, and I looked up and some kids were moshing by the front of the stage and some of them were the bald skinheads, with their blue and green bomber jackets on, and they were kind of shoving each other and slamming hard into the scrawny punk kids and it was almost the end of the song, and finally some lanky punk kid with a green mohawk shoved a bigger straightedge kid and *wham!*—like that—the straightedge kid hauled off and socked the punk kid in the eye. In a moment, the punk kid's friend, a little blue-haired fireplug of a girl in a black leather jacket, went up and spat in the straightedge kid's face. The straightedge kid laughed and spat back, hitting the girl on the forehead. The girl went fucking nuts, lunging at the straightedge kid, and then some other punk kids started getting into it, the punks and skins throwing off their jackets and swinging at each other until the song stopped and the singer, Kevin Seconds, looked up and said, "OK, OK, tonight we walk out of here together, punks and skins, we all walk out of here together," and I had no idea what he meant but I liked that he had said it. And it fucking worked. The punk kids and skinhead kids kind of relaxed and went back to dancing, without killing each other, and this one fat straightedge kid even helped this one punk girl off the floor and it was a very strange moment for me, I guess.

After the show, Gretchen got in line to buy some merchandise, a T-shirt, I think, and she said, "These guys, this band, they make all of their own stuff."

"So?" I said.

"So, that's fucking cool."

"Why?"

"Because they want to do it themselves, you know, without like record labels and everything telling them what they can say. You know, so like they're not owned by the corporations. You know, D.I.Y."

"That's cool," I said. "What the fuck does it mean?"

"Do-it-Yourself," Gretchen said. "It like means they stand for something, you know. They're not like fucking Guns n' Roses."

"Guns n' Roses stands for shit," I said.

"What?"

"I dunno. Having fun and everything."

"You don't get it," she said. "These guys, they want you to, like, think." I looked over at the table full of T-shirts and records and buttons and stickers and thought, *Why haven't I heard of this shit before?*

As we were waiting in the merchandise line, Katie, the very short girl from the mall, ran up to me, hugged me like we were old pals, and said, "I got to go, my mom's waiting. Here, I made this for you," and she slipped a mix-tape into my hand, hugging me again and running off. She was like a blur with blue hair. The tape was just a regular-looking cassette, except she had taped a picture of herself on it, a photograph of her as a kid dressed up as like a pink ballerina or fairy, with the words *For Brian* on the cover, in silver glitter.

"Who was that?" Gretchen asked.

"I dunno. The girl that gave me the flyer."

"She made you a tape?"

"I guess so," I said, and slipped it into my pocket, like that, not even knowing what I was in store for, but looking around at everything and feeling very, very strange.

The tape was fucking amazing. I mean, I listened to the tape for days, for fucking weeks, even rewinding the tape over and over to listen and really try to understand the lyrics, you know, and the girl, Katie, who I never saw again, well, she had typed up a track listing with the songs and band names and even some of the lines she must have liked—

Seeing Red by minor threat
"My looks they must threaten you
To make you act the way you do"

Think Again by minor threat
"Ignorance, it set your standards.
Intelligence, that don't work in your brain."

Nazi Punks Fuck Off by the dead kennedys
"You ain't hardcore cos you spike your hair
When a jock still lives inside your head"

We've Got A Bigger Problem Now
    by the dead kennedys
"Nigger knockin' for the master race
Still you wear the happy face"

Jock-O-Rama (Invasion of the Beef Patrol)
    by the dead kennedys
"Jock-O-Rama—Save my soul
We're under the thumb of the Beef Patrol"

—and I kept thinking about that one moment at the show, with all these different kids who weren't that different and the singer telling them to walk out together. I had been to shows before—you know, Mötley Crüe, Guns n' Roses, even Metallica, all with Mike, all at stadiums with like thousands of people—but never in a small club like that, and, well, it wasn't the same, I mean we were all packed in close and singing and dancing and, well, never, never did anyone ever say anything like that, you know, about walking out together. Like I said, I thought about it for weeks, because for some reason it really meant something to me, because, well, I had never thought about it before, but like music, well, maybe it could change some things, like even for me.

eight

The only time Gretchen saw me naked, or almost naked, she laughed at me and said I was built like an eleven-year-old girl. We were in my room in the basement, and she had just about finished shaving my head. She had brought her own clippers over and they had conked out while my head was only halfway done, so she had to use scissors and my dad's straight razor to finish the rest.

"Gretch, be careful with those, huh?" I said, squirming in the metal folding chair. At the time, I was only in my tighty-whitey underwear and my room was cold because it was in the basement, so I was fucking freezing.

"No problem, ya douche-bag, just relax," she replied, and as soon as her soft white hands began to touch the delicate hairs along the back of my neck, all I could do was relax. No, that was not true—I began to get a monster-size erection. In the tighty-whitey underwear there was nowhere to hide it, so I jumped up and said, "OK, I'm done," and she said, "Half your head still has, like, hair on it," and I said, "That's fine," and she looked at me and said, "Look at you. You look like an eleven-year-old girl. Do you ever think about like working out?" and I said, "Well, at least I'm not fat," which immediately afterwards I knew I should not have said, and she said, "Yeah. Yeah, at least you're not fat," and then she left, storming out of my room, running up the stairs, even leaving her black vinyl purse. In a couple of minutes, she knocked on the bedroom door, and right away I said, "I'm sorry," and she said, "If you ever say something like that to me again, I'll kick your bitchy little ass."

"OK," I said.

"Let me finish cutting your fucking hair," she said.

"OK." I took a seat back down in the metal chair, pulling one of my dirty black T-shirts over my crotch. Gretchen turned on the clippers but they were still broken, so she took out the scissors again and began running her small hands through my hair, her fingers gently stroking the skin beside my ear. She worked for a while, singing some cute song I didn't recognize to herself, but like years later, sitting on some other girl's couch beginning to make out, I suddenly realized it was "Love Song" by the fucking Cure. Anyway, Gretchen was singing and I could feel her hot breath on my neck and I was trying hard not to get hard but not having much luck with it, and then she took the can of shaving cream sitting on my dresser and squirted some into her palm and began rubbing it along my neck, really slow, laughing, saying, "This smells good, like a man," and I nodded and laughed too, and then she took my dad's straight razor and very softly, very carefully, began shaving my neck. In a moment she cut me pretty bad, by accident, and I screamed like a girl, and she shoved me back in the chair and grabbed one of my mom's white towels and was holding it there to stop the blood, and I said, "Is my fucking head still attached?" and she said, "Uh, yeah. Don't be such a pussy," and she kept holding the towel there and I felt around and she slapped my hands away and lifted the towel and leaned close to look, and then she did it. I had my eyes closed, still feeling the sting of the razor cut, and out of nowhere, all of a sudden, I felt Gretchen kiss the back of my neck very gently and say, "See, it's not so bad at all."

What happened next was a total surprise, but I lost it and shot up out of the folding chair, turned, and grabbed Gretchen by the shoulders and just started kissing her like fucking mad. I mean I grabbed her and French-kissed her and had her pinned up against my wall and she was kissing me back, but really—I mean, *really*—and she had her eyes closed and was kind of laughing, but I was serious as hell, and I slid one arm behind her back and laid her down on the corner of my bed, and I just climbed on top of her, Gretchen still kind of laughing, us kissing these long, wet kisses, me lifting up her T-shirt and actually touching her skin, and I moved my hand up her side to her breasts, and her pulling me closer and rubbing my bare head, and I started going right for her pants, and she had on these kind of tight plaid slacks with like a hundred fucking zippers and everything, and I started unzipping the real zipper and I got my hand down her pants and I could feel the soft fabric of her panties, which I could see were pink, and I could feel the soft, strange hair, and she had her eyes closed and wasn't laughing anymore and was holding the back of my head with one hand and digging into my pants with her other, and as soon as she touched me down there, that was it: I came right in my underpants in like five seconds. Gretchen pulled her hand out and I looked up at her and she was looking at me and, like, kind of saying, *OK, now what?* and I just got up and ran into the bathroom to wash up and, well, to freak out. When I came back out a few minutes later, her purse was gone and she had split and I knew I had finally blown it with her, and I figured it had all finally been settled just like that. Like shit.

nine

We were sitting on our skateboards, rolling back and forth behind a parked Chevy minivan at the mall. First of all, Nick said, you need to get your nose broke. *Why?* I asked. Because if you get it broke once, no one will be able to kick your ass. *Really?* I asked. Well, unless they've had their nose broken once before too. But most dudes haven't. If you look at all the big dudes you know, most of them haven't. *Why?* I asked. Because they were like probably always big and no one ever fucked with them, you know? So they probably have never had to take a good punch. Which is awesome for guys like us. That's what makes it even, he said. Them not having ever had their noses broken and you already having your nose broke. *I still don't get it,* I said. It will completely incapacitate you, he said. Your eyes swell up and get all full of tears and you can't fucking breathe and blood is, like, pouring down your face and down your throat and you feel like puking and it's an all-around very bad experience. *And that's what I want?* I asked. Yes, he said. Because then you'll be unstoppable. And you'll never have to worry about taking anyone's shit ever again. You'll never have to worry about losing a fight because you'll always know. You will always fucking know. *Are you thinking about going to prom?* I asked him. No, he said. Hell fucking no. That is an event designed just to make you look stupid. *I want to go,* I said. You are better off getting your nose broke, he said.

ten

From the moment I did get my nose fucking broke, but backwards now, here's what it must have looked like: A ton of hot red blood pouring up my chin, slipping back around the corner of my lips, up, up, up my nostrils. Blood, in very tiny specks and drops, rising like magic from the front of my Misfits "Die, Die, Die My Darling" black T-shirt. My teeth tightening themselves, the gritty-tasting enamel slipping magically back in place. My fucking stomach relaxing, my guts pulling themselves back together. The bridge of my nose deflating, like a balloon losing its air, folding back to its original straight shape. Me coughing, but backwards, the sound going back inside and down into my lungs with the blood. My eyes opening. My mouth sliding apart. My head snapping back into place at the top of my neck. Me falling forward off a crummy green dumpster. Some tough straightedge girl with a red Chelsea haircut in a blue-jean skirt and a Life Sentence T, uncovering her face. A big, dopey-looking kid in a T-shirt with a black X magic-markered in the middle of it, beside her, taking back his look of pain and disgust then his yelling. The dude, the straightedge guy who hit me, in his black field pants, red suspenders, and a white T-shirt pulling a heavy right hand from the middle of my face, his arm lacing through the air and arcing back through space, then down, down, down to his side. Him taking a step back. Me taking a step back. Him taking another step back to the side. Me taking a step to the opposite side. A car horn honking in reverse from down the alley, the sound of it being sucked back under the hood of a green Chevy van as it passed. Some punked-out teenagers walking hand in hand, but backwards, from the back-alley entrance of the juice-bar club Off the Alley, their faces changing from disgust to looking happy. An airplane flying backwards, tail end first, overhead. The girl in the Life Sentence T-shirt shaking her head and saying, "Ssa sih kcik, taht kcuf," her finger pointed at me but then dropping down to her side, her walking backwards, right beside the straightedge dude in the white T. A glob of my spit sliding back together, up the dude in the white T and red suspender's shirt, then flying back through the air into my mouth. Me swallowing the spit back down. Me pointing angrily at him and his shirt. Me pointing at the dude, not looking at his arms or chest or fists, just his shirt. Him flipping me off, stopping, walking backwards, back across the long narrow alley. Me shooting the kid a very dirty look, saying, "Uoy kcuf," as loud as I can with my eyes. Me staring at the kid, walking with his five or six straightedge friends, shaking my head and beginning to get very fucking angry. Nick pointing to the kid in the white "Punk's Dead, You're Next" hand-made T-shirt with his bald head and red suspenders. Me asking Nick what happened, seeing his torn-up black nylon jacket. Me seeing Nick's mouth full of blood, him leaning against the club's black brick wall, holding his ribs. Me finally finding Nick outside the club, my ears ringing from the lousy Misfits cover band, the last notes of the song "Some Kinda Hate" being carried back into my ears.

Then, very quickly, backwards from that night to earlier that afternoon: me storming out of Gretchen's car, swearing. Her refusing to look at me, explaining why it was never going to happen between us, never ever, never. Me feeling sick to my stomach, then excited, hopeful, dreaming of what might happen between us. Us listening to the song "Horror Business," sitting in Gretchen's car, not saying anything, very close, me very close to kissing her soft, glittery pink lips, but neither of us saying a word or moving. Me putting my hand on her hand, turning the radio down, from loud to quiet. I am trying to come up with some way to get her to sit in the car with me. Gretchen laughing. Me pointing at her neck. I see a small tiny mole on Gretchen's neck that, more than anything else, demands that I make some move to try and kiss her again. Gretchen turning off the ignition, getting out of the car. Me watching her cross the parking lot. Me sitting on the hood of Gretchen's fantastic Ford Escort, after school that day, just lying there smiling. I am thinking about Gretchen again and how badly I really want her. Me watching her walk backwards, back from across the parking lot, back to her high school side entrance, slipping back inside. Me staring. I look over at the door, waiting for Gretchen. Looking back from the parking lot of Mother McCauley, I am, like always, thinking of how to get Gretchen to like me and how today, like the day before, anything might happen for me.

eleven

We were going to visit my grandma because she had been put in this retirement home and it was like the first time in months my fucking family were all in the van together and no one was fucking talking because, you know, my parents' marriage was like over, and my dad was driving, stone-faced, and my mom was sitting beside him silent in the passenger seat, and Alice was sitting beside me in the first row of backseats, and Tim was all stretched out on his own bench because he was all long legs and elbows, and my nose was still swollen as shit, big and sore, and one of my eyes was black and blue and I had told my folks I had wiped out on my skateboard, and my mom began talking but I stopped listening, though I think my dad might have known I was lying somehow, and, well, at that moment, in the van, he was kind of mumbling, flipping through the stations and for the hell of it I popped open my Walkman, slid the Misfits' *Legacy of Brutality* tape out, and handed it to my dad. "Try it, you'll like it," I said, and he kind of sighed, then smiled, sliding it into the tape player. Right then "Horror Business," one of my favorites, kicked on and the guitar was ringing and the drums keeping the beat and Glenn just began singing, "Too much horror business," and then my dad coughed and popped it out. He handed it back to me, smiling, saying, "It's just a little too loud for me," and I felt my face get all red and I was very furious for some reason—I mean really fucking upset—really fucking angry even though it was no big deal. I thought, *Like why the fuck should I care what my dad thinks of my music?* and, *What difference does it make anyway?* But I did care and it did make a difference and I couldn't figure out why, really.

twelve

We did this thing in the mall parking lot where one of us pretended to get hit by a car as we were skating around, kind of scaring the driver into giving us some money. It was Nick's idea again, mostly. It was best to start off with an open wound. That was just way more believable. To do this, Nick would either try to do a move he knew he couldn't pull off, like ollying onto one of those sharp stone benches and landing on his knees on purpose, or he would take his keys and scrape up his shins until they were raw and bloody. Since my face was still swollen and black and blue and weird-looking, I didn't have to do much to look wounded. If I had to, I could scrape my knuckles on the cement and hold my hand and look up with my swollen hand and kind of mutter, *Why? Why? I am an orphan and all I wanted to do was enjoy my special day on my skateboard*, kind of guilting them into feeling bad for me. Nick, on the other hand, was way more courageous. He would actually take the hit, flying full speed into the back end of a station wagon or minivan, us always totally aware of some poor suburban mom behind the wheel, yelling at her kids as she tried to back out. It had to be a mom. No one else would feel bad for running us down. Most of the time, Nick was the one who would get hit. I would stand on my board at the end of the long row of cars and watch, to make sure no security guards cut in. If I saw one coming, I'd whistle and Nick would pull himself to his feet and cruise away to safety.

Usually it would go like this: Nick would skate out and slam himself against the back of the car and lie face down, because it was easier not to laugh and blow the whole thing. The mom would scream, the kids would scream, the mom would throw the minivan into park, fling open the driver's side door, leap out, and stand over

Nick, already crying, "Oh God, oh God, oh God, I wasn't even looking." If the mom said that, you knew you had a winner. Most, if not all, started balling; one lady even bent over Nick and began gently stroking his bald head, whispering nice things to him like, "Oh, I'm so sorry, you'll be OK, you'll be OK," which he said was slightly erotic. The key was this however: Nick would turn over, wipe the drool from his mouth, kind of sit up, fall back down, sit up again, look up at the lady, and say, "I'm so sorry," and if the woman was crying, that would do it. In a matter of minutes, Nick would explain that he was riding to the bus stop to get to work, because his dad had left and he had to help with the bills and now he might get fired and he couldn't even walk to the bus stop, and he'd limp around a little to show he couldn't even walk. The woman would hold her hand over her heart, under her crocheted sweater with kittens on it, dig into her purse, and demand Nick take some money so he could get a cab to work. He averaged about twenty bucks a fall, which was smart because he wasn't too greedy. Once, some very over-eager mom demanded that she take him home, and he looked at me over his shoulder and shook his head, and the woman, well, she saw it—the look—and she started getting upset, and so we just skated away. None of the other moms ever caught on; no one for a moment thought what we were doing was a scam. Mostly because of Nick's bloody knees and uncontested falls.

Every so often one of the fat-ass security guards would come out, recognize us in our Halloween masks if we were wearing them, and then chase us away for a while. The thing was, the mall parking lot was just too big. I mean, it went all the way around the mall and we were on skateboards and these dudes, in their shiny blue polyester uniforms, fake silver badges, and gun belts armed with nothing but walkie-talkies, were almost all overweight and on foot. We would skate away—or I would, while Nick would skate right toward them, sliding past in a quick figure-eight and almost running them down before hopping the curb and disappearing behind some old ladies with shopping bags in their hands.

We never made a lot of money that way, getting hit by cars, but the cash we did make we'd split and go and spend on import records and cassettes. I got this one Misfits import from Germany, *Nothing to Loose*, the spelling kind of weird for the songs like the title, but it had some live tracks and demos I had never heard before, which was cool. I guess, more than anything, it was like being with Nick, listening to him talk about the government and bands and, well, doing something, even if it was faking trauma, that I liked the best, I guess.

thirteen

OK, it was a big lie—*stay together for the kids, you know, for appearance*—because fuck those kinds of appearances. My older brother Tim, who was just about to graduate high school, and my little sister Alice, who was a freshman, and me, we all were hoping our parents would get split finally. I guess I had been expecting it for a while, coming home every night and seeing my dad crashed out on the couch, weird and lonely and snoring, and then he started disappearing days at a time, and then one night I was heading out to this other punk show at Off the Alley and this great band, Screeching Weasel, was supposed to be playing a secret show there, and I had heard about it through Nick who had gotten a flyer from this record store and he was going to pick me up in his shitty green 1985 Caprice but he was running late, and I was walking out of my room and I had stolen my dad's combat boots back because he had just put them up in the garage in the same place I had found them and so I was wearing them and my dad was sitting on the couch, and the TV was on but he wasn't watching it, and I thought there was going to be trouble again. But my dad was looking down at his hands, which were folded in his lap, and he wasn't wearing his glasses, he was holding them in his hands like he was praying—maybe he was, I guess—and when I came out he looked up and smiled, but a real painful kind of smile, and his hair was dirty from work and he still had his blue factory uniform on, and I said, "See you later, pops," and started up the stairs, and he said, "Brian," and I said, "Yeah?" and he said, "Take care of those boots, will you? Those are special to me," and I stopped and nodded and looked down at the black combat boots and I said, "Sure thing, Dad," and he lowered his head and said, "Um, Brian," and I turned and faced him and saw he was crying and I didn't know what the hell to do because

I had never seen the man cry, except the one time at his own dad's funeral, and that one was so quick I was never sure if I remembered it the right way or not. My dad looked down at his folded hands, nodded, wiped his eyes, and then stood, putting out his arms like he wanted me to hug him, so I did, starting to cry a little too, I guess, and I put my face against his shoulder which smelled like Tootsie Rolls, and he sucked back some tears and said, "I've got to leave you guys, Brian, I'm so sorry," and I said, "I know, Dad," really crying hard for some reason, and then he said, "Please, I don't want you guys to hate me," and I said, "I could never hate you, Dad," and he said, "I just can't be here anymore," and I said, "I know, Dad, I get it," and he said, "I won't be here tonight when you get back," and I nodded and he patted me on the shoulder, then sat back down on the couch, staring down at his hands. I ran like hell up the stairs and out into the night, my hands shaking.

I didn't end up going to the show. Nick and I just drove around all night, which was really nice of him. We didn't talk, we just drove around listening to Naked Raygun, which Nick had started getting into because they were from Chicago. Them and, well, Big Black, who were more techno-sounding because they had a drum machine instead of a drummer.

When I finally came home, my dad's car was gone and he wasn't down on the couch and the house was very, very quiet, and I thought about calling up Gretchen to tell her what happened, but it was still real weird between us because of the make out session and everything, and so instead I put in the mix-tape she had made me, the one about her mom dying, Carol, and I listened to that over and over, and even though I was only listening to punk now and the tape, well, it was mostly sissy kind of Smiths songs, I ended up rewinding that side all night anyway.

fourteen

Resurrection Cemetery on Roberts Road was supposed to be haunted too. There was this story about a traveling salesman who was driving past one night and this young girl in a white slip came out of the dark and he almost ran her down with his car and he pulled over and saw she was only wearing a slip and kind of noticed she looked like she had been robbed or raped or whatever, and he asked her for her name and she said it was Mary and she kind of reminded the traveling salesmen of his daughter, and he asked her if he could drive her home, and she got in, and he dug into the backseat and put this shawl around her shoulders, which was his daughter's, and he like drove her home, and she thanked him and began to hand the shawl back to him, and he said, *No, it's all right*, and she ran up to this house and disappeared inside, and you know the whole ghost-story thing, he went back the next day to see if she was all right and the mother answered the door and said the girl, Mary, had died like five years before, on the exact same night, but Nick, who told me the story, didn't know what night it was exactly.

We took his car, the green 1985 Caprice, over to the cemetery at like midnight on this weeknight—because my dad was really gone now and my mom, well, she would begin talking to me and all I would hear was this silence, the kind of totally complete death-like silence that had been running between her and my dad already, and at home I felt like I was really invisible, maybe because I wanted it that way, so I had started doing whatever the fuck I pleased and I had decided I would stay out as late as I wanted, even during the week—so we parked in the forest preserve about a half-mile away and walked over and stood before the wide, iron cemetery gates that simply said RESURRECTION, and there along one of the gates was the spot where supposedly Mary's hand had forced it open, because there was a kind of indentation like the shape of someone's hand, though I wasn't really convinced, and Nick and I started walking inside and I started hoping there were such things as ghosts because it would kind of give me hope, knowing some people got second chances or that the end wasn't the end or that resurrection could really happen and you could go through the worst of it and come out something else—changed somehow, untouchable, invulnerable—because I was like a ghost now, or that's how I had been feeling anyway, and it made me happy to believe there was somehow maybe some other chance for me.

fifteen

In the few minutes before fifth period, like two weeks before senior prom, Bobby B. got expelled for putting this other kid in the hospital because he hit the kid in the head with a baseball bat and the kid lost, like, vision in one of his eyes and it would be, like, permanently damaged for the rest of his life and everything. I felt let down for some reason. It was totally fucking unbelievable to me. One day Bobby B. was strutting down the hallway of Brother Rice, flipping off the Holy Brothers behind their backs, smoking in the bathroom, getting high after lunch, copying test answers off of the weaker kids around him, spitting in the water fountains, pissing in the bathroom sinks, taking the freshman class' lunch money, ditching sixth period to go hang out in the school parking lot to rev up his van and crank "Dream On" by Aerosmith on its stereo, greasing his hair down to hide under the back of his collar, selling dope to the juniors, making obscene tongue gestures at Miss Lannon while she was writing a new Spanish word on the blackboard, shooting milk out his nose in the cafeteria, and giving me the devil sign in the hallway. I mean, like, one day he was my friend, and the next day I saw Coach Alberts, who used to play college football, a big, big man with a square chin and shiny silver whistle around his neck, shoving Bobby B. down the hallway by his neck. It was right before fifth period and classes were changing and Bobby B. tried to knock Coach Alberts's hand off his neck, but the coach was just too big and he kept shoving Bobby B. down the hall toward the dean's office, and I looked up and saw him and he rolled his eyes and kind of shook his head, as if to say, *Dude, I have no clue why they're hassling me now,* but by then everybody pretty much knew what happened the night before—the upperclassmen anyways—and so a lot of people had just been waiting to see what the school administration would do and this was it. Expulsion. Like two weeks before his senior year was going to end. That was it.

OK, what happened was this: The night before, a Thursday night, some dudes from Brother Rice, our school, and this other Catholic boy's school, Mt. Carmel, were supposed to fight these other kids from the rich, preppy boy's school, Marist. I didn't even know why for sure, really, but it had something to do with some kid, Derek Duane, this baseball player–type jock from our school, getting the fuck beat out of him by two Marist kids the weekend before at some stupid prep party in the suburbs. I mean, it was all pretty sketchy why all these meatheads and stoners decided to fight each other, I guess. I mean, most of them were seniors and about to graduate like in two weeks. Who the fuck really cared? But Gretchen had heard about it from Kim and Bobby B. had told me himself during school, just saying, "There is going to be a serious ass-beating tonight at Oak Lawn Park. Bring a tire iron or something," and I nodded, having no idea what the fuck he meant really, but I walked up there by myself and saw Gretchen, all alone, sitting on the hood of her car and I sucked in a breath, trying to, like, smile and not seem all awkward and nervous, and then I went up and stood beside her, not saying anything, just watching to see what would happen, I guess. She was wearing a blue jean jacket and her boots and a plaid skirt and she was looking really cute and I almost started off by saying that and I got flustered and walked up and waved instead.

"What's up?" I said, nodding in her direction like eight hundred times.

"What's up?" she asked back, her cheeks kind of going red.

She wouldn't look me in the eyes and I was feeling nervous and so I said, "Oh, you know, nothing."

"Cool," she said.

"Yeah," I said. "I haven't seen you in a while."

"Yeah."

"Yep," I said. I kind of kicked the tire of her car and started to say, "Gretchen, about the other day—" when she cut me off.

"Please, just fucking stop talking about it."

"But, I mean . . ."

"Duh. It was stupid. Just don't say another word about it or I'll fucking lose my shit. Seriously."

"OK," I said. "No problem. But if you do want to talk about it . . ."

"No," she said. "Not ever. Seriously."

"OK," I said, and turned to look back at the park. Like everything, the park was kind of run-down, small, right in the middle of a residential area, street after street of nice little houses, brown brick bungalows mostly, some newer ranch-style houses, just a regular kind of neighborhood, except that Oak Lawn Park was where the kids from Marist, usually hung out. There were some redwood picnic tables and a swing set and metal slide and sandbox and then some paths to walk on and, at the corner of the park, a basketball court. Both of the basketball hoops had metallic chain nets. It was real warm that night and almost felt like summer, and Gretchen and I were just sitting on the hood of the Escort. There were like fifteen cars parked along the curb all around the park already, some kids waiting, leaning against their vehicles, some watching from their front seats. There were rough-looking dudes sitting on the swings, maybe eight or nine kids in red and white Marist nylon varsity jackets with big M's on the right side of their chests, with different sports written on their backs—wrestling, football, baseball—and they were sitting there with their hands in their pockets, some standing and smoking. I guess they were the ones who were going to be doing the fighting if there was any. They didn't look any different from the sport-os at our school, really. They had the same cro-mag build and bullish facial expressions, like maybe they were contemplating what they were going to say or do.

Out of nowhere came Bobby B.'s purple wizard van. I could see it rolling down the street, the engine hissing and rumbling. It was blaring "White Room" by Cream, where the song is loud and the guitar is kind of distorted and full of wha-wha, and it kind of begins with this Spanish matador riff, with the drums pounding like a conquistador—*bump–badda-ba-bum–badda-ba-bum–badda-ba-bum-da-da-bum-da-dad-bum*—and the purple metallic flake of the van was glistening because it had rained earlier that day, and the wizard airbrushed on the side—his dark blue cloak rippled with wind, his mouth open as if casting a spell, his wooden staff outstretched, churning and exploding with pure purple and white lighting—seemed to look vaguely ominous instead of just weird and goofy, his dark hood covering his triangular face like the cowl of death. The purple wizard van pulled up right beside the swing set, the sliding side door opened, and about eight or nine kids jumped out, shouting, some of them with wood two-by-fours, some of them carrying baseball bats. They didn't have varsity jackets on. They were not really jocks, I didn't think. They were mostly the stoners, the burnouts, the hoods, in their jean jackets, a few older dudes like Tony Degan, who was wearing a beat-up black baseball hat, and, of course, Bobby B., who had left the wizard van running, the headlights still burning, casting shadows all along the jungle gym set. It had begun raining again, just white and silver flickers of it in the field of light, the radio still blaring Cream as Bobby B. hopped out of the driver's side, carrying a narrow, whitish-yellow baseball bat, down low, almost touching the ground, then charging right up to the biggest Marist kid there, a bruiser with a square head in a puffy red and white wrestling varsity jacket. Bobby B. lifted the bat and swung in one quick fluid motion, catching the corner of the bigger kid's face, knocking him flying completely off his feet. It made this sound, loud and cracking but kind of soft too. The big kid went down, slumping onto his side as Bobby swung again, hitting him over the shoulder. Nobody else fucking moved—none of the other kids. They just looked at the big kid on the ground who was knocked out—or worse—and I think I almost vomited. None of the kids did anything for a while, they kind of just stared at the big kid on the ground and then at Bobby B., who was still holding the bat, pointing it from kid to kid. "What the fuck," someone whispered, and then some Marist dude charged Bobby and started hitting him. Tony Degan punched the kid in the back of the head just before some other Marist jock pounded Tony in the side of the ear. I had never seen anything like it before in my fucking life. It was fucking madness. They all began punching each other and fighting.

From the hood of the superbad Escort, Gretchen and I just watched, not doing anything, just fucking staring. "Let's get the fuck out of here," she said, hopping off and starting the car quick. I looked over my shoulder and kept on watching and Gretchen was starting to pull away and I got inside the Escort and I could see her face was wet with tears and all she kept saying was, "What the fuck? What the fuck was that?" over and over and over again.

sixteen

On the way to the mall to drop Kim off at work after school the next day, everyone was quiet as hell. I was riding in the backseat but feeling like Gretchen did not want me there, like she had been surprised to see me show up waiting at the car in the first place. It was very weird for everybody. Finally, Kim cleared her throat and turned to Gretchen and said, "Um, did you know your boyfriend got arrested last night?"

"I know."

"What?" I asked.

And then Kim said, "He got his stupid ass thrown in jail with Bobby."

"I know," Gretchen muttered with a whisper.

"What do you mean you know?"

"I was there, with Brian. We saw it happen," Gretchen said.

"You were there too?" she asked me. "Why didn't you guys tell me you were going?"

"I dunno. I just went," she said.

"Well, what I heard was there were these like ten kids from Marist and like ten kids from Rice and the kids from Rice kicked their asses."

"Yeah. That's pretty much what happened."

"So. Are you worried?" Kim asked.

"Worried? About what?" Gretchen replied.

"I dunno, that Tony was hurt or something?"

"No, I dunno. I dunno. He didn't look hurt when we took off."

"What do you mean? You didn't stay?"

"No, I fucking went home. I didn't want to watch," Gretchen said.

"Well, are you supposed to see him later?" Kim asked.

"Yeah, he was gonna stop by tonight. My dad is working late. I don't know if I want to see him."

"Well, Bobby got his hand sprained," Kim announced.

"Yeah? He seemed like he was OK."

"I think he got expelled," I said from the backseat, quietly.

"What? What for?" Kim asked.

"He, like, blinded some kid from Marist."

"That's fucking bullshit," she said. "They would have done the same thing to him, if they could have. Those kids from that school are fags."

"Dude," I said. "He went up and hit this kid in the head with a fucking baseball bat."

"Was he the only one with a bat?" she asked.

"No," I said.

"So there," she said.

"But he was the only one who hit anyone," I said.

"Jesus," she said. "Jesus, that fucking sucks."

"Uh, yeah," I said. "For the blind kid."

We pulled up to the mall by the blue food court vinyl canopy. Kim got her bag together and began getting out. "Well, fuck, call me later, Gretchen, and tell me what fucking happened." Kim hopped out of the car and straightened her skirt, looking back inside the car as I climbed into the front seat.

"Sure," Gretchen said, staring off into the distance. "See you later."

"Hey, Gretchen, you OK?" Kim asked, leaning in through the window.

"Yeah, I'm OK," she said, and we drove in silence, the two of us, for a very long time. She tried the tape player but it was not working and so it was just the two of us sitting in total silence for a very long time; Gretchen knocking me out with her American thighs, me kind of hoping.

"So, um, are you still thinking about going to the prom?" she asked. "Or did they cancel them both finally?"

"No, the junior one is still on. The administration made them pick two theme songs and like work them together. It's going to be like, 'Make this Wonderful Night Last Forever,' which doesn't even make sense, but that's all right, I guess."

"What's happening with the seniors?"

"I dunno," I said, and I didn't because, well, I felt like it wasn't any of my fucking business really, and also, even if I did think it was wrong, what the hell was I going to do about it anyway? "I guess I'm going. I mean, I want to go. I mean, I haven't asked anyone. Mike Madden, I talked to him, and he said he could fix me up with this one girl, but I dunno. Like I said, I really don't want to go with someone I don't know."

"Yeah," she said, not getting it but nodding. "Hey, what are you doing now?"

"Going home, I guess. Why, are you meeting Tony?"

"I don't know," she said. "I don't know."

"That's cool. If you want to drop me off by my place . . ."

"Do you want to watch a movie or something?"

"Seriously?" I asked. "Like old times. That would be the best."

At Gretchen's we were watching *Night of the Living Dead*, a favorite of ours—you know, the original black-and-white zombie movie—and we were sitting in her basement which was pitch dark, and she was lying on this dark brown leather sofa which was very sticky and ugly and I was sitting on the floor in front of her, leaning back against the front of the couch. The lights were all off, except the TV, which was black-and-white and everything, and I was thinking about turning around and trying to attack Gretchen and fantasizing about us getting it on, you know, on the leather sofa, just reaching up under her Catholic school-girl skirt and well, you know, but then I started really watching the movie, like paying attention, and I dunno, it was like taking on a whole different meaning to me, because of the separate proms and the brawl and Bobby B. getting arrested and expelled and that one kid getting sent to the hospital. There was this one scene where the hero, this young black dude, and the heroine, this kind of high-strung white girl, are like hiding out in this old farmhouse trying to avoid being strangled by the hundreds of zombies, right, and it turns out that in the cellar or basement of the farmhouse, well, there are all these other people, white people, and they were hiding down there and they knew what the fuck was going on upstairs but they didn't help the black guy and white chick, and so the black guy starts yelling at this dude who is kind of middle-aged and blue collar, the leader of the white people who were all chicken-shit, and the white dude says something like, *"We were in a safe place. Are you telling me we were supposed to leave our safe place just to help someone out?"* and I couldn't believe he was saying that, you know, because it was all like school and shit. Everyone—all the kids at school and the teachers and the administrators and their parents, everyone—knew there was trouble, that the black kids were being made to feel like they didn't count, like they didn't belong, and that they were fucking fed up with feeling like that, so they were going to do it themselves, have their own prom. But no one, none of the teachers or parents or other students, were doing anything to get involved. Why? Because who wanted to get involved in that shit when sticking your neck out might mean you were gonna get your ass kicked? Not me. But, so here's the really fucked-up thing: At the end of the movie, all of them, all the people—I mean the survivors, not the zombies, even the black guy and white chick—all of them get killed by the military at the end, and that made me think too, you know? It was all about action. *Action*. That if you knew something was wrong and didn't stand up for what was right, well, not only do the people who are being treated like shit suffer, but so do you somehow; no matter how hard you try, you can't separate your life from other people's lives, so you've got to act, do something. I thought about it throughout the whole movie, wondering maybe if there was something, anything I could do, and getting nowhere by only wondering.

At the very end of the movie, they show these still photos of the zombies and of the survivors who had been shot, and there's like a fake radio news reporter and everything. Well, I turned around and looked up at Gretchen and she was looking at me, and she kind of shook her head, no, no, and I turned back, facing the TV, and then she leaned forward on the couch, putting her hands over my eyes, and in a minute we were kissing all over again. She was on top of me, laughing and saying, "Shhhh," and, "Please don't talk," and I nodded and pretended to zip my lip and she climbed off the couch, sitting in my lap, her legs wrapped around me, facing me, as she sighed and began kissing me, very slowly, very gently. "This doesn't mean anything," she said, and I nodded, reaching up the back of her shirt. I ran my hands up and down her sides and kissed her ear and neck, breathing hard there, and she pushed me back against the front of the sofa. We kind of dry-humped like that for a few minutes, and I reached up to pull off her panties but she said, "No," and I tried again and she said, "No," like I was a little boy, and we kept pushing ourselves together, rocking, until I came, digging my hands into her hair.

"We have to stop doing this," she said, standing up, groaning, covering her face.

I said, "Yeah," then, "No," and she shook her head, folding into the couch, kicking her legs.

"I'm going to leave," I said, hoping she'd say, *No, please stay*, but she just nodded and I knew if I didn't go through with it—you know, leaving—then it would seem like I was totally in love with her, which I might have been. I looked at her once more, said, "Later," and bounded up the stairs, happy and totally, completely confused, which was almost worse than if nothing had ever happened maybe.

seventeen

Bad things happened at school. In between third and fourth periods, Mr. Alba, the tall, kind of funny senior Religion teacher shouted at this kid, Keith Parsons, for spitting in the hallway. When Mr. Alba demanded that the kid, who was a senior—squat, thick-necked, a football player and sometime burnout—clean it up, the kid said, "I'm not touching it. That's what we have janitors for," and started to walk away. Mr. Alba grabbed Keith by the back of the neck, maybe grabbing him too hard, I dunno, I wasn't there, but the kid, Keith Parsons, just snapped, punching Mr. Alba in the mouth. Mr. Alba tripped back into some lockers, and since it was between classes, tons of kids saw it, which was kind of weird and funny and a little sad, I guess. The whole school was very uptight. After Bobby B. got expelled, the whole separate senior prom thing was in the newspapers and it looked like it was really going to happen, the black seniors booking their own hotel and their parents helping them put it together, which I thought was cool, but the entire school seemed like it was ready to fucking blow, I guess, fights in the hallways and threats and shouting and this black kid, Ray Love, being suspended for calling Bro. Mooney a "cracker." It was a very strange fucking feeling.

Later the same day I saw Rod in the hallway and he was looking sad and glum, his dark face kind of greenish.

"What's up?" I asked.

"I hate this fucking school," he said.

"Why?"

"Look," he said, and pointed to the back of his white dress shirt, which said *FAG* in big black letters.

"How'd that happen?"

"Mick Stephens wrote it on my back during Physics class."

"That's what you get for taking honors classes with seniors," I said. He nodded and walked off, frowning at the ground.

Since I had study hall fourth period, I was in no rush. I ambled over to my locker and started putting my other books away when I saw fucking John McDunnah walk past, grinning at me, with his two sport-o friends. I even fucking think he winked at me. And I don't know what the fuck came over me. I don't know if it was one thing or everything— all the Misfits songs in my head, being pals with Nick, already having my nose busted once, my dad leaving, my mom an unmistakably unhappy and deafening silence in my life, wanting Gretchen so bad but never able to really be with her, Bobby B. getting expelled, seeing Rod as beaten as he was, or all, maybe all of those things, I dunno— but I just shoved my locker closed, slammed the lock into place, and started following the three of these meatheads down the busy hallway. I saw where they turned down senior hall, where they stopped so John McDunnah could sneak some cigarettes out of his locker, and where they went after that, the second floor bathroom. I had been fucking dreaming of kicking that guy's ass for so long—I didn't know how, really, maybe by, like, magically learning karate or somehow punching him in the nose and, like, mortally wounding him that way—that I almost ran up to him and started swinging, but then I stopped and figured something out: John McDunnah was always going to be bigger than me. He was always going to be stronger, broken nose or not; what the fuck could I do to him, to tear him apart, to hurt him?

That's when I really started thinking. He'd always be able to kick my ass—in like a hundred years, even. I would never be able to get to him. I'd never feel the satisfaction of letting him know I wasn't just some pussy, some fucking target; that I was a fucking person, you know, that I counted for something. But then I thought maybe that was OK. Maybe it was a fucking waste of time to even try to get him, I mean he was who he was, you know. He was like this certain kind of person and *what was I going to do to change that?* Now I was thinking. I was really thinking.

I got this idea to start putting big pictures of kittens in his locker. That day I ditched study hall and went down to the library and scoured the fucking card catalog and I was in luck, because there was a book called *Kittens*, honest to God—*Why? Why would there be a book called* Kittens *in an all-boys' Catholic school?* I did not know or care. But I hurried down the stacks, found it, drifted off to one of the library's remote corners, and started tearing pages from it. I took a pen and a magic marker and started writing these little messages in those cartoon bubbles, like the different kittens were saying them, like, "John is my friend," and, "John always remembers to feed me," and, "John scratches my belly," and I was practically fucking peeing my pants from laughing to myself so hard. Then I tore out a few more pages and made some more messages, the baby kittens becoming a little more philosophical, like, "Be nice, John, like me, a nice kitten," and, "If you hurt people, it makes me cry," and I drew a tear under this gray kitten's eye, and then my best one of all time, this photo of like fifteen white furry kittens all lying on top of each other, to which I added, "Every time you hurt someone, John, one of us dies," and I drew a small pair of X's over one of the cats' eyes.

Then, still laughing to myself, I strode out of library and stuck one of the pictures in the vent of his locker, just one, the one of a small tabby sleeping beside a red ball of yarn, saying, "John is my friend." I wanted to wait to see him check it out and be totally confused and weirded out, but I thought that might give it away if he happened to see me.

That became my thing then—for like the rest of the school year. In between second, third, fifth, and sixth periods, I began sticking torn-out photos of kittens, puppies, ponies, and baby seals in John McDunnah's locker, hoping it would somehow, somehow make him think about how he fucking acted, you know? But really, I guess, really, I just did it for me.

eighteen

After school I was sitting on the hood of the Escort and Kim and Gretchen were smoking. Gretchen was acting like everything was cool and nothing had ever happened and so was I then. I had my arms folded over my chest and was acting like I was in a great mood, even smoking a cigarette to show how cool I was with everything.

"So, Brian, what's the deal with prom and shit?" Kim asked me, blowing her fucking smoke in my face. I could see my own reflection in her big, black, bug-eye sunglasses. "Are you still going?"

"I dunno. I guess. I still got to find a date."

"So you're really going?" Kim asked.

"To the junior prom? Yeah, I mean the junior prom is OK. It's the senior one that's kinda fucked up," I said.

"So what's the fucking deal with that?" Kim asked.

"I dunno. I guess the black kids, the seniors, are pissed, so they're having their own prom," I said.

"That's fucking stupid," Kim said.

"Yeah it is, but not for the reason you think it is," I said.

Kim took off her sunglasses and turned around, staring at me. "And what would that be?"

"I think it's fucking bullshit that just because you're white, you get everything you fucking want," I said. "That, I think, is fucking stupid."

"What?" Kim asked, staring at me like my head was on fucking fire.

"I think it's fucking shit," I said. "They just wanted to be, like, fucking accepted or whatever. It was like their song. Fuck, think about how important your fucking music is to you, you know? Fuck. They just wanted to feel like they were part of it, you know?"

"They seem like a bunch of babies," Gretchen said. "They didn't get their way, so now they're ruining it for everybody."

"No, that's not it," I said. "You don't get it. You feel like you don't belong and you get fucking sick of it, so you do your own fucking thing."

We pulled into the mall parking lot a little later, right by the big blue canopy for the food court, and Kim started getting out. "I got to go, chumps. Until we meet again, lover," Kim said, winking at me.

"Get fucked," I said, turning away. I climbed into the front seat and slid the seat belt into place. "She always acts like such a fucking jerk."

"You fucking love it," Gretchen said.

"I dunno. I used to, maybe. Maybe I wish she didn't have to act so rude all the fucking time."

"Rude? She doesn't act rude."

"Sure she does," I said. "She thinks it makes her adorable. She's been doing it since junior high. She thinks no boys will like her if she is nice. She's got to put on this act all the time: punk rock Kim. Yeah. She's not ever like a real person anymore hardly."

"Well, you're in a fucking mood, aren't you?" Gretchen asked.

"I guess," I said. "I just kind of realized this shit, you know?"

"Like what?" she asked.

"I think a lot of these punk kids we know are fucking poseurs," I said. "I think most of them, they just do whatever, you know, to fit in. It's like a totally mindless act. Like Kim—it's all about fucking fashion."

"What the fuck are you talking about?" Gretchen asked, raising her eyebrows at me.

"I'm talking about how you two guys are like the most close-minded people I know," I said. "You don't even know what punk is about, you know? You just dress like it, because you were like a loser and it, like, gave you someone to be after junior high, something to belong to, you know?"

"What the fuck are you talking about?"

"You and all those other kids we knew from junior high. I mean, fuck—do you think I forgot Dave Lattel had a *Grease* lunchbox?"

"What?"

"The movie *Grease* with John Travolta? He had a *Grease* lunchbox all through grade school because he said he liked John Travolta's hair. And he was way into GI Joe and Transformers. He used to tell people to call him "Dave-o-Tron" and he'd make that Transformer sound and pretend he had become a jet and fly around. And that was like in seventh grade. And now, now, now he's punk? It's like you and Kim. Kim used to be a cheerleader for god sakes. She used to date Barry Nolan who was on the basketball team. And suddenly all you guys were all hard-core."

"Whatever, dweeb."

"You're just like the jocks. Just because you have blue hair doesn't make you fucking better than everyone else."

"What?"

"Just because you have blue hair and fucked-up clothes doesn't mean you're better than everyone else. Because you know what? You're just conforming to someone else's code. Even though you don't wear khakis or sweaters or whatever, but to me all you guys look the same. You think you're so individualistic, but you're not. You guys— you and Kim and all the rest—you're like anti-snob snobs. But you're just as mean as the preppy kids. You're all just as fucking lame."

"Oh really?"

"No, I dunno. I didn't mean to call you a poseur. I just . . . I just wish you guys knew that people like you for who you are. You could, like, be yourself. But someone, well a guy, some dick like Tony Degan, well, he doesn't even care about who you really are. I know, I'm a guy."

"You are? I thought you were a hermaphrodite."

"I'm a guy and I know what guys think. All they care about is having sex with you."

"So all you care about is having sex with me?" she asked, and my face got very red very instantly.

"No, no, I just meant you're my friend and I really care about you."

"Oh, shut up before you make me puke."

"I'm sorry. Maybe I shouldn't have said anything. But, well . . . well, kids grow up so fast today," I said, smiling.

"Get out! Get out of my car!" Gretchen shouted, pulling up in front of my house. I turned and watched her pull away, thinking, *I said too much, I open my fucking mouth too much*, and that I'd be lucky if I ever saw her again because it felt like something had just ended for me.

nineteen

So I wish I could say I didn't go to junior prom at all. I wish I could say I was like, "Fuck you, you racist American institution." Heck, I wish I could say I took Gretchen, even. But I didn't. Because I was a dumb teenager and all I wanted was to feel like I fit in, or at least look like I fit in—which when I look back now is the stupidest thing and the most basic thing anybody ever needs, maybe. So I let my hair grow out for the next two weeks—for the stupid fucking pictures, you know—and I asked this girl, Kelly Connors, who Mike Madden helped set me up with, who was the little sister of one of Erin McDougal's friends, you know. Well, this girl Kelly Connors was very short with curly orange hair and she had asthma and was like allergic to everything, like even grass, and when I went to pin the white corsage on her pink dress she said, "I'm sorry. Roses give me a rash," and me and two other marching band dudes I hardly knew rented a limo, and me and Kelly danced to all the stupid dances and all I remember was the last one, which was, of course, "Wonderful Tonight" by Eric Clapton, because, like usual, I had this massive erection, and poor Kelly Connors kind of noticed it and I just shrugged and kept on dancing. Mike Madden was there with Erin McDougal and we talked for a while and I told him about my dad splitting, and then Mike and Erin got in a fight and ended up leaving, and like that, in a matter of the briefest of awkward moments, the junior prom was pretty much over for me.

twenty

After prom in the limousine, the limousine we had rented, me and the two other loners I knew from band class, well, I did something very bad. I fingered Kelly Connors right in front of everybody, just switching off the interior light and pinning her to the backseat and I thought I might have had sex with her that night, but I wasn't sure; all the while the other kids and their dates kind of whispered and one girl said, "This is disgusting. I want to go home," and I didn't even care, because I felt like I had something to prove, because I did. I had to prove what a desperate asshole I was, really. I wanted to show everyone how cool I was, I guess, and what better way than mauling your date in front of a bunch of strangers? Perfect.

After Kelly had been dropped off in front of her house, with her pink dress halfway up her thighs and her makeup all over her face and a rash spreading all over her chest, and the other two band dorks had taken their dates home and said goodnight, I was riding alone in the back of the limousine, feeling alone and lonely, and laughing to myself about the terrible night I'd had, thinking about the stupidity of it, of trying so hard to impress somebody, anybody, of just trying so hard to seem like I fit in, and I thought about that girl Kelly's rash even and was feeling lousy about that too now. Then I thought, *You know who would get a kick out of all this? Gretchen*.

The limousine driver, who was black—because it was just like the Dead Kennedys said, *there really was an international conspiracy, and you never saw white people doing shit jobs anymore*—turned to me, his face long and shiny, him taking off his chauffeur cap as he said, "Did you have a nice night, kid?"

"No, it was kind of shitty," I said.

"Yeah, I went to my prom and it was shitty too," he said.

"Yeah. How come?" I asked.

"I didn't understand it then, but I wish I had spent more time hanging with my boys, you know? Instead, I was all up on some girl I never even talked to again."

"Yeah, I hear that," I said, and then I asked, "How much longer do I got left, before you got to drop me off."

"You guys rented it until seven a.m. It's only six now."

"Can you go by and pick up a buddy of mine?" I asked.

"Sure, pal, whatever you want. Where to?"

I thought if Gretchen was home and if she'd listen, I'd tell her I was sorry and ask her to please, please, please come out with me.

And so that's what happened. We drove around together in the back of the rented limo for an hour and maybe it was because I was tired and it was so late—or so early—but Gretchen was in her pajamas and leaning back in the big leather seats and we were cruising along Lake Shore Drive and eating breakfast from McDonald's and it was like nothing bad in the world had ever happened to me.

halloween night
october 1991

"This day anything goes, I remember Halloween"
—"Halloween"
Glenn Danzig, The Misfits

We went to Laura's Halloween party because we figured we were seniors now and it would be the last Halloween we'd all be together for. Gretchen went as a kind of zombie cheerleader and she looked very hot to me, all done-up in this red and white uniform, her hair in pigtails, but with black circles around her eyes, and I went as a mummy, which was kind of half-assed because all I did was at the last minute wrap myself up in toilet paper. I kind of wrapped my face up a little, but I couldn't see really, and by then I had grown my hair out and was not combing it and it was kind of this poofy, random mess, and I couldn't get the toilet paper to stay tight against it because it kept breaking, so I just did my body, arms, legs, neck, and forehead, mostly.

OK, so the party was in Laura's basement, Laura, the redhead who had sometimes fooled around with Bobby B. when Kim and Bobby B. had been dating, but all that was over now, and apparently Kim and Laura were now like best friends. Laura was having this party, and she had bought her mom and dad this gift certificate for Sybaris, this couples spa motel with, like, hot tubs in the room, to keep them away for the night, and, well, she had gone all out and had decorated her entire basement which like everyone else's in the neighborhood was one long rectangle but with fake brown paneling, and she put up orange and black streamers and crepe paper and cut-outs of cats and ghosts and monsters and there were like five carved jack-o'-lanterns, all lit up and everything, and all kinds of spooky food, like a green brain-shaped Jell-O mold and orange and black M&M cupcakes on a table in the corner, and Laura's dad was a cop and didn't ever mind kids drinking in the basement as long as they were staying put for the evening, so there were cases and cases of PBR and Old Milwaukee stacked by the back basement door, which were going quickly. Also, Laura had, like, some crap goth music playing, either Bauhaus or Siouxsie and the Banshees, but it was OK because the spooky mumbling and whininess fit, I guess.

There were like thirty or so kids there, mostly seniors, because, well, believe it or not, we really were seniors now. Most of the kids who had come were wearing pretty generic costumes: a ghost, which was just a kid in a white sheet with holes for eyes; a hobo, which was some other dude who wore crummy clothes and blacked out a tooth; and a coach, which was some guy in a football jersey with a whistle around his neck. Then there were kids who were wearing big rubber plastic masks of President Bush and Darth Vader and Frankenstein, and there were like one or two girls who didn't really have costumes on but had like glitter in their hair and on their faces, then there were like five kids who didn't have any costumes at all and said they had come as "seniors," which was kind of dumb after the third or fourth kid said it, and then, of course, there was Tony Degan, in his white "I'm with Stupid" T-shirt with the arrow pointing to some random kid beside him, and I guess, as his costume, Tony was wearing a black patch over one of his eyes. When Gretchen and I walked downstairs, Tony had his arm around this small stoner chick with buck teeth, Jill, a sophomore dressed like a witch, and I watched Gretchen head over to him and, like usual, start yelling and I smiled and went over and grabbed a beer and checked out the rest of the party. There were all kinds of kids, kids I didn't know or didn't recognize in vampire makeup or fake mustaches and the like, and, well, like a few kids who had gone all out with their costumes, who must have been planning their costumes for months, seriously. Like of course, there was Laura, whose party it was, who was this really tall, freckled, lovely redhead, dressed as an entire kissing booth. Like I said, she was kind of known for being easy, fooling around with anybody, especially Bobby B., and she was always breaking up with some guy we knew and then going off with someone else the same night, and she had this big brown cardboard box and she was standing inside it and there was a sign along the top that said, "Kisses $1.00," and guys were going up, handing her money, and she was laughing and making out with them. Then there was like this other guy at the party we knew, Bill, a chubby stoner, who would try to sell you fake acid—little pieces of paper which were just that, only paper—and he was dressed up as Batman, but in a costume he had made himself out of, like, sweatpants and a baby blue blanket, so he was like Fat Batman, and he was like dancing but he really couldn't dance, and he was a big kid, I mean, fat, because his costume didn't fit and you could see his big belly hanging over his black sweatpants.

OK, then there was this kind of tall girl dressed as the Tooth Fairy and at first I thought it was this girl Lucy, but Lucy had cut her hair real short and this girl had long flowing brown hair with a lovely gold tiara atop it and this small black mask concealing her identity and all. She had this ornate gold dress on and a gold wand and a necklace full of small white teeth and a golden satchel full of money. She was very gently touching her wand to all the kids present and, goofing around, everyone was acting like they immediately fell asleep.

The Tooth Fairy came right up to me, smiled, and took my hand. Then she dug into her magic satchel and pulled out a funny-looking quarter and put it into my palm. I looked at it and it wasn't a quarter at all, but some funny kind of foreign coin.

She smiled, blinking at me, and said, "That one is from Greece."

"Thanks," I said.

"I give out coins to children all over the world," she said.

"That must get confusing," I said.

She nodded and said, "It does."

"Well, thanks," I said.

"This will be the last gift I give you," she said.

"What?"

"This will be the last time I come visit you because you're not a child anymore."

I laughed and wondered who the hell she really was under the mask.

I put the Greek coin in my pocket and smiled nervously. I kind of walked away, toward the orange and black pyramid of cupcakes, and looked at her and she waved at me, nodding, and I suddenly felt very strange for some reason, like it really was the end of my childhood or something. I sat there for a moment staring at everyone at the party and all of a sudden it hit me, really. It was like the last Halloween party I'd ever go to in high school, and Halloween, well, I guess that was always like my favorite holiday as a kid because, you know, you got to dress up and be someone else, and I looked around and here were all these kids—sixteen, seventeen, eighteen years old—all in different costumes and everything, and like I said, something right there ended for me.

It was like I saw all these kids, but like how they looked every other day, the different kinds of kids, you know, like *the stoners* like Bill or Mike Madden, who I had seen just the other day and who was now mostly high all the time, or at least every time I saw him, always sitting in his stone-washed jean jacket in the backseat of an El Camino he was trying to rebuild, getting stoned in the parking lot after school, and I'd wonder where he'd be in a year; or *the punk kids* and *goths* like Kim or Laura or Gretchen, dyeing their hair or wearing their spiked bracelets or Clash T-shirts, still very concerned with keeping up their weirdo punk appearance; or *the jocks, the sport-o's, the athletes* in their varsity jackets, backwards baseball hats, and professional sports team jerseys; or *the nerds, the geeks, the pussies,* kids like Rod, wherever he was at that moment, in their *Star Trek* T-shirts, dressed in dorky, plain clothes their overprotective mothers had picked out for them; or *the gangster wanna-bes* in baggy pants, gold chains, and oversized shirts; or *the rich prude girls* in very tight Esprit sweaters, who stuck their noses up so high and drove around in their brand-new convertibles; or *the sluts* in low-cut bodysuits and skirts so short you could see how hard they were trying to be noticed by somebody, anybody; or *the oldest teenagers in the world*, those kids who weren't kids anymore but wouldn't ever let go of high school, dudes like Tony Degan, who would never really age, in his ironic "I'm With Stupid" T-shirt, constantly looking wise and amused but now looking a lot less cool; or *the ghosts*—the ones who had, for whatever reason, disappeared and stopped hanging out with us before they could finish growing up, like Bobby B. in his military fatigues because he had joined the Army after being expelled a few months back. All these kids, all these people were trying to pretend they were the people they wanted to be by how they dressed, just to fit in, just to be accepted and to belong to something, and, well, I got it all suddenly.

It would always be a put-on, high school or not, for the whole rest of the world, for the rest of our lives. You couldn't ever guess who someone was by the way they looked because, good or bad, the way they looked was always just a costume or an act. It was Halloween every day, for most people anyway, just to feel like they weren't alone, to belong, just to keep being happy maybe. Maybe everyone else might go on thinking that people were just what you saw—*the clothes, the haircuts, the cars*—but not me, even though it seemed the whole world kind of worked that way: a put-on, only interested in the appearance of things like your class, your race, whether you were a girl or a boy, all the stuff you couldn't really change anyway. It seemed really hard to grow out of that; maybe all you could do was try your best, try not to judge people from the way they appeared to be, I guess. I decided I might try to do that, try not to make decisions about everyone by what I saw because of how small and wrong that was, but it seemed that was just the way my brain worked, that all I could do was keep trying, keep trying, keep trying. I thought maybe that's what growing up might do for me maybe, which was kind of scary.

I guess I started feeling kind of strange, and then I saw Gretchen in the corner of the basement still arguing with Tony Degan who, like I said, wasn't wearing a costume but had on a black eye patch; I maybe felt like I didn't want to be myself suddenly, I didn't want to be a senior and at the end of it all anymore, I just wanted to keep being a kid and keep being stupid, because not being a kid was weird. That's all I had ever been, really, and now someone was asking me to be someone else suddenly, and I pounded a PBR quick, then another, the cold foam charging down my throat, then smashed the can against my forehead, and a sophomore, Lenny, someone's little brother, saw me do it and clapped his hands and said, "Bad-ass!" and I nodded toward him and walked past Gretchen, who looked like she was crying, her black zombie eye makeup running down her soft cheeks, still shouting at Tony. I walked right past her and up to the Kissing Booth girl, Laura, and dug into my back pocket, opened my wallet, and said, "How much do I get for twenty bucks?" and she laughed and took my hand and I ended up making out with her fiercely in her own kitchen upstairs.

After ten minutes of serious groping, during one point I was biting her wrist, Laura blinked at me and said, "Brian Oswald. Wow," and I didn't have an answer to that, but I said, real cool, "Do you want to show me your room?" and she nodded and we were just about to head upstairs when I saw Gretchen, whose face looked like black spiderwebs, lines and crisscrosses of mascara. I let go of Laura's hand and watched Gretchen walk out back and sit on the small cement porch.

It was over between her and Tony, finally, and it had been coming for some time, months maybe, and I could tell because she had not gone back downstairs to kick that other girl's ass, which was like kind of amazing to me, considering, like, she had finally just given up on him, and also she was really, really crying, shaking her head, and now she was sitting on Laura's back porch, her knees pulled to her chest, smoking, and really, really crying, and, well, right there I decided I would go out and sit beside her and tell her I was sorry—for her, for everything—and then be ready for whatever might happen after that.

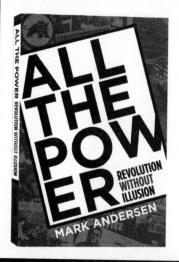

Joe Meno is a fiction writer from Chicago. He is the author of two novels, *Tender As Hellfire* (St. Martin's 1999) and *How the Hula Girl Sings* (HarperCollins 2001), and the winner of the 2003 Nelson Algren Award for short fiction. He is a professor of creative writing at Columbia College, Chicago, the cofounder of *Sleepwalk* magazine, coeditor of *Bail* magazine, and a columnist for *Punk Planet* magazine.

Praise for *Hairstyles of the Damned*

A selection of the Barnes & Noble Discover Great New Writers Program

"Meno gives his proverbial coming-of-age tale a punk-rock edge . . . Will appeal to alterna-adolescents and adults alike."
—*Publishers Weekly*

"Don't let anybody kid you: High school was hard and always will be. Joe Meno knows that, and in his new novel *Hairstyles of the Damned*, he writes in the most authentic young voice since J.D. Salinger's Holden Caulfield." —*Daily Southtown*

"Meno's language is rhythmic and honest, expressing things proper English never could. And you've got to hand it to the author, who pulled off a very good trick: The book *is* punk rock. It's not just *about* punk rock; it embodies the idea of punk—it's pissed off at authority, it won't groom itself properly, and it irritates. Yet its rebellious spirit is inspiring and right on the mark." —*SF Weekly*

"What makes *Hairstyles of the Damned* compelling is Meno's ability to create the rhythm of teen-speak without pandering, and his ability to infuse the story with pop-culture references. A good read for those wanting to remember their youthful mischief."
—*Tablet*

"Meno's recounting of first concerts, first loves, and the first tragedies of adolescence are awesomely paired with the heavy backbeat of late 80's subculture. The contagious foot tapping that is symptomatic of a good record is the same energy that drives you as you follow Meno's narrative." —*Fresno Famous*